To Dimitri
from Grandad
with love
X mas 2000

THE CLEFT

and Other Odd Tales

By Gahan Wilson from Tom Doherty Associates

Still Weird

Gahan Wilson's Even Weirder

The Cleft and Other Odd Tales

THE CLEFT
and Other Odd Tales

GAHAN WILSON

A TOM DOHERTY ASSOCIATES BOOK
NEW YORK

THE CLEFT AND OTHER ODD TALES

Copyright © 1998 by Gahan Wilson

This book is printed on acid-free paper.

A Tor Book
Published by Tom Doherty Associates, Inc.
175 Fifth Avenue
New York, NY 10010

Tor Books on the World Wide Web:
http://www.tor.com

Tor® is a registered trademark of Tom Doherty Associates, Inc.

Library of Congress Cataloging-in-Publication

Wilson, Gahan.
    The cleft, and other odd tales / Gahan Wilson. — 1st ed.
        p.   cm.
    "A Tor book."
    ISBN 0-312-86574-0
    1. Fantastic fiction, American.   2. Horror tales, American.
I. Title.
PS3573.I4569538C58   1998
813'.54—dc21   98-24426
                                                                    CIP

First Edition: November 1998

Printed in the United States of America

0   9   8   7   6   5   4   3   2   1

Contents

THE CLEFT

and Other Odd Tales

The Cleft

The monastery was located atop a huge mountain formed of one enormous rock thrusting upward at a slight angle from the surrounding plain. The top of the mountain stood a full hundred feet high. Its tilted upper surface had posed endless problems for the architects and the resulting building was at the same time both oddly beautiful and amusing to see.

If asked why this sacred edifice had been erected in such an unlikely place, a monk would explain that the eleventh Patriarch, passing by on a journey to the north, saw the Holy One in the form of shining gold standing atop the mountain pointing at the stern rock under his sandaled feet and that the Patriarch had heard Him say: "Even here, in this peculiar place, shall the Truth be known."

There was only one mode of access to the monastery from the plain beneath, and this was by way of a shallow cleft which meandered up the side of the mountain from its base to its peak. Because it zigzagged at reasonable angles and because its rough surface provided sufficient traction, the cleft formed a crude but usable natural stairway. It was, however, only wide enough to allow for the passage of a single user at a time; this limitation had led to a meticulous etiquette that had been elaborated on and added to through the centuries until the pilgrims' passage up or down the mountain was not only physically taxing but one which demanded spiritual and ritualistic exercises of extreme complexity, surrounded by a multitude of harsh enforcements.

In the early period a simple instruction by a monk stationed at the foot of the cleft sufficed to give the novice climber enough information to make his way to the top in full confidence he was ascending with complete correctness.

First the aspiring climber was instructed to listen quietly for a moment in order to hear whether a huge gong standing at the cleft's head was ringing. If he did not hear the gong he was to sound one note on an identical gong situated by his side at the cleft's foot. If he then heard the gong above ring once in reply he knew the cleft was clear for ascent, but two ringings gave warning that a personage was about to begin the process of descent and that the cleft was therefore in full use and that he would have to wait.

Once the signals indicated the way was clear, the climber was handed a small, portable gong in order to perform the secondary precaution of ringing it every fifth step along the way up and told to listen carefully for the next five steps just in case there was a reply to be heard from a descending party who was somehow on his way down in spite of the previous business with the two large gongs. If he did hear such a thing he was to turn around immediately and return to the base of the cleft as it was understood that people going down always had priority over people coming up since it was considerably more difficult for the descenders to retrace their steps, particularly if they were aged or otherwise infirm.

This simple procedure worked admirably and it is not unreasonable to speculate that it would have continued to work well up to the present day if it had been left alone, but as the good monks of the monastery found their attention drawn to the process again and again, since it was in constant usage with them, they simply could not resist adding elaborations to it.

For example, when a visiting abbot scoldingly observed that there was not a single image of the Holy One throughout the entire length of the cleft, the monks placed statues of Him at both the cleft's base and head and carved a bas-relief of Him into its middle. Some decades later it occurred to another abbot that incense should be burnt at each one of these points, and yet a third abbot composed three prayers, one to be intoned at what had come to be called the Upper Lord, one for the Middle, and one for the Bottom or Welcoming Lord.

The accumulation of these improvements seemed to cry out for the construction of a temple at each stopping place, so a lovely little one was duly set up at each place of the Three Lords, the middle one being an absolute masterpiece of cantilevering.

Of course once these edifices had been erected it seemed obvious that they called for the devising of more elaborate rituals, but the creation of each new rite only led the way to another of increased subtlety and depth, and as this process continued with the passing of time the necessary proprieties en route became so involved and required so much apparatus that no one but an advanced adept could be expected to work his way through them in a manner which would be pleasing to the increasingly watchful and ever more astoundingly expert authorities.

The answer to this was to create an entire subclass of priests whose sole duty was to see to it that the rituals of the cleft were always scrupulously performed. Anyone wishing to mount or descend it had to be accompanied by at least two of these priests attending, one to read the appropriate prayers and incantations and commit the proper sacrifices, the other to carry the large quantity of scrolls, costumes, gongs, banners, incense burners, and other equipment which was now absolutely vital for the execution of a satisfactory passage.

There were many expansions of cleft ceremonies for special occasions, the most elaborate recorded being the visit of a particularly devout and especially high-ranking dignitary in which the ascent and descent of the cleft took no less than thirteen days, required the services of some 2,438 persons, not counting the said dignitary's own personal staff and choir, and called for the sacrifice of armies of goats, uncounted wicker baskets stuffed with doves, and an elephant. This last sacrifice had to be performed at the foot of the mountain once it was realized the creature could not be fitted into the cleft itself.

A month or so after the possible excesses of this last event, at the first light of a bright morning in the spring of the year, an unlettered monk began pushing an enormous bundle wrapped in ragged fabric from the scullery, where he worked, to the edge of the mountain directly opposite the cleft.

As a growing number of other monks watched in fascination, their brother pounded several huge stakes into cracks in the rock, tied a thick rope extending from the bundle firmly around them, then pulled aside the stitched and tattered covering to reveal an enormously long rope worked into large knots at regular intervals. He kicked the rope off the edge of the mountain and stood watching calmly as it tumbled its full length and its bottom end dangled less than a foot above the ground of the plain beneath.

Saying not a single word, the scullery monk climbed down the rope, going hand over hand from knot to knot, and when he reached the ground he walked away without a backward glance, leaving his brothers above to watch him dwindle to a dot and eventually vanish into a far gully. He never returned.

The monks silently and rather furtively studied their present Patriarch, who had come among them quietly during this strange procedure. They had observed, with growing trepidation, a wide variety of expressions cross his face and were both vastly relieved and somewhat astonished when he finally broke out with a large, beaming smile.

Clasping his hands before him, and bowing in the direction the scullery monk had taken, he declared to the other monks that their brother was a precious example to them and that they must never forget what he had taught them.

Then, in order to begin the long task of commemoration which would continuously accrue over the endless centuries to come, he solemnly ordered that the stakes which held the rope's upper end be thickly coated in the purest gold.

Phyllis

A fter this nice gentleman catches my eye in the bar mirror a couple of times and sees I don't flinch away in spite of he's giving me The Look, he comes over, kind of unsteady, and asks me would I mind if he bought me a drink, Miss, and I tell him It's a free country and I will have a double Scotch, thank you. So pretty soon we're talking away like anything you could want to mention and in spite of what we are talking about is not concerned with sex, directly, his hand keeps brushing my knee. But I don't jerk away, only sort of shift over so as to let him know I am not stuck-up but I am not the kind of girl with which you can rush things, if you know what I mean.

It turns out his name is Eddie and he is a salesman in from Chicago here for the convention. He says as how they usually have the convention in Chicago but he is just as glad they are having it here this year as it gives him a chance to get away.

After we have a few more drinks he asks me do I live around here and I tell him I live just next door in the third-floor back with Phyllis. He says he wouldn't think a pretty girl like me would want to bother with a roommate and I tell him there is no bother at all with Phyllis and we have been together ever since Daddy died.

Eddie says we sound like a regular team and I say we are, kind of, but we each live our own lives. He asks me Is she like you? and I say Oh heavens no, we are altogether different and in fact it would be hard to imagine two girls who are more different than Phyllis and me. Take like I am always going around all the time, like in bars and like this, but Phyllis she just stays up in the apartment practically for all day.

He asks me What does she do up there? and I say Oh, she just sits up in her corner all the time and knits. Eddie asks me What does she knit? and I say Oh, she just knits, is all.

We have a couple of more drinks and Eddie asks how about we buy a bottle and go up to my place and sort of talk where it's private, if Phyllis wouldn't mind, and I say Sure, why not?

So he gets a bottle and we head up the stairs with him all the time asking me You sure Phyllis won't mind? and me telling him she doesn't mind at all. We get into the living room and I take off my hat and Eddie fixes a couple of drinks at the sink and then he sits down on the sofa beside me and hands me my drink but I put it on the table and say I have had enough for a while and he looks at me and he guesses so has he and puts his drink on the table next to mine and we start doing this and that on the sofa.

Well we have hardly got started when he gets this worried expression on his face and says No offense, Honey, but what is that funny musty smell? I tell him Oh, it isn't anything, and put my arms around his neck, but he still looks worried and asks me No, but what is it? So I say For Pete's sake, it is only Phyllis, and he sits up and says What do you mean?

Well what can I do but sit up and tell him Well that is the way she smells, is all, and it isn't that she isn't clean or anything and we even tried perfume once but it only made it worse. It is not her fault that Phyllis smells that way.

Eddie has some of his drink and asks me Is she sick or something? and I say No she has been that way ever since I met her when Daddy died and left me an orphan and without her I honestly don't know what would have happened to me so if she smells a little it is hardly for me to complain.

I can see it will be No Go for a while so I turn on the radio with some nice quiet music and Eddie fixes a couple more drinks and eventually we get back to fooling around on the sofa again but we haven't hardly more than just got going when so help me up he sits with that worried expression on his face all over.

Well what is the matter now? I ask him, and he says What was that noise for cryeye? Boy I am getting more than just a little tired with him but I say Forget the noise and come back to Mama, but he says It came from over there, and he points to Phyllis' door.

I can tell you I am getting plenty exasperated with him but I sit up and say It is only Phyllis so ignore her. He says It sounded like somebody scratching on the door with a bunch of dry twigs for cryeye, what is she doing scratching on the damn door? I tell him How should I know? And it certainly doesn't take much to get your mind off of certain things after all the big eyes down at the bar. He says Don't get mad, Baby, it's only that it kind of startled me is all.

So I tell him All right, then, just forget it and come back here and let's have some fun, but he says he thinks he could use another drink and he goes over and fixes one but all the time he keeps his eyes on Phyllis' door. Then he starts to come back to the sofa but then he stops by the end table and looks down and points to the floor and asks What the hell is that?

What the hell is what? I say, and I am by now feeling very irritated with him altogether. That stuff, he says, still pointing at the floor. So I lean over the arm of the sofa and look down and say Oh that is only some of Phyllis' knitting.

He says It don't look like any knitting I ever saw. He says It looks like a bunch of fluffed-up dirty Kleenex. Then he bends down and touches it and when he straightens up it has all stuck to him except where it's still stuck to the floor.

For God's sake, he says, It's all sticky! I tell him Of course it is, you dope, if it wasn't sticky it wouldn't work. He looks at me and his face goes pale and he drops his drink and begins to pull at Phyllis' knitting to try to get it off him but it won't break and he just gets himself more tangled up.

Well, I say to him, I had hoped we could have had some fun but have it your way, and I walk over to Phyllis' door and open it and out she comes.

I am hardly ready for bed by the time she is all done with Eddie and there is only that mummy thing she leaves. Well, I say to her, I hope you enjoyed him as he was a complete waste of time as far as I'm concerned. But I can tell from the bored way she cleans her forelegs with her fangs that she also considers he was pretty much a washout.

The old man sniveled and stared at him with his eyes all round and bulging like a scared little boy's.

"I'm not going to hurt you, old timer," Nolan told him.

The old man studied the Inspector a little longer, then he pulled in a deep, wavering breath to get some air, and spoke.

"They took'm," he wheezed, and I could see Nolan fight not to turn his face from the stink pouring out of the old man's mouth. "They took m'arms!"

"See?" hissed Mancini. "It's the same stuff all these people been telling us, I swear to God. Only it's so crazy we haven't been passing it on, see?"

Nolan sighed.

"Who took your arms, old timer?"

The bum blinked and gaped around with his boiled eyes as if he were trying to spot the answer somewhere on the sidewalk.

"I dunno. I was asleep down there." He bobbed his head toward the nearby subway entrance. "Sleeping by the token booth where it's safe, you know? But it wasn't, 'cause I woke up and m'arms was gone, and it never even hurt. It don't even hurt now, mister."

He blinked and tears spurted out of him.

"Oh Jesus!" he wailed. "Oh Mommy! Was I bad? Is that why they done it? Is that why they took'm?"

"It's just like the other stuff we've been hearing from these people," whispered Mancini, then turned and snapped up at his partner: "Isn't it, Parkhurst, goddammit?"

"Yeah," Parkhurst answered him, after a pause. "Fuck."

"See?" cried Mancini in triumph, backed for a second time. "It's always the same kind of shit, Inspector, but who could be-lieve it?"

Leavings

I was not happy when I saw the looks on the faces of Officers Mancini and Parkhurst because I could see right off we had a couple of cops way out of their league and floundering, and enough difficult things had already happened to put Inspector Nolan in a bad mood, and here it was only eight-fifteen in the morning.

I drove more or less up to the curb, with a police car you don't have to be all that precise, and Nolan stepped out of the car. He blew on his big hands against the chilly, dirty Eighty-sixth Street wind, crammed them into his pockets when that didn't work, and by then I was standing next to him and we were both looking down at the sobbing man.

He was an old, worn-out bum, hunkered up on a little bit of concrete located just inside the doorway of a failed shop where the two patrolmen had crammed him in order to keep civilians from stepping all over his body. He had a weird, shriveled look, and you could smell the poor bastard from a yard off.

"Alright, Sergeant Mancini," said Nolan, "We haven't got all day here, for Christ's sake. What's it all about?"

His voice had a real edge to it, so I suppose the old man's sobbing was getting to him the same as it was to me.

"I hate to bother you with this, Inspector," Mancini said, dry-mouthed and shooting occasional glances over at his partner for signs of reassurance, but not getting any. "Only this is the first time I know maybe all this craziness is for real."

"It's cold, Mancini," said Nolan. "Get to the point."

Mancini bent down, then took hold of the sleeves of the old man's coat and flapped them one by one like raggedy flags, all the time looking back up at us over his shoulder. The old man winced each time Mancini touched him, then his sobbing broke off and he gave a soft, short little howl like a dog might make.

"Jesus!" I said.

Nolan gave me a quick look, then frowned down at Mancini.

"Alright," he said, "So the poor bastard hasn't got any arms."

"They end like right here," Mancini said, tapping his own shoulders and looking back and forth from Nolan to me as if he was afraid we might not understand what he was trying to say. "Smooth as a whistle, see? Like his skin was polished. No scars at all. Parkhurst and me, we looked. Didn't we, Parkhurst?"

Parkhurst glared into the street, not saying a word.

"Come on, Parkhurst, goddammit," Mancini shouted at him.

"You got to back me up on this! It's like the poor old shit was born that way, right?"

"Maybe he *was* born that way, Mancini," said Nolan, after a pause. "Babies do get born without arms all the time, these days. It's the price of progress. What's your fucking point?"

Mancini swallowed, then blurted it out.

"That's just it, Inspector," he said, talking in a rush. "We know goddam well he wasn't born that way, Parkhurst and me, because just yesterday we damn near busted him for stealing a couple of pineapples offen the Greeks' vegetable stand down the street there. He run near half a block with those pineapples before we got him, and he was using arms to hold the goddam things, two of them, just like you and me got! Isn't that right, Parkhurst, goddammit?"

Parkhurst only screwed up his mouth a little tighter.

"This has got to be bullshit, Mancini," said Nolan.

"Ask my goddam statue partner, there, if it's bullshit!"

Parkhurst still never looked at us, but I could see his lips move. Then they moved again and we could make his voice out.

"Yeah, alright," he said. "Like Mancini says. He had arms."

Mancini heaved a big sigh of relief and then looked around, justified.

"Alright?" he said. "There it is. The man had arms. They wasn't much, okay? Just like the rest of him. But he had arms. So it means that all these other stories these bums been telling us, maybe they're true."

Nolan was hunched down, now, carefully patting the old man's greasy coat around its shoulders.

"Shit," he said, "there's not even any stumps."

Leavings

I was not happy when I saw the looks on the faces of Officers Mancini and Parkhurst because I could see right off we had a couple of cops way out of their league and floundering, and enough difficult things had already happened to put Inspector Nolan in a bad mood, and here it was only eight-fifteen in the morning.

I drove more or less up to the curb, with a police car you don't have to be all that precise, and Nolan stepped out of the car. He blew on his big hands against the chilly, dirty Eighty-sixth Street wind, crammed them into his pockets when that didn't work, and by then I was standing next to him and we were both looking down at the sobbing man.

He was an old, worn-out bum, hunkered up on a little bit of concrete located just inside the doorway of a failed shop where the two patrolmen had crammed him in order to keep civilians from stepping all over his body. He had a weird, shriveled look, and you could smell the poor bastard from a yard off.

"Alright, Sergeant Mancini," said Nolan, "We haven't got all day here, for Christ's sake. What's it all about?"

His voice had a real edge to it, so I suppose the old man's sobbing was getting to him the same as it was to me.

"I hate to bother you with this, Inspector," Mancini said, dry-mouthed and shooting occasional glances over at his partner for signs of reassurance, but not getting any. "Only this is the first time I know maybe all this craziness is for real."

"It's cold, Mancini," said Nolan. "Get to the point."

Mancini bent down, then took hold of the sleeves of the old man's coat and flapped them one by one like raggedy flags, all the time looking back up at us over his shoulder. The old man winced each time Mancini touched him, then his sobbing broke off and he gave a soft, short little howl like a dog might make.

"Jesus!" I said.

Nolan gave me a quick look, then frowned down at Mancini.

"Alright," he said, "So the poor bastard hasn't got any arms."

"They end like right here," Mancini said, tapping his own shoulders and looking back and forth from Nolan to me as if he was afraid we might not understand what he was trying to say. "Smooth as a whistle, see? Like his skin was polished. No scars at all. Parkhurst and me, we looked. Didn't we, Parkhurst?"

Parkhurst glared into the street, not saying a word.

"Come on, Parkhurst, goddammit," Mancini shouted at him.

"You got to back me up on this! It's like the poor old shit was born that way, right?"

"Maybe he *was* born that way, Mancini," said Nolan, after a pause. "Babies do get born without arms all the time, these days. It's the price of progress. What's your fucking point?"

Mancini swallowed, then blurted it out.

"That's just it, Inspector," he said, talking in a rush. "We know goddam well he wasn't born that way, Parkhurst and me, because just yesterday we damn near busted him for stealing a couple of pineapples offen the Greeks' vegetable stand down the street there. He run near half a block with those pineapples before we got him, and he was using arms to hold the goddam things, two of them, just like you and me got! Isn't that right, Parkhurst, goddammit?"

Parkhurst only screwed up his mouth a little tighter.

"This has got to be bullshit, Mancini," said Nolan.

"Ask my goddam statue partner, there, if it's bullshit!"

Parkhurst still never looked at us, but I could see his lips move. Then they moved again and we could make his voice out.

"Yeah, alright," he said. "Like Mancini says. He had arms."

Mancini heaved a big sigh of relief and then looked around, justified.

"Alright?" he said. "There it is. The man had arms. They wasn't much, okay? Just like the rest of him. But he had arms. So it means that all these other stories these bums been telling us, maybe they're true."

Nolan was hunched down, now, carefully patting the old man's greasy coat around its shoulders.

"Shit," he said, "there's not even any stumps."

The old man sniveled and stared at him with his eyes all round and bulging like a scared little boy's.

"I'm not going to hurt you, old timer," Nolan told him.

The old man studied the Inspector a little longer, then he pulled in a deep, wavering breath to get some air, and spoke.

"They took'm," he wheezed, and I could see Nolan fight not to turn his face from the stink pouring out of the old man's mouth. "They took m'arms!"

"See?" hissed Mancini. "It's the same stuff all these people been telling us, I swear to God. Only it's so crazy we haven't been passing it on, see?"

Nolan sighed.

"Who took your arms, old timer?"

The bum blinked and gaped around with his boiled eyes as if he were trying to spot the answer somewhere on the sidewalk.

"I dunno. I was asleep down there." He bobbed his head toward the nearby subway entrance. "Sleeping by the token booth where it's safe, you know? But it wasn't, 'cause I woke up and m'arms was gone, and it never even hurt. It don't even hurt now, mister."

He blinked and tears spurted out of him.

"Oh Jesus!" he wailed. "Oh Mommy! Was I bad? Is that why they done it? Is that why they took'm?"

"It's just like the other stuff we've been hearing from these people," whispered Mancini, then turned and snapped up at his partner: "Isn't it, Parkhurst, goddammit?"

"Yeah," Parkhurst answered him, after a pause. "Fuck."

"See?" cried Mancini in triumph, backed for a second time. "It's always the same kind of shit, Inspector, but who could be-lieve it?"

Nolan stood, and I could see it was to get away from being that close to the crazy relief in Mancini's face.

"Who the hell could believe some bum telling him he's just missing some part of him, only there's no blood and no scars, for Chrissake?" Mancini asked us, talking a little wilder all the time. "Missing ears, goddam noses—all that. Who's going to believe this sort of shit?"

Parkhurst cleared his throat, still looking away from us.

"One man came up to our car and told us he didn't have his stomach no more," he muttered. "Then he died."

"You think we're going to pass that on to those creeps on the meat wagon?" Mancini asked us, standing. "Say, I tried that once when we picked up this old bag lady working her way right down the middle of Lexington Avenue in front of all the taxis and trucks, dropping her packages and whatever, and she's screaming they stole her eyes! I told them what she said and the son of a bitch really gave it to me, you know? 'She never had no eyes, asshole!' he tells me. Fuck that. Who's going to ask for that?"

Nolan dusted his coat off carefully even though it had never touched the sidewalk, then he turned to Parkhurst.

"You're backing this up, Parkhurst?" he asked.

Parkhurst finally looked over at us.

"Once we came across what we figured was this nut case trying to play a busted guitar for quarters," he said. "He didn't have any fingers or thumbs. His hands was only a pair of little flippers, like a seal. He told us yesterday he could have played us anything we wanted. Another guy he didn't have no inside to his mouth at all. No teeth, no tongue, no nothing."

Nolan stared at him and sighed.

"Once you've got started you're kind of hard to stop, aren't you, Parkhurst?" he said.

"The worst one was this guy who wasn't missing anything at all, see? He had everything. Only the pieces didn't match up," Parkhurst said.

Nolan looked over at me, and I looked back at him, and we both moved in a little closer to Parkhurst, like we were walling him off from the street. Parkhurst didn't notice any of this, but Mancini did, and his eyes widened and he swallowed.

"Tell me about this one," Nolan said. "I really want to hear about this one."

Mancini had gotten all shifty. He took hold of Parkhurst's arm.

"Forget that one," he told his partner. "We was wrong about that one."

"Oh, yeah?" Parkhurst said, jerking his arm away, really angry with Mancini. "The hell we was! You wanted me to tell them about it, so I'll tell them about it!"

He turned back to us.

"We saw him down to the far end of the uptown platform down there in the subway, right? The lower level, where the express trains stop. It was maybe around four in the morning. He was kind of waddling away from us, only he had to move at angles, first this way, then that way, on account of he was all lopsided."

"He's wrong about this," Mancini said, looking at us with a serious expression. "Look, I'll talk to him about this, I promise. I'll look after it."

"You shut up," Parkhurst said to him, and then he turned to us again. "He wouldn't answer to me, this guy, so I took hold of his shoulders, see? And it was awful, I can't tell you why, except one of his shoulders was big and the other was small, and it felt awful. When I got him turned around I saw he wasn't able to talk on account of his head didn't match his neck so the throat couldn't work right. He got enough air for breathing, see? but not enough for talking."

"Hey, fellows, just forget this," Mancini said.

He looked at the Inspector, then at me, then back at the Inspector.

"I'll take care of it," he said, stepping in front of his partner, trying to block him from us. "He hasn't caught on, he's a little slow, Parkhurst, but he's okay, he'll play along. I'll talk to him. It'll be alright."

Nolan had written an address on a slip of paper. He handed it carefully to Mancini.

"You two take the old man to this place," he said to Mancini. "The people there will know what to do. Don't leave the place, alright? That's an order, understand? You be sure to wait until we turn up. Don't go anywhere."

"Say, listen," Mancini said, looking sick. "We don't have to do any of this. We'll just leave the old bastard here where we found him, what the fuck? I mean, who gives a damn about someone like him anyways, right? I'll take care of Parkhurst, Inspector, I swear to God. *There won't be any problem!*"

It was too late for all that because we were back in the car, now, Nolan and me, and I'd already started the engine. Parkhurst, standing in back of Mancini, was looking confused. I started the car rolling and Mancini reached out like he wanted to take hold of it and stop it, but of course he knew that wouldn't help at all, and so when we drove off he was just holding his hands up there in the air in front of him, touching nothing.

The first time Reginald Archer saw the thing, it was, in its simplicity, absolute. It owned not the slightest complication or involvement. It lacked the tiniest, the remotest, the most insignificant trace of embellishment. It looked like this:

A spot. Nothing more. Black, as you see, somewhat lopsided, as you see—an unprepossessing, unpretentious spot.

It was located on Reginald Archer's dazzlingly white linen tablecloth, on his breakfast table, three and one half inches from the side of his egg cup. Reginald Archer was in the act of opening the egg in the egg cup when he saw the spot.

He paused and frowned. Reginald Archer was a bachelor,

had been one for his full forty-three years, and he was fond of a smoothly running household. Things like black spots on table linens displeased him, perhaps beyond reason. He rang the bell to summon his butler, Faulks.

That worthy entered and, seeing the dark expression upon his master's face, approached his side with caution. He cleared his throat, bowed ever so slightly, just exactly the right amount of bow, and, following the direction of his master's thin, pale, pointing finger, observed, in his turn, the spot.

"What," asked Archer, "is *this* doing here?"

Faulks, after a moment's solemn consideration, owned he had no idea how the spot had come to be there, apologized profusely for its presence, and promised its imminent and permanent removal. Archer stood, the egg left untasted in its cup, his appetite quite gone, and left the room.

It was Archer's habit to retire every morning to his study and there tend to any little chores of correspondence and finance which had accumulated. His approach to this, as to everything else, was precise to the point of being ritualistic; he liked to arrange his days in reliable, predictable patterns. He had seated himself at his desk, a lovely affair of lustrous mahogany, and was reaching for the mail which had been tidily stacked for his perusal, when, on the green blotter which entirely covered the desk's working surface, he saw:

He paled, I do not exaggerate, and rang once more for his butler. There was a pause, a longer pause than would usually have occurred, before the trustworthy Faulks responded to his master's summons. The butler's face bore a recognizable confusion.

"The spot, sir—" Faulks began, but Archer cut him short.

"Bother the spot," he snapped, indicating the offense on the blotter. "What is *this*?"

Faulks peered at the ◖ in bafflement.

"I do not know, sir," he said. "I have never seen anything quite like it."

"Nor have I," said Archer. "Nor do I wish to see its likes again. Have it removed."

Faulks began to carefully take away the blotter, sliding it out from the leather corner grips which held it to the desk, as Archer watched him icily. Then, for the first time, Archer noticed his elderly servant's very odd expression. He recalled Faulks' discontinued comment.

"What is it you were trying to tell me, then?" he asked.

The butler glanced up at him, hesitated, and then spoke.

"It's about the spot, sir," he said. "The one on the table-cloth. I went to look at it, after you had left, sir, and, I cannot understand it, sir—it was *gone*!"

"Gone?" asked Archer.

"Gone," said Faulks.

The butler glanced down at the blotter, which he now held before him, and started.

"And so is *this*, sir!" he gasped, and, turning round the blotter, revealed it to be innocent of the slightest trace of a ◖.

Conscious, now, that something very much out of the ordinary was afoot, Archer gazed thoughtfully into space. Faulks, watching, observed the gaze suddenly harden into focus.

"Look over there, Faulks," said Archer, in a quiet tone. "Over yonder, at the wall."

Faulks did as he was told, wondering at his master's instructions. Then comprehension dawned, for there, on the wallpaper, directly under an indifferent seascape, was:

Archer stood, and the two men crossed the room.

"What can it be, sir?" asked Faulks.

"I can't imagine," said Archer.

He turned to speak, but when he saw his butler's eyes move to his, he looked quickly back at the wall. Too late—the was gone.

"It needs constant observation," Archer murmured, then, aloud: "Look for it, Faulks. Look for it. And when you see it, *don't take your eyes from it for a second!*"

They walked about the room in an intensive search. They had not been at it for more than a moment when Faulks gave an exclamation.

"Here, sir!" he cried. "On the window sill!"

Archer hurried to his side and saw:

"Don't let it out of your sight!" he hissed.

As the butler stood, transfixed and gaping, his master chewed furiously at the knuckles of his left hand. Whatever the thing was, it must be taken care of, and promptly. He would not allow such continued disruption in his house.

But how to get rid of it? He shifted to the knuckles of his other hand and thought. The thing had, he hated to admit it, but there it was, *supernatural* overtones. Perhaps it was some beastly sort of ghost.

He shoved both hands, together with their attendant knuckles, into his pants pockets. It showed the extreme state of his agitation, for he loathed nothing more than unsightly bulges in a well-cut suit. Who would know about this sort of thing? Who could possibly handle it?

It came to him in a flash—Sir Harry Mandifer! Of course! He'd known Sir Harry back at school, only plain Harry, then, of course, and now they shared several clubs. Harry had taken to writing, made a good thing of it, and now, with piles of money to play with, he'd taken to spiritualism, become, perhaps, the top authority in the field. Sir Harry was just the man! If *only* he could persuade him.

His face set in grimly determined lines, Archer marched to his telephone and dialed Sir Harry's number. It was not so easy to get through to him as it had been in the old days. Now there were secretaries, suspicious and secretive. But he was known, that made all the difference, and soon he and Sir Harry were together on the line. After the customary greetings and small talk, Archer brought the conversation around to the business at hand. Crisply, economically, he described the morning's events. Could Sir Harry find it possible to come? He fancied that time might be an important factor. Sir Harry would! Archer thanked him with all the warmth his somewhat constricted personality would allow, and, with a heartfelt sigh of relief, put back the receiver.

He had barely done it when he heard Faulks give a small cry of despair. He turned to see the old fellow wringing his hands in abject misery.

"I just blinked, sir!" he quavered. "Only blinked!"

It had been enough. A fraction of a second unwatched, and the was gone from the sill.

Resignedly, they once again took up the search.

Sir Harry Mandifer settled back comfortably in the cushioned seat of his limousine and congratulated himself on settling the business of Marston Rectory the night before. It would not have done to leave that dangerous affair in the lurch, but the bones of the Mewing Nun had been found at last, and now she would rest peacefully in a consecrated grave. No more would headless children decorate the Cornish landscape, no more would the nights resound with mothers' lamentations. He had done his job, done it well, and now he was free to investigate what sounded a perfectly charming mystery.

Contentedly, the large man lit a cigar and watched the streets go sliding by. Delicious that a man as cautious and organized as poor old Archer should find himself confronted with something so outrageous. It only showed you that the tidiest lives have nothing but quicksand for a base. The snuggest haven's full of trap doors and sliding panels, unsuspected attics and suddenly discovered rooms. Why should the careful Archer find himself exempt? And he hadn't.

The limousine drifted to a gentle stop before Archer's house and Mandifer, emerging from his car, gazed up at the building with pleasure. It was a gracious Georgian structure which had been in Archer's family since the time of its construction. Mandifer mounted its steps and was about to apply himself to its knocker when the door flew open and he found himself facing a desperately agitated Faulks.

"Oh, sir," gasped the butler, speaking in piteous tones, "I'm so glad you could come! We don't know what to make of it, sir, and we can't hardly keep track of it, it moves so fast!"

"There, Faulks, there," rumbled Sir Harry, moving smoothly into the entrance with the unstoppable authority of a great clipper ship under full sail. "It can't be as bad as all that, now, can it?"

"Oh, it can, sir, it can," said Faulks, following in Mandifer's wake down the hall. "You just can't get a *hold* on it, sir, is what it is, and every time it's back, it's *bigger,* sir!"

"In the study, isn't it?" asked Sir Harry, opening the door of that room and gazing inside.

He stood stock still and his eyes widened a trifle because the sight before him, even for one so experienced in peculiar sights as he, was startling.

Imagine a beautiful room, exquisitely furnished, impeccably maintained. Imagine the occupant of that room to be a thin, tallish gentleman, dressed faultlessly, in the best possible taste. Conceive of the whole thing, man and room in combination, to be a flawless example of the sort of styled perfection that only large amounts of money, filtered through generations of confident privilege, can produce.

Now see that man on his hands and knees, in one of the room's corners, staring, bug-eyed, at the wall, and, on the wall, picture:

"Remarkable," said Sir Harry Mandifer.

"Isn't it, sir?" moaned Faulks. "Oh, isn't it?"

"I'm so glad you could come, Sir Harry," said Archer, from his crouched position in the corner. It was difficult to make out his words as he spoke them through clenched teeth. "Forgive me for not rising, but if I take my eyes off this thing, or even blink, the whole—oh, God *damn* it!"

Instantly, the

vanished from the wall. Archer gave out an explosive sigh, clapped his hands to his face, and sat back heavily on the floor.

"Don't tell me where it's got to, now, Faulks," he said, "I don't want to know; I don't want to hear about it."

Faulks said nothing, only touched a trembling hand on Sir Harry's shoulder and pointed to the ceiling. There, almost directly in its center, was:

Sir Harry leaned his head close to Faulks' ear and whispered: "Keep looking at it for as long as you can, old man. Try not to let it get away." Then in his normal, conversational tone, which was a kind of cheerful roar, he spoke to Archer: "Seems you have a bit of a sticky problem here, what?"

Archer looked up grimly from between his fingers. Then, carefully, he lowered his arms and stood. He brushed himself off, made a few adjustments of his coat and tie, and spoke:

"I'm sorry, Sir Harry. I'm afraid I rather let it get the better of me."

"No such thing!" boomed Sir Harry Mandifer, clapping Archer on the back. "Besides, it's enough to rattle anyone. Gave me quite a turn, myself, and I'm used to this sort of nonsense!"

Sir Harry had developed his sturdy technique of encouragement during many a campaign in haunted house and ghost-ridden moor, and it did not fail him now. Archer's return to self-possession was almost immediate. Satisfied at the restoration, Sir Harry looked up at the ceiling.

"You say it started as a kind of spot?" he asked, peering at the dark thing which spread above them.

"About as big as a penny," answered Archer.

"What have the stages been like, between then and now?"

"Little bits come out of it. They get bigger, and, at the same time, other little bits come popping out, and, as if that weren't enough, the whole ghastly thing keeps *swelling,* like some damned balloon."

"Nasty," said Sir Harry.

"I'd say it's gotten to be a yard across," said Archer.

"At least."

"What do you make of it, Sir Harry?"

"It looks to me like a sort of plant."

Both the butler and Archer gaped at him. The

instantly disappeared.

"I'm sorry, sir," said the butler, stricken.

"What do you mean, **plant**?" asked Archer. "It can't be a plant, Harry. It's perfectly flat, for one thing."

"Have you touched it?"

Archer sniffed.

"Not very likely," he said.

Discreetly, the butler cleared his throat.

"It's on the floor, gentlemen," he said.

The three   looked down at the   thing with re-
flectful expressions. Its longest reach was now a little over
four feet.

"You'll notice," said Sir Harry, "that the texture of the carpet does not show through the blackness, therefore it's not
like ink, or some other stain. It has an independent surface."

He stooped down, surprisingly graceful for a man of his
size, and, pulling a pencil from his pocket, poked at the thing.
The pencil went into the darkness for about a quarter of an
inch, and then stopped. He jabbed at another point, this time
penetrating a good full inch.

"You see," said Sir Harry, standing. "It does have a complex kind of shape. Our eyes can perceive it only in a two-
dimensional way, but the sense of touch moves it along to the
third. The obvious implication of all this length, width, and
breadth business is that your plant's drifted in from some
other dimensional set, do you see? I should imagine the original spot was its seed. Am I making myself clear on all this? Do
you understand?"

Archer did not, quite, but he gave a reasonably good imitation of a man who had.

"But why did the accursed thing show up here?" he asked.

Sir Harry seemed to have the answer for that one, too, but Faulks interrupted it, whatever it may have been, and we shall never know it.

"Oh, sir," he cried. "It's gone, again!"

It was, indeed. The carpet stretched unblemished under the three men's feet. They looked about the room, somewhat anxiously now, but could find no trace of the invader.

"Perhaps it's gone back into the dining room," said Sir Harry, but a search revealed that it had not.

"There is no reason to assume it must confine itself to the two rooms," said Sir Harry, thoughtfully chewing his lip. "Nor even to the house, itself."

Faulks, standing closer to the hallway door than the others, tottered slightly, and emitted a strangled sound. The others turned and looked where the old man pointed. There, stretching across the striped paper of the hall across from the door was:

"This is," Archer said, in a choked voice, "*really* a bit too much, Sir Harry. Something simply must be done or the damned thing will take over the whole bloody house!"

"Keep your eyes fixed on it, Faulks," said Sir Harry, "at all costs." He turned to Archer. "It has substance, I have proven that. It can be attacked. Have you some large cutting instrument about the place? A machete? Something like that?"

Archer pondered, then brightened, in a grim sort of way.

"I have a kris," he said.

"Get it," said Sir Harry.

Archer strode from the room, clenching and unclenching his hands. There was a longish pause, and then his voice called from another room:

"I can't get the blasted thing off its mounting!"

"I'll come and help," Sir Harry answered. He turned to Faulks, who was pointing at the thing on the wall like some loyal bird dog. "Never falter, old man," he said. "Keep your gaze rock steady!"

The kris, an old war souvenir brought to the house by Archer's grandfather, was fixed to its display panel by a complicatedly woven arrangement of wires, and it took Sir Harry and Archer a good two minutes to get it free. They hurried back to the hall and there jarred to a halt, absolutely thunderstruck. The

was nowhere to be seen, but that was not the worst— the butler, Faulks, was gone! Archer and Sir Harry exchanged startled glances and then called the servant's name, again and again, with no effect whatever.

"What can it be, Sir Harry?" asked Archer. "What, in God's name, has happened?"

Sir Harry Mandifer did not reply. He grasped the kris before him, his eyes darting this way and that, and Archer, to his horror, saw that the man was trembling where he stood. Then, with a visible effort of will, Sir Harry pulled himself together and assumed, once more, his usual staunch air.

"We must find it, Archer," he said, his chin thrust out. "We must find it and we must kill it. We may not have another chance if it gets away, again!"

Sir Harry leading the way, the two men covered the ground floor, going from room to room, but found nothing. A search of the second also proved futile.

"Pray God," said Sir Harry, mounting to the floor above, "the creature has not quit the house."

Archer, now short of breath from simple fear, climbed unsteadily after.

"Perhaps it's gone back where it came from, Sir Harry," he said.

"Not now," the other answered grimly. "Not after Faulks. I think it's found it likes our little world."

"But what *is* it?" asked Archer.

"It's what I said it was—a plant," replied the large man, opening a door and peering into the room revealed. "A special kind of plant. We have them here, in our dimension."

At this point, Archer understood. Sir Harry opened another door, and then another, with no success. There was the attic left. They went up the narrow steps, Sir Harry in the lead, his kris held high before him. Archer, by now, was barely able to drag himself along by the bannister. His breath came in tiny whimpers.

"A meat-eater, isn't it?" he whispered. "*Isn't* it, Sir Harry?"

Sir Harry Mandifer took his hand from the knob of the small door and turned to look down at his companion.

"That's right, Archer," he said, the door swinging open, all unnoticed, behind his back. "The thing's a carnivore."

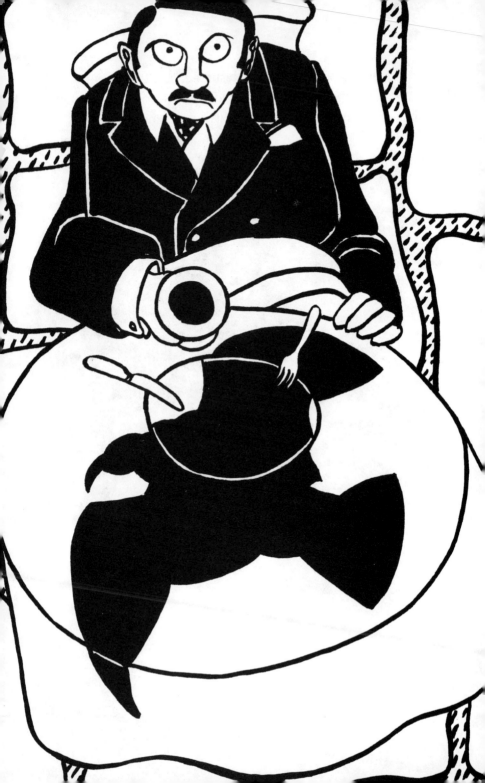

Sea Gulls

have been sitting here, throughout this entire morning, watching the gulls watching me. They come, a small group at a time, carefully unnoticeable, and squat on various branches of a large tree opposite the hotel veranda. When each shift of them have gaped their fill of me, they fly away and their places are taken at once by others of their disgusting species.

Outside of their orderly coming and going, the deportment of these feathered spectators of my discomfort has been calculatedly devoid of anything which might excite the attention of anyone lacking my particular and special knowledge of their loathsome kind. Their demeanor has been more than ordinarily ordinary. They are on their best behavior, now that they have sealed my doom.

I stumbled on their true nature, and I curse the day I did,

by a complete fluke. It was, ironically, Geraldine herself who called my attention to that little army of them on the beach.

We had been sitting side by side on a large, sun-warmed rock, I in a precise but somewhat Redonesque pose, Geraldine in her usual, space-occupying, sprawl. I was deep in a poetic revery, reflecting on the almost alchemical transition of sand to water to sky while Geraldine, my wife, was absorbed in completely finishing off the sumptuous but rather overlarge picnic the hotel staff had prepared for our outing, when she abruptly straightened, a half-consumed jar of *pâté* clutched forgotten in her greasy fingers, and suddenly emitted that barking coo of hers which never has never failed to simultaneously startle and annoy me throughout all the years of our marriage.

"Hughie, look!" she cried. "The gulls are marching!"

"What do you mean, 'marching'?" I asked, doing what I could to conceal my annoyance.

"I mean they're marching, Hughie," she said. "I mean they *are* marching!"

I looked where she pointed, the *pâté* jar still in her hand, and a vague complaint died unspoken on my lips as I observed that Geraldine had been scrupulously correct in her announcement. The gulls were, indeed, marching.

Their formation was about ten files wide and some forty ranks deep, and it was well held, with no raggedness about the edges. A line of five or so officer gulls marched at the army's head, and one solitary gull, I assumed their general, marched ahead of them.

The gull general was considerably larger than the other birds, and he had an imposing, eaglelike bearing to him. His army was obviously well drilled, for all the gulls marched in perfect step on their orange claws, and seemed capable of neatly executing endless elaborate maneuvers.

Geraldine and I watched, fascinated, for as long as ten minutes, observing the creatures wheeling about, splitting and rejoining, and carrying out whole routines of complicated, weaving patterns. The display was so astoundingly absorbing that it took me quite some time to realize the fantastic impropriety of the whole proceeding, but at last it dawned on me.

"This will never do," I observed in a firm, quiet tone, and carefully placing my cigar on the edge of the rock, I selected a large, smooth stone and hefted it in my hand.

"Hughie!" Geraldine cried, observing the rock and the look of grim determination on my face. "What are you planning to do?"

"We must discourage this sort of thing the instant we see it," I said. "We must nip it in the bud."

I shot the stone into their midst and they scattered, squawking in a highly satisfactory fashion. I threw another stone, this one rather pointy, and had the pleasure of striking the general smartly on his rear. I turned to Geraldine, expecting words of praise, but of course I should have known better.

"You should not hurt dumb animals," she said, regarding me gently but mournfully as a mother might regard a backward child. "Look, you have made that big one limp!"

"Gulls are birds, not animals," I pointed out. "And their behavior was far from dumb. It was, if you ask me, altogether too smart."

My cigar had gone out so I lit another one, using the gold lighter she had given me a day or so before, and I was so piqued at her that I was tempted to ostentatiously throw it away as casually as I would a match, but she would only have forgiven me with a little sigh and bought me another. I would only be like an infant knocking objects off the tray of his high chair, its bowls and cups replaced with loving care. I had learned, through the years, that there really was no way to get one's rage through to Geraldine.

That night, as we were having dinner on the terrace of the hotel, Geraldine stared out into the darkness and once again drew my attention to an odd action on the part of the gulls. This time her tiny little bark caught me with a spoonful of consommé halfway to my lips, and when I started at the sudden sound, a shimmering blob of the stuff tumbled back into the bowl with a tiny plop.

"The gulls, Hughie," she said, in a loud, dramatic whisper as she reached out and tightly clutched my arm. "See how they are staring at you!"

I frowned at her.

"Gulls?" I said. "It's night, my dear. One doesn't see gulls at night. They go somewhere."

But then I peered where she had pointed, and I saw that once again she was right. There, in the branches of the tree which I have mentioned before, were in view perhaps as many as thirty gulls staring at us, or more precisely at me, with their cold, beady little eyes.

"There must be hundreds of them!" she whispered. "They're everywhere!"

Again she was quite correct. The creatures were not only in the tree, they were perched on railings, stone vases, the heads of statues, and all the various other accoutrements with which a first-class, traditional French seaboard hotel is wont to litter its premises. They were all, to the last gull among them, staring steadily and unblinkingly at me.

"Do you think," I whispered very quietly to Geraldine, "that anyone else has noticed?"

"I don't believe so," she said, and turned to openly study the people sitting at neighboring tables. "Should we ask them if they have?"

"For God's sake, no!" I said, in a harsh whisper. "What do you think it looks like—being singled out by crowds of gulls to be stared at? How do you think it makes me *feel*?"

"Of course, Hughie," she said, loosing her hold on my arm and patting my hand. "Don't you worry, dearest. We shall just pretend it isn't happening."

Halfway through the wretched dinner the gulls flew off for mysterious reasons of their own, and when it was through I made my excuses and left my wife to attend to herself while I took a thoughtful little stroll.

I had some time ago sketched out the broad design of what I intended to do during our visit to this hotel, had, indeed, begun to plan it the very day Geraldine suggested we come here to celebrate our wedding anniversary, because it had dawned on me fatally and completely and quite irreversibly, even as she spoke, that we had already celebrated far too many anniversaries and that this one should definitely be our last.

But now it was time to put in the fine details, the small, delicate strokes which would spell the difference between disaster and success. Eliminating Geraldine would serve very little purpose if I did not survive the act to enjoy her money afterward.

I wandered down to the canopied pier where I knew the hotel moored several brightly painted little rowboats, and even a couple of dwarfish sailboats, for the use of their guests. I knew full well that the sailboats would strike Geraldine as being far too adventurous, so I concentrated on examining the rowboats.

I was pleasantly surprised to discover that they were even more unseaworthy than I'd dared to hope. I quietly tested them, one after the other, and found that the boat at the end of the pier, a jaunty little thing with a puce hull and a bright gold stripe running around its sides, was especially dangerous. I felt absolutely confident the police would have no trouble at all in convincing themselves that any drowning fatality associated with this highly tippy boat had been the result of a tragic accident.

Just to make sure—I have been accused of being something of a perfectionist—I climbed into the tiny craft, pretended I was rowing, and then suddenly made a move to one side. The boat came so close to capsizing that I had considerable difficulty avoiding unexpectedly tumbling out of it then and there! I exited the craft carefully, with even more respect for its deadliness, and started walking up the path leading back to the hotel, whistling a little snatch of a Chopin mazurka softly to myself as I went.

The path took a turn by a kind of miniature cliff, which concealed it from almost all points of view, and when I reached this point the mazurka died on my lips as I saw that the ground before me was lumpy and grayish in the moonlight as though it was infested with some sort of disgusting mold, but then I peered closer and saw that the place was horribly carpeted with the softly stirring bodies of countless sea gulls.

They were crowded together, so tightly packed that there was absolutely no space between them, and every one of them was glaring up at me. The menace emanating from their hundreds of tiny eyes was, at the same time, both ridiculous and totally terrifying. It was also positively sickening, and for a brief, absolutely ghastly moment I was afraid that I would faint and fall and be suffocated in the soft, feathery sea of them.

However, I took several very deep breaths and managed to still the pounding in my ears and to steady myself. With great casualness, very slowly and deliberately, I reached into my breast pocket and withdrew a cigar. I lit the cigar and blew a contemptuous puff of smoke at the enormous crowd of gulls at my feet.

"You have exceeded your position in life," I told them, speaking softly and calmly. "You have overstepped your natural authority. But I am on to you."

I drew on the cigar carefully, increasing its ash, and when I'd produced a good half inch, I tapped the cigar so that the ash fell directly and humiliatingly on the top of the head of the remarkably large gull standing directly in front of me. Of course I had recognized him as the general. He did not stir or blink; nor did any of the others. They continued to glare up at me.

"Whereas you are merely birds," I continued, "and scavenger birds at that, *I* am a human being. I am not only smarter than you are, I am stronger. If you attack me, I will simply shield my eyes with my arm and walk away, and soon other humans will see me and come to my aid."

I took another long pull at my cigar and looked away from them, as if bored.

"I guarantee you," I went on, "that I will not panic. I will survive, merely scratched, to see that you, and a great number of your kin, pay dearly for attacking your betters. Pay painfully. Pay with your lives."

I paused a little in order that my words might sink into their narrow little heads, and then I began to walk casually along the clearing path, gazing upward and smoking dreamily as I did so. I did not even watch to see how they slunk, in cowed confusion, out of my way.

The next morning, during breakfast, while I was having my second coffee and Geraldine her second herbal tea, I proposed brightly that we take a short row in the cove. I approached the whole thing in a very airy, casual fashion, but made it clear I would be saddened and a little hurt if she did not accept my whimsical invitation. Naturally I knew the whole idea would strike her as childish and that she would do it only to indulge me. She, herself, would never dream of instigating anything childish, of course. That, in our marriage, was understood to be my function.

To my relief—one never knew with Geraldine, never—she accepted with almost no perceptible hesitation. She even suggested we do it without further ado, seeing as how the sun was bright and the waters of the cove presently smooth and placid. We rose from the table and went directly to the gaily beflagged pier.

We were the first arrivals for water sports that morning and the little puce boat with its gold stripe bobbed fetchingly as it waited for us in the water. In a rather neat piece of seamanship, I managed to get both Geraldine and myself aboard it without her realizing how tiltable a craft it was. Smiling and chatting about how extremely pleasant everything was, I rowed us to an isolated part of the cove behind a rise of the shore which put us out of sight of our fellow vacationers.

Once I had reached this point I let go of the oars, took firm hold of the sides of the boat, and gave it the tipping motion I had practiced with such great success the night before. I was highly discomfited to discover that the little craft had somehow achieved a new seaworthiness.

"Hughie," she asked, "What on earth are you trying to do?"

I looked up at her, perhaps just a little wild-eyed, and suddenly realized that it must be Geraldine's considerable bulk which was stabilizing the boat. I would have to exert a good deal more effort if I was to upset it successfully. I began to shake the boat again, this time with markedly increased determination. I was uncomfortably aware that I had begun to sweat noticeably and that damp blotches were beginning to spread from the armpits of my striped blazer.

"Hughie," she said, a vague alarm starting to dawn in her eyes. "Whatever you are doing, you must stop it now!"

I glared at her and began to shake the boat with a new energy verging on desperation.

"I've asked you not to call me Hughie," I told her, through clenched teeth. "For *years* I've asked you not to call me Hughie!"

She frowned at me, just a little uncertainly, and had opened her mouth to say something further when, with a gratifyingly smooth, swooping motion, the little puce boat finally tilted over.

For a moment all was blue confusion and bubbles, but then my head broke water and I saw the boat bobbing upside down on the sparkling surface of the cove a yard or two away from me. There was no sign whatsoever of Geraldine so I ducked my head down under the water, peered this way and that, and was pleased to observe a dim, sinking flurry of skirts and kicking feet speedily disappearing into the darker blues far below the bright and cheery green hues flickering just under the surface.

I swam up to the little inverted craft, took hold of it, surveyed the coastline to see if it was empty of witnesses, and saw this was, indeed, the case. Several gulls were circling overhead, but when I glared up at them and shook my fist in their direction, they flew away with an almost furtive air. I cried for help once or twice for effect, then pushed off from the side of the boat and swam for the shore where I staggered, gasping, up onto the hotel grounds into the view of my astonished fellow guests.

At first the investigation proceeded almost exactly along the lines I had envisioned it would. The general reaction toward me was, of course, one of great pity and everyone, the police included, treated me quite gently. It never appeared to occur to anyone that the business was anything other than a tragic accident.

But then things began to take an increasingly odd turning as the authorities, after a highly confident commencement, found themselves unable to locate Geraldine's cadaver, and by the time I was judged able to sit warmly wrapped on the veranda and overlook their activities, they had become seriously discouraged.

I watched them as they carefully and conscientiously trailed their hooks and nets up and down the cove and in the waters beyond, observing their scuba divers bob and sink repeatedly to no effect, and seeing them all grow increasingly philosophical as Geraldine's large body continued to evade them. There was more and more talk of riptides and rapid ocean currents and prior total vanishments.

Toward the end of this period I was on the veranda con-
suming a particularly subtle *crêpes fruits de mer,* and rather
regretting the repast had almost come to an end, when the
chain of events began which have led to my present distasteful predicament.

Startled by a sudden flurry of noise, I looked up to see a
large bird perched on the railing, which I had no difficulty in
recognizing as the general of the gulls. As I gaped at the creature, he hopped from his perch over to my table, gave me a
fierce glare, dropped something which landed with a clink
upon my plate, and then flew away emitting maniacal, gullish
bursts of laughter.

When I saw what the disgusting beast had dropped amidst
the remains of my *crêpes* my appetite departed completely
and has not, to be frank, ever been quite the same since. I recognized the object instantly for what it was—the wedding ring
I had given my late wife—but to be absolutely sure, I rubbed
the ring's interior clear of sauce with my napkin and read what
she had caused to be engraved there years ago: "Geraldine
and Hughie, forever!"

I carefully wiped the remaining sauce from the ring, and
deposited it in the pocket of my jacket. I heard another burst
of crazed, avian laughter and, looking up, observed the general of the gulls leering at me from a far railing of the veranda.
I determinedly returned to my *crêpes* and made a great show
of appearing to enjoy the remainder of my dinner, even to the
extent of having an extra *café filtre* after dessert. I then
strolled in a languid fashion down to the beach for a little con-
stitutional before retiring.

It was a quiet, clear night. The Mediterranean was smooth
and silvery under the full moon, and its waves rolled softly

and almost soundlessly into the sand. I gazed up at the sky, checking it for birds, and when I was absolutely sure there were none to be seen, I threw the ring out over the water with all the strength I could muster.

Imagine my astonishment when with a great rush of air the general of the gulls soared out over my shoulder from behind me and, executing what I must admit was a remarkably skillful and accurate dive, reached out with his orange claws and plucked the ring from the air inches above the surface of the water. Emitting a final, lunatic laugh of triumph, he flew up into the moonlight and out of sight.

That night I was awakened from a very troubled sleep by a sound extremely difficult to describe. It was a soft, steady, rhythmic patting, and put me so much in mind of a demented audience enthusiastically applauding with heavily mittened hands that as I pushed back my covers and lurched to my feet in the darkness of my room, my still half-dreaming mind produced such a vivid vision of a madly clapping throng in some asylum auditorium that I could observe, with remarkable clarity, the various desperate grimaces on the faces of the nearer inmates.

I groped my way to the curtains, since the sound seemed to emanate from that direction, and when I pulled them aside and looked out the window a muffled shriek tore itself from my lips and I staggered back and almost fell to the carpet, for I had suddenly given myself all too clear a view of the source of that weird, nocturnal racket.

There, hanging in the air in the moonlight directly outside my window was the large, sagging body of my wife, Geraldine. She looked huge, positively enormous, like some kind of horrible balloon. Water poured copiously in silvery fountains from her white lace dress, and her bulging eyes, also entirely white, gaped out like prisoners staring through the dark, lank strands of hair which hung down in glistening bars across her dripping, bloated face.

The sound I had heard was being made by the wings of the hundreds of gulls who were holding Geraldine aloft by means of their claws and beaks, which they had sunk deeply into her skin and dress, both of which seemed to be stretching dangerously near to the ripping point. She was surrounded by a nimbus of the awful creatures, each one flapping its wings in perfect rhythm with its neighbors in a miracle of cooperative effort.

Sitting on her head, his claws digging almost covetously into her brow, was the gull general. For a long moment, he watched me staring at him and at the tableau he had wrought with obvious satisfaction and then he must have given some command for the gulls began to move in unison and the lolling, pale bulk of Geraldine swayed backward from the window and then, lifted by the beating of gleaming, multitudinous wings, it wafted upward and inland, over the dark tiles of the roof of the hotel and out of my line of vision.

I had breakfast brought up to my room the next morning for I anticipated, quite correctly as it turned out, a potentially awkward visit from the police and preferred it to take place in reasonable private surroundings.

I had barely finished my first cup of coffee and half a brioche when they arrived, shuffling into my room with an air of obvious uncertainty, the inspector looking at me with the downward, shifting gaze which authority tends to adopt when it is not quite sure it is authority.

It seemed that a local farmer hunting just after dawn for

a strayed cow had come across the body of Geraldine. It had been tucked into a small culvert on his property and rather ineffectually covered with branches and leaves and little clods of earth. One particularly unpleasant feature about the corpse was that it had been brutally stripped of the jewelry which Geraldine had been seen to be wearing that morning. Her fingers and wrists and neck had been deeply scratched by the thief or thieves who had clawed her gold from her, and the lobes of both her ears had been cruelly torn.

The police could not have been more courteous with me. Their community's main source of income originates from well-to-do vacationers, and the arrest and possible execution of one of them—myself, for instance—because of murder would be bound to produce all sorts of unfortunate and discouraging publicity. They were vastly relieved at the taking of Geraldine's baubles since it suggested not only the sort of common robber they could easily understand and pursue enthusiastically, it gave their imagined culprit a clear motive for spiriting the body away from the water and later trying to hide it.

Taking my cue from them, I confessed myself astonished and saddened to learn that my wife's drowned corpse had been so grossly violated and wished them luck in apprehending the villain responsible as soon as possible. The lot of us, from differing motives, were considerably pleased to have the affair resolved so amicably, and after shaking hands all around and giving them permission to look over my suite—an action understood by us all to be a mere formality—I took my leave of them and assumed my present situation on the veranda.

Just now I've noticed that in the midst of the latest shift of gulls taking their places to observe me from the overlooking tree is the general himself, and since I gather that signifies something of considerable import is about to transpire, I've cast a sidewise glance at the doors opening out onto the terrace from the hotel's lobby.

Sure enough, I see the approaching police, all of them wearing expressions of unhappiness and great regret. Worse, I see the unmistakable glint of gold in the inspector's cupped hands. The gulls obviously paid another, quieter, visit to my rooms last night in order to leave my dead wife's pretty things behind in some craftily selected hiding place. Perhaps the general did it personally. It would be like him.

Now I have risen, a *demitasse* held lightly in one hand, and strolled slowly over to the railing of the veranda. There is a considerable drop to the rocks below and if I tumble directly from here to there it will surely put a quick and effective end to a very rapidly developing unpleasant situation so far as I am concerned.

I have stepped up onto the railing, which is a very solid structure built wide enough to hold trays of nightcaps or canapés and any number of leaning lovers' elbows. The police are calling out to me in rather frantic tones and I hear the soles of their large shoes scuffling and scraping on the stones of the veranda as they rush desperately in my direction.

My eyes and the general's are firmly locked as I step out into space. He lifts his wings and, with an easy beat or two, he rises from his branch.

Our paths cross in midair.

He can fly, but I can only fall.

The Casino Mirago

At the end of a very long chain of many things gone most astonishingly wrong I found myself booked out of season under an assumed name in the grandest suite of a Hotel Splendide located on the coast of Portugal.

My luggage, clothing, and papers effectively proclaimed me to be a minor member of an ancient family of power which had the very good fortune not only to have retained the bulk of its wealth, but to have added considerably to it as the centuries had passed.

The contents of my briefcase, an extravagant amount of money in various denominations and currencies and a stack of passports bearing different names, indicated my actual situation rather more directly. I was, in fact, a desperate fugitive trying to avoid the police of a number of different countries.

I had spent the last several weeks dodging across Europe, hiding out in the obscure, ofttimes exceptionally dismal sort of nooks and crannies favored by criminals on the lam. I was both physically and mentally exhausted and felt I had run completely out of feasible options.

I was quite literally at my wits' end and, to put it bluntly, had chosen this extravagant suite as a suicide site because I had no intention of letting the triumphant authorities discover my pathetic corpse in the sort of rat hole I had lately been frequenting.

After the porter had hung my clothes and stashed my bags I sat alone on the silken coverlet of my vast bed and contemplated the small bottle of poison I had acquired in Berlin, regarding it with something very close to affection. I had been assured it was not only instant and foolproof but that it actually possessed a rather pleasant strawberry flavor which I might enjoy in that tiny microsecond my taste buds functioned before the stuff did me in.

I uncorked the little container and had half raised it to my lips when it occurred to me that the combination of my owning this fatal elixir and my complete willingness to use it put me very effectively beyond the reach of the law. I need only conceal it about my person in some accessible fashion and I would have the means of instantly escaping any approaching official agent, even if he'd come close enough to clap his hand upon my shoulder.

After shining over me for a moment like the depiction of a heaven-sent ray in an El Greco painting of a newly inspired saint, this simple insight wafted me into a remarkably improved frame of mind.

I sang some of my favorite songs as I took a very pleasant shower, the poison bottle resting next to a bar of delicately scented soap provided by the hotel, and washed the real and imagined grime of my recent flight from my tired body and let the water's warmth ease the tension somewhat from my muscles. I then dressed for dinner, clipping the bottle neatly behind my left lapel, sauntered down the broad marble staircase to the ground floor, and settled myself comfortably in the Splendide's elegant little salon.

If one is of a quiet frame of mind, there is an undeniable charm about luxury resorts when they are thoroughly out of season. True, the weather tends to be on the dark, wet side, and diverting activities are decidedly at a minimum, but the visitor is compensated by an enormous increase in attention on the part of the staff, and there is something soothing about sharing the facilities with a small handful of people whose schedule is pretty much a matter of their own choosing rather than a great, milling multitude who must take their vacations *en masse* as dictated by various middle-class considerations.

I gazed unobtrusively over my apéritif at the little group presently seated in the salon and decided they were an excellent example of the sort of people one encounters in such places when the seasonal types are forced to labor in their offices and banks. They were all interesting to look on and to speculate upon, and a number of them possessed unusual, not to mention downright eccentric attributes which promised much in the way of diversion and entertainment.

The most immediately noticeable person present was an elegant elderly woman whose large, pale neck and arms were beautifully and amply bejeweled and whose brilliantly white hair was magnificently, not to say lovingly coiffed. Her fingers sparkled charmingly with many diamonds as her hands danced this way and that through the air while she described some incident which, judging from the consistent laughter of the gentleman seated to her immediate right, must have been hilariously amusing.

The laughing man was also elderly, and also elegant. His upright posture and the clipping of his iron-gray hair and beard suggested a soldierly past, and the sparkling of a magnificent medal dangling from a broad ribbon under his white tie suggested he'd been given considerable recognition for the same. His blue eyes darted alertly in my direction now and then from almost my first glance and I saw he was not a man to observe unobserved. I would not have relished being an enemy officer attempting a sneak upon his flank.

But both these intriguing individuals swiftly dimmed to unimportance, so far as I was concerned, once I'd noticed the presence of the quiet young woman who was seated next to them and formed the third member of their little group.

She immediately struck me as being extraordinary, but it took me any number of furtive glances before I was able to put my finger on what it was about her that was both so intriguing and mysterious as to be, without any exaggeration, utterly hypnotic.

She was almost, but not quite, the most beautiful woman I had ever seen in my life, and I include in that count not only those I had observed and marveled at in the flesh, but the most legendary charmers of the films, not to mention the supreme exquisites represented in marble and paint during the Renaissance and in antiquity.

Understand it was not that beauty itself, it was the *excruciating nearness of the miss* which so completely overwhelmed me. The tension between her actual state and her nearly achieved perfection put me into a condition of utter fascination which I had not experienced since I was a little child. Suddenly, and with the most remarkable, heartbreaking clarity, I could simultaneously remember gaping in the Christmas window of a department store at a madly desired toy and gazing open-mouthed at Disney's Snow White as she was discovered sleeping by the seven dwarfs.

I was abruptly roused from this trance, for such it was, by the sudden, shocking realization that the young woman in question was gazing back at me, eye to eye, and by a gentle but decidedly authoritative touch upon my shoulder. I looked up and saw that the military gentleman was standing by my chair and looking down at me with a strange mixture of amusement and pity on his strong old face.

"We noticed you sitting here alone, old chap," he said, speaking in a deep, oddly accented voice. "We wondered if you should like some company."

"I should indeed," I said, barely avoiding a stammer and managing a credible smile.

"Excellent," he said as I stood, and he led me over to the two women, who were now both studying me with a forgiving, kindly air.

"I am Brigadier General Vasillos Konstantinides," he said, executing a courtly bow. "This is the Baroness von Liechtenburg, and this is Mademoiselle Denise Chandron."

I introduced myself, using the distinguished name I had borrowed for the purposes of evading the law, and we settled into a pleasant little chat. They were old friends, these three, who stayed at the hotel often, "this time of year," as they put it.

Eventually we carried our conversation into the dining room, and though it was unfailingly interesting, I was ever most conscious of, and most grateful for, the close proximity of the absolutely fascinating Miss Chandron.

Toward the end of the meal I detected a certain awkward-
ness on the part of my new acquaintances. More and more
they cast unobtrusive glances at one another and I caught an
increasing air of thoughtful indecision on all their parts amid a
growing number of conversational pauses. There was no
doubt of it, some sort of unspoken question had begun to
hover in the air.

"I can't tell you how much I've enjoyed talking with you," I
said, "and I very much hope we might do it again, perhaps
even tomorrow night, but I must confess I'm quite exhausted
from my journey. Please excuse me, I hate to tear myself
away, but I think it would be extremely wise of me to retire
early."

The shared relief discreetly concealed under their murmured regrets and consolations showed me I had undoubtedly
done the right thing. They had all been hesitating uncomfortably on—but not quite able to cross over—the edge of some
decision. My exit was gratefully accepted and I was assured
that we would, indeed, assemble in the salon the following
evening.

I had breakfast in my room before the French windows
which looked out on a small, private balcony beyond. In season the windows would have been opened to allow a sun-
warmed sea breeze, but I rather enjoyed them as they were,
closed and snug against a gentle autumnal drizzle.

I spent a lazy hour or more bathing and dressing and then
began again to descend the marble staircase, this time with a
book under my arm. My plan was simple and pleasant: I intended to find some quiet corner and read the book, or doze
over it, until lunch.

My tranquil mood was jarred, as was my elbow, when a

group of porters bustled by me on the stairs bearing a chair with some difficulty. On the chair sat a grotesque figure, a hunched woman who was heavily veiled and whose thin limbs seemed to be bent at every angle possible, as were the clawed fingers she held tangled in her lap.

The poor creature must have been in considerable pain for she moaned constantly as the porters carried her, and as she passed by me, the gray mound of veiling covering her face turned in my direction and she emitted a kind of keening wail which froze me where I stood so that I looked down still as a statue after her and her bearers as they completed their descent, passed through the lobby, and exited from the Hotel Splendide through its tall, crystal-paned doorway into the rain falling beyond.

I did find exactly the sort of quiet corner that I'd hoped for, but I derived very small enjoyment from my reading, not through any fault of the little book I'd brought, but because of the repeated interceding vision of the distorted woman in the chair which kept floating between its pages and my eyes.

That evening when I arrived at the little salon I found the Baroness von Liechtenburg and General Konstantinides sitting beside one another exactly where I had seen them the night before and chatting in a sprightly way with one another. They looked remarkably better than I remembered them, more than merely well rested; it almost seemed as though they'd both shed years.

Their brightening at the sight of me seemed hearteningly genuine and the General stood and took my hand firmly in a large, strong grip and bade me sit by them just in time for a gliding waiter to take my order for an Amontillado.

"Let me put you out of your misery at once regarding Miss

Chandron, my poor fellow," said the Baroness, patting my hand and giving me the kindest smile possible, "for I see you are anxiously looking about for her. Unfortunately, she will not be with us this evening. Let me comfort you in a small way at least by telling you that she was most insistent I make it clear to you that she hopes very much to see you again and regrets the necessity for her departure, which was extreme."

"She lost heavily at the Casino, I am afraid," said the General with a sigh. He took a sip of his sherry and brightened somewhat. "But I am sure she will be back next year and, I am confident, have much better luck. Doubtless you will see her then."

"Oh, yes," said the Baroness, looking around the salon. "We shall all be back next year. Without doubt. All of us."

I expressed my regret at Miss Chandron's absence, and that regret was genuine in the extreme—so genuine, in fact, that it quite surprised me. I had realized in a vague sort of way that I had taken a fancy to Denise, but until my heart lurched so within my chest at the news of her absence, I had no idea how much she had come to mean to me in that short time which we had spent together.

From the growing concern in my friends' eyes it dawned on me that I must have gone completely silent for far too long a time, and in an effort to break it I stirred myself to ask them about the casino they'd mentioned, though I really was not even slightly interested in the subject.

"Ah, yes," said the General, "that's why we come here, you see. For the Casino, altogether for the Casino. It only opens this time of year. The regular one, the one that caters to the seasonal people, is closed, of course. The Casino Mirago only functions these last two weeks of autumn. Only these last two weeks."

"We naturally assumed that you were also here for the purpose of playing at the Casino, and of course we thought of asking you to join us last night," said the Baroness. "But we supposed you'd already made arrangements, as most people do, so we weren't quite sure how to proceed. We should have bulled ahead and simply asked you to come along, of course."

"Perhaps, though," the General murmured reflectively, more to himself than to me, "it was just as well you weren't there, as things worked out. It was quite distressing."

"But tonight," the Baroness said brightly, "would you like to come with us tonight? I think you would fit in quite well at the Casino, you know? I'm sure of it. You seem—I don't know exactly why—you seem to have the *air* for it."

"We should be delighted to have you come as part of our company," said the General. "They are somewhat hesitant when it comes to new faces, but we shall usher you in, never fear."

"You must come with us and try your luck," said the Baroness with a finality which was past all resistance.

My acceptance of their kind invitation opened a sort of floodgate and our dinner conversation was dedicated entirely to the topic of the Casino Mirago, which appeared to be a genuine obsession with both my companions. Every year they came and every year they gambled, and very heavily it seemed. I thought of the ridiculous amounts of money in my briefcase upstairs and decided I could imagine no more fitting fate for it than to throw it away at the tables of an odd and eccentric gaming establishment such as was being described to me by my two new friends.

It seemed that the Casino Mirago had been in operation for an extraordinarily long period of time and that generations upon generations of important and occasionally downright legendary people had tried their luck with its croupiers through the years. But in spite of its great age and the dedication of its regulars, its reputation was, in fact, highly restricted.

The very existence of the Casino was a great secret which was firmly and carefully guarded by an extremely jealous clientele and as I ate my dinner and heard more and more hints of the wonders of this apparently fabulous establishment, it dawned upon me that I was extremely lucky, and could be, perhaps, extremely unlucky, to be receiving this initiation into its mysteries.

"It takes considerable nerve, the Casino does," the General said, studying me closely over the candles burning discreetly in our dinner table's silver candelabra. "But I have the most peculiar conviction, just as the Baroness expressed, that you are exactly the right sort of chap for the spot."

"I must confess," I said, thinking of the vial of poison clipped to the underside of my lapel, "that from what you've said of it, there is nowhere on this planet I can think of which fits in better with my present mood."

We traveled in the General's limousine, a fine old Bentley captained with consummate artistry by an elderly chauffeur named Sweeney, who had the bright eyes and beak of an eagle, or perhaps a vulture. The glow of the General's cigar shone and dimmed with almost a regular pulsing on my left while the Baroness, who had heretofore languidly puffed only the occasional long cigarette, chain-smoked relentlessly on my right.

The rain and its attendant mists had blown away completely and as we drove alongside the sea a bright, clear moon coasted over it, glinting the low, slow waves and gliding so smoothly and steadily beside the car that I could almost fancy it was watching us.

I could easily sense the excitement building in both my friends. Now and then the General or the Baroness would try to ease their tension by breaking the waiting silence with some odd story or practical hint concerning the Casino Mirago.

"You buy your chips with money, of course, as in any ordinary place of its kind," observed the Baroness after puffing into life perhaps her dozenth cigarette. "But you may choose to take your winnings in a great variety of forms."

"Ah, yes, that's the grand thing," murmured the General, giving a firm nod which made the glowing coal of his cigar describe two neat little arcs a half foot in front of his face. "That's what sets the Casino Mirago totally apart from all the competition, you see. You need only specify, dear fellow. Only specify and they'll give it to you. It's really quite remarkable. But it does take some getting used to. Ah, yes."

"The really important rule to bear in mind is that once you've decided what you're playing for, that's what you lose," said the Baroness, and as her dark eyes turned in my direction I could see a reflection of the full moon shining brightly in each of her pupils. "*That's* what you lose."

When I confessed I did not quite grasp her meaning she gave a soft, nervous laugh.

"You will understand when you see the others coming and going," she said. "That sight will make it all come clear to you."

"And here is your chance to see it," said the General, "for we have arrived at last."

I saw a pale building grow larger as the Bentley glided into a curving drive and eased to a halt before a row of tall doors with light streaming through the elaborate etching of their panes. Simultaneously with the chauffeur Sweeney stepping around to let us out of the car, the two central doors were swiftly and smoothly opened by attendants costumed in purple uniforms heavily decorated with golden buttons and braidings so that we entered at once in a sweep and I only had a chance for the most cursory glimpse of the Casino's exterior.

The building was covered with marble which was fish-belly pale, smooth enough to glisten, and every inch of the stuff was carved in a complicated riot of Neptunes and mermaids swimming lustily through festoons of seaweed crowded with shells and alive with the paralyzed writhings of stone sea horses and eels. Obviously the intent of all this heavy-handed gaiety was to create a festive display, to make a kind of architectural wedding cake, but in the moonlight and the autumn cold and with the salt air blowing over all, it seemed to me more like mortuary art and put me in mind of some dismal, if gaudy, tomb.

The interior was another confusion of rococo carvings, but these were old nymphs and satyrs executed in plaster and thickly coated with gold paint which had become dulled and dusky through the years. They pranced and posed around countless murals of their betters: divers pagan deities painted in once bright oil colors long gone sooty and dim. These old gods stood with their toes poking over clouds flaking plaster and they gazed down at the gaming mortals beneath them with smiles and gesturings which struck me as sinister and possibly contemptuous.

A tall, astoundingly thin man in white tie and tails glided toward us and brushed aside the fawning attendants so that he might take personal charge of the General and the Baroness, who were obviously both old and highly valued regulars of the Casino. I was introduced and accepted and doubtless permanently noted as he guided us almost reverently through a series of outer rooms filled with gamblers playing a greater variety of games than I had known existed.

It became ever clearer that the Casino Mirago catered to a highly eccentric, not to say bizarre, clientele. The usual grim seriousness which underlies the mood of all gambling places, however jolly their superficial air may seem, was here most extraordinarily heightened. The customers all played with such highly focused attention that it seemed their gazes would burn holes into the green felt lining the card tables and singe the ivory dice as they flew. I had never before in all my life seen so much desperate intensity.

A good many of the players appeared to be ill, a number of them shockingly so, and not a few of these were afflicted so severely that I was astounded that their care givers had permitted them their ill-advised expedition to this crowded and stressful place.

At one point I saw what I believe was the oldest man I had ever observed being guided, perhaps it were better to say carried, by three of the purple-clad attendants.

His head was totally hairless and its flesh was such a cascade of wrinkles that the definition of his face was almost completely obscured by the complicated patterns of its saggings and wattlings. His little feet in their shiny patent leather pumps turned pathetically this way and that over the thick carpet as the attendants dragged him along hurriedly and with little ceremony.

I found myself shuddering when his limp body was brushed against mine as they dragged him past us, and I could see the wrinkled gap of his drooling, toothless mouth working obscenely and actually smell his sour, winy breath as I heard his high, thin, piping voice monotonously reciting, over and over and over again, the same series of numbers.

The General looked after him, shaking his head sadly, but not without a trace of sardonic amusement.

"I believe he is reviewing his bets," he whispered to me.

On the other extreme of age, and perhaps even more grotesque, was the sight of a child, a young boy, throwing a kind of fit by the side of a dice table while the spectacularly beautiful woman who was clearly his companion desperately tried to calm him, but with a total lack of success. The boy was weirdly attired in impeccable evening clothes which were at least three sizes too large, and as I watched, he heaved the dice clumsily onto the numbered table before him, observing them bounce with a lunatic glee in his crazily bright young eyes.

The woman looked up and saw me staring. She started to reach out toward me as if to grasp my arm, but her gesture faltered as we passed her and she began to weep and to wave her hands aimlessly in the air.

"He won't stop!" she wailed hysterically. "Why won't somebody make him stop?"

As we penetrated deeper and deeper into the establishment the rooms grew smaller and more elegant until we arrived at a jewel of a chamber which contained but a single roulette table whose wheel sparkled magically as it spun under a gorgeously subtle chandelier.

Our host seated us carefully at three empty chairs which had apparently been waiting just for ourselves; at his nod there was no question of credit and the croupier pushed a sizable stack of counters toward each one of us across the green baize.

The croupier's skin was as smooth and of the same bone color as the little ivory ball he tossed at his wheel. His face was completely devoid of expression, save for an ever vigilant watchfulness, and all his gestures were so quick and efficient that his hands and arms seemed to blur as they moved. He never stood but remained fixed to his chair like one of those mechanical fortune-telling gypsies you sometimes come across in old, failing amusement parks sitting dustily in their glass boxes.

"Mesdames, messieurs, faites vos jeux," he intoned like a priest at his service, and set the wheel spinning.

The roulette wheel was a kind of masterpiece, as skillfully crafted as a bejeweled egg made for a czarina, and I would not have been in the slightest surprised to learn that it had been executed by the hand of Fabergé himself.

The colors of it seemed to flicker and shift subtly in tone as you watched it whirl; only its sparkling gold bandings—looking like the lines of magical circles holding demons and angels in check—remained constant. Unlike any other roulette wheel with which I had played, this one moved with total silence; no matter how smartly the croupier spun it, the thing whirled without a sound from the start of its rotation to the finish.

The ball, on the other hand, made an almost fiendishly

penetrating kind of clatter which brought to mind the rappings of bony knuckles and the chatterings of fever victims' teeth, and I confess that throughout my gaming I always found myself holding my breath like one afraid of being overheard in some dark place during the whole time it danced and bounced from one number to the next.

At first I gambled in a somewhat dilettantish sort of way, not following any particular pattern and frankly more interested in my fellow gamblers than the results of my betting, but then I felt the Baroness' gaze upon me and turned to her and saw her studying me with some amusement.

"Have you decided to wager for money or for more important things?" she asked me, and I am afraid I looked at her a trifle blankly.

"Surely you have understood by now," she continued, with just a trace of impatience. "That ancient fellow expiring of old age as they dragged him away? The child turning into a baby before your eyes?"

She bent a little closer to me.

"Take a quiet look at the General beside you," she whispered softly. "Obviously he is winning. Wouldn't you say he is now at least a decade younger?"

I turned my head surreptitiously to steal a glance at General Vasillos Konstantinides and I am afraid my eyes must have literally bulged as I observed that the Baroness was quite right and that the old gentleman appeared to have dropped at least a good tenth of a century. He turned to me and grinned hugely with a whole new brightness in his eyes.

"It is an extraordinary place, is it not?" he asked me, and with a hearty puff at his cigar he enthusiastically resumed his gambling.

I turned back to the Baroness and stared with astonishment down at her upturned face as she regarded me with an
ironic smile.

"Now you finally appear to have got it," she said dryly, after
a little pause. "The penny seems to have finally dropped."

"But how is it done?" I asked in a cracked whisper.

"Exactly as I told you, dear boy," she said. "You make up
your mind what you want and then you gamble for it. You
don't have to tell anyone, you just go ahead and do it. It's as
simple as that."

Then she paused and leaned forward and I saw the jewels
on her fingers sparkle under the chandelier as she took hold of
my arm and held it in a tightening grip.

"But you absolutely must remember what I told you back in
the car," she said, with extreme solemnity. "That if you lose,
you lose in those same terms you've set."

Her grip continued to tighten until it became positively
painful. I could feel her nails digging into the fabric of my
sleeve and one or two of them actually penetrating my flesh.

"That woman you saw this morning," she said, "that poor,
bent, moaning creature they were carrying down the staircase
in a chair, was Mademoiselle Chandron. She was born horribly
deformed, you see. She had been betting against it all this
week and she'd been winning. Those were her terms. Last
night she lost. Rather horribly, I'm afraid."

The Baroness studied me carefully for a long moment, then
she nodded, apparently satisfied at her instructions, gave me
a final, almost motherly, smile of encouragement, let go of my
arm, and went back to her game.

I looked up at the croupier to find he was regarding me
with the same sort of intensity as a poised and swaying cobra

regards a fakir from its basket and somehow I summoned the courage to stare back at him.

Apparently, at a previous point all unknown to my conscious mind, I must have carefully formed the whole structure of my special wager for I found I had it ready for him then and there. He read it somehow, gave me a small, cool, barely noticeable nod, and then once more spun his wheel.

As this totally different game advanced I began to empathize increasingly with the profound seriousness of my fellow wagerers. There were tuggings in my gut now which I had never felt before, there was a bottomless depth of awful apprehension in my belly deeper than any I had previously known.

More and more my mind, my whole being, focused in on the spinnings and respinnings and spinnings again of that pretty wheel with its flashing gold bandings and its constantly changing tones, and the cracking and chittering of that smartly tossed ivory ball made me jump and wince like a child frightened by a boogie man under the bed.

But I was winning more and more, steadily and regularly, and I could feel the shape of what I was after growing realer and solider each time the croupier pushed more chips toward me with his little golden rake. Soon, very soon, if my luck held, if I could only maintain this constant improvement, it would all come true with a kind of click whose first echoings I could almost hear. It would suddenly tumble into place and be there, done and completed and solid. It would be a holdable fact and I would have it truly. It would be mine.

Then I heard a horrible hollow gasp and turned to see the Baroness folding in on herself beside me like a collapsing spring.

"Take hold of her, sir," whispered the General urgently into my ear.

I turned to him and was astonished to see he was now nearly as young as myself.

"Help her at once, man," he said, "or she'll fall from her chair!"

I grabbed her near arm with both my hands and was appalled to feel the change in it. I had held that arm before, helping her rise in the salon, escorting her along with Denise into the dining room of the Hotel Splendide, and it had been firm and full with smooth, resilient skin.

Now that skin was limp and porous and hung loosely as an oversized sleeve from an arm which had shriveled to something little more than bone and stringy muscle. I gaped at her and saw that in the last half hour or so her whole body had undergone the sort of ghastly shrinking which was ordinarily produced only by long months of some monstrous wasting disease.

"She has lost badly," said the General. "We must make a sizable wager from her funds at once. She hasn't the time to drag it out."

He reached across me to her pile of counters and hastily shoved forward something more than half of them just in time to catch the new spinning of the wheel.

"*Rien ne va plus,*" said the croupier, and we both watched the hopping of the bone-pale ball with a terrible intentness and we both cursed when it landed wrong.

I was now holding the Baroness with both arms, cradling her against me, and I could actually feel her body shrinking as the wheel slowed to a stop.

"There's not much left of her," I said.

"Cancer," said the General. "I thought she'd beaten it. I thought she was betting on something else altogether. I suppose she was trying to make sure she'd cleaned it out of her body.

He reached across me again and pushed what was left of her counters onto the board. She lost again.

"Oh, damn," said the General, very softly. "Oh damn, damn, damn."

It only took one of those purple-clad attendants to lift her, chair and all. I reached up and touched the General, who had stood in order to follow after her.

"I've got to finish," I said.

He glanced down at me and nodded.

"Of course you do, old fellow," he said, scooping up his counters. "We'll both be waiting in the Bentley."

He glanced down at his chips.

"I'd give you these to play with," he said. "But we can't transfer them from one of us to another. It's one of their damned rules, you see."

I nodded and he pushed them all through the little slot cut into the table in front of the croupier to receive his tips.

"*Pour votre service,*" the General said to him and the croupier mechanically gave him one of his little bows.

"*Merci beaucoup,*" he said.

It was no time at all, I think only three more bets, before I felt something go absolutely right inside me and knew for certain that I had won. I pushed a generous tip into the slot, but did not follow the General's example and leave all my remaining chips as I did not care overmuch for the croupier.

"*Merci beaucoup,*" he said, giving me the same exact bow he had bestowed on the General.

We took what was left of the Baroness to the hospital. After some hours I yielded to the General's kindly insistence I be driven back to the hotel and left him with her, sitting next to her bed in the dimly lit room. I hope to see them both again sometime, but one never knows. There is so much luck involved in that sort of thing.

The next morning, after a very nice breakfast, I passed through the tall front doors of the Hotel Splendide for perhaps the very last time and made my way leisurely down its steps to the Rolls Silver Ghost patiently waiting for me with my family crest, the crest of that legendarily distinguished and wealthy family I had claimed to belong to and now actually did belong to, painted very discreetly on both its rear doors.

The chauffeur greeted me with considerable deference as I had been wise enough to improve my situation with that family in the terms of my bet from being an obscure member of the clan to being its oldest son and, therefore, the major inheritor of its practically uncountable holdings. I would be, upon the death of my elderly mother, one of the richest men in the world. I was presently something like the tenth richest man in the world.

With a deep bow, a much better bow I may say than anything the croupier of the Casino Mirago had to offer, my chauffeur opened the door of my Rolls and I prepared to enter it in order to sit next to my wife, the former Denise Chandron, and give her the kiss I had been aching to bestow upon her for what now seemed a very long time as I loved her very deeply because—among the many other marvelous and wonderful things about her—I knew she would be exactly as beautiful as she wanted to be. The terms of the bet I had made at the Casino Mirago had left all that entirely up to her.

The Frog Prince

A h, so, again the same dream," sighed Doctor Neiman, without any trace of accusation, making a note
among many other notes in his notebook. "Always
the same dream."

Frog rolled the tiniest bit to the right on the couch, selecting another part of the ceiling to look at, the part with the
crack which ran out of the edging of plaster flowers like a
questing tendril, perhaps his favorite part.

He was aware that the continuing emanation of sweat from
his armpits was once again soaking itself into the twin bunching of his shirt underneath the tweed jacket, making the material into two hard, swelling, highly uncomfortable lumps.

There was so much moisture in him! Saliva, as always, had
nearly filled his mouth and he would soon have to swallow,
silently, as silently as possible, since Doctor Neiman often in-
corporated Frog's frequent gulpings into his little analytical

summations near the ends of their sessions. Frog always felt particularly vulnerable when it came to gulpings. With reason, of course, with reason.

And then there was the constant wetness in his eyes which would increase and brim and finally spill over the edges of his heavy, puffy lids and roll down his round, pale cheeks each and every time he spoke or thought of sad or moving things, which was often. Not to mention the constant moisture on his palms which turned them into little, pale suction cups and made them cling alarmingly to the soft leather of the couch, or the ever renewing dampness of his socks so that the unending process of evaporation taking place continued to bring uncomfortable and unnerving coolness to the wide bottoms of his feet.

Sometimes, lying there, he wondered if he was making visible rivulets and pools underneath himself on the surface of the couch. Sometimes he wondered if it had got so bad it was running off the couch's sides and darkening the thick oriental carpet, and that only Doctor Neiman's professional politeness was preventing him from making some totally understandable comment about the potential damage this flood of sweat and tears and drool—yes, even drool!—represented to his property.

Again and again he would turn on the couch—always just the tiniest little bit—and think these thoughts, and each time he moved he would anticipate and listen, with repressed winces, for the squishings and squelchings which he never heard, thank God!

But when he finally rose to leave at the end of his session and was not able to resist the impulse to look back down at the couch and see if the damage done by the flood of moisture from his round body was anywhere near as bad as his imagination conjured, he would observe, with perhaps the smallest wisp of disappointment, that the couch had not been reduced to a sodden, dripping mass, that it seemed startlingly dry, and that the only visible trace of all that steady gushing seemed to be a faint dampness on the disposable paper cover on the pillow—a dim round spot representing his head with a short, wide, vertical tail underneath it representing his neck, the whole thing vaguely suggesting the sun reflected in water more or less as it would be done if painted by Edvard Munch.

"The king in your dream," Doctor Neiman said, frowning and making another note, perhaps underlining it. "You say you feel he is your father?"

His father, yes! his father. Holding him high in his heavy, hard metal gauntlets, holding him over the battlements of the topmost tower so that they could look down upon their kingdom together and see the glinting of gold, the long banners flapping, the dust rising from the wide earth road and settling on the gaudy wrappings of the horses; holding him high so that he could clearly hear the trumpets, the loving cheers from the crowd, the drumbeats! The king had been, indeed, his father.

But then had come the spell, and the separation, and the desperate, unsuccessful hunting which had once come so close, so terribly close that he had felt the water shaking, the whole pool trembling, as the hoofs pounded the soft earth of its round shore, could even see the ripples caused by nearness of the trumpets' high, brassy notes.

Worst of all had been the horribly brief glimpse of a rider larger than all the others, bound in golden armor, wearing a long, billowing, red cape, and calling out his name over and over in a cracked, frantic lion's roar.

Not that he hadn't loved the pool, loved the modulations of its greenness as he swam this way and that underwater; loved digging into the cool, soft, receiving blackness of its bottom mud; loved to squat waiting on the smooth warmth of its lily pads, letting the hunger lazily grow and watching the buzzing bugs circle overhead, their wings sparkling in the sunlight, until they came too close.

It was a warm July day and he had fed particularly well and was swimming just below the surface with wide, easy strokes when he saw a great, bright pinkness shimmering ahead of him through the water, a blur of color so dazzling that his limbs stopped moving where they were and only his momentum pushed him through the water, closer to that vast glowing, in a dreamy, hypnotized, forward drifting.

The wide, round, golden bulging of his eyes with their long black slits strained past aching to absorb the sight of this gorgeousness as it came nearer and nearer, and he sank into a trance far, far deeper than his tiny pond.

Then the pinkness moved, faceted by the water into an enormous, glittering wall of multitudinous shades of rose and pale reds, and he realized how huge, how tremendous the thing that made it must be, and backed away speedily, sculling to the security of the far end of the pond and a cluster of willow roots where he cowered behind the slimy stems a moment, gathering himself and letting his heart slow so that its pounding didn't frighten him quite so much.

But the pinkness continued to fascinate him absolutely, and he found himself slowly and carefully raising his head, keeping his eyes the highest part of him until they gently and very quietly broke the surface of the water and he found himself staring directly at a beautiful woman kneeling by the side of the pond and smiling intently into its mysteries.

The pinkness had been her face and neck and shoulders and arms leaning over the surface of his pond. The rest of her was clad in a long green dress flecked with gold, and had blended with the water. Her hair was a piled mass of gold and Frog knew that was what he had taken for the sun.

He realized, then and there, that he would love her always and forever, hopelessly and beyond redemption. Clinging to the smooth curving of a willow root with his tiny, emerald feet, he stared at her with a helpless wonder for long, uncounted minutes, and his ordinarily unnoticed blood stirred strangely within him and seemed to warm him and he almost half believed that he could sense it taking on a redness in his veins.

It began to dawn on him, watching her make one precious, unforgettable, irreplaceable move of her body after another, that he had been alone in his quiet little pond for a long, long while. He observed her slim, pale, perfect fingers trail along the surface of the water and was astonished to realize how far ago that day of hoof poundings and harsh trumpet blasts and hoarse shoutings of his name must have been. He watched her darling arm straighten as she stretched forward to gently nudge a floating leaf and was amazed to see how faint and dim and blurred with time the recollections of his castle and his father's face had grown in his mind.

With an incredible effort, he tore his eyes from his beloved and let himself slide noiselessly down the willow root to the soft, yielding mud at the bottom of the pond, and then he walked on the tips of his toes over the vagueness of the mud's dim, uncertain surface until he came to a little heap of algae-covered rocks. He moved the rocks gently to one side and then carefully dug into the bit of mud which they had marked. At first his gropings only found deeper mud and a terrible anxiety swept through him, but then he clawed just a little farther and felt a flood of enormous relief when the pale little pads on the ends of his front feet made contact with a smooth, hard, curving surface.

He reached down, and when all his green fingers were curled around the object hidden underneath the mud, he pulled mightily with every bit of strength in his stout little body and at last, with a wet sucking and a dark, swirling cloud of mud, he pulled out his treasure.

It was a lovely, large ruby carved beautifully into the shape of a heart, and as he gently stroked the mud from its surface, it glowed brightly, even here, in the deepest, darkest corner of the pond. It had stayed with him, he had no idea why or how, through his losses and transformations, and through all the endless eons which had passed over him since.

He had always suspected there was something wonderful and magical about it; it had always been a great source of hope, and now, holding it with a clear plan forming easily and effortlessly in his mind, he was sure of it. He knew, in the deepest part of his speckled green body, that he and it had been waiting together in this lonely pool all along, through all these stretching years, for just this moment.

He fondled it, clutched it to his breast, hugged it fiercely, and then, gripping it as firmly as he could with all his might in both his tiny front feet, he kicked his way up through the whole height of the pond to the underside of a large lily pad.

He peered carefully and cautiously out from under the pad,

and when he was sure his beloved's gaze was thoroughly absorbed elsewhere, he climbed over the pad's edge and sat on its exact center. He arranged his small body carefully, folding the roundness of his legs neatly along his sides and spreading the toes of his feet in order to show off their webbing to its best advantage. Then, lifting his head just so in order that the curve of the bulge of flesh under his chin might echo exactly the swelling of his belly in the classic frog mode, he held the heart-shaped ruby up in both paws, toward her, and waited patiently, breathing tiny, anxious breaths, and gazing at her with his wide, adoring eyes.

She turned and saw him and at first she only smiled affectionately with a slow parting of her lovely red lips at the sight of the little fat, green creature, but then a look of curiosity grew in her eyes as she noticed the heart-shaped ruby and the oddly human way he held it, and then her curiosity in turn changed to wonder when she saw the tiny golden crown which rested on the flat, green-speckled top of Frog's head.

Very carefully, doing all as gracefully as he possibly could, Frog bent and placed the ruby on the pad before him. Then he made a formal little bow, stepped back, and waited again.

The ruby glistened on the lily pad, looking more like a drop of liquid than a solid thing. The beloved reached out in its direction, moving gently, keeping her eyes on Frog to make sure she was not startling him, and touched the ruby cautiously with the tip of the softly curving, delicately pink nail of her forefinger. Only after she saw Frog solemnly blink his bulging, golden eyes and nod approvingly did she take hold of the ruby between her finger and thumb and lift it from the leaf's waxy surface.

She held it up before her face, turning it as she did so, and her lovely eyes widened as she watched the sun shine through its heart-shaped redness in endlessly wonderful ways. Frog watched from his lily pad, confident that the magic would work on its own, that his salvation was approaching, that this endless time of solitude was coming to its end and that all of it had served a purpose.

Eventually her gaze traveled slowly from the ruby to the little frog and a look of understanding crossed over her face. She took the heart-shaped jewel between her fingertips and pressed it to the center of her chest, just above the parting of her breasts, and as she and Frog watched together, it sank gently into her flesh.

She sat a moment longer, her fingers resting quietly over her beating heart, and then she leaned forward and gathered Frog's small body up in her sweet hands and lifted him closer and closer to the full, round swelling of the softness of her lips.

"And this is where you wake up," sighed Doctor Neiman, making yet another note in his little book. "Always, this is where you wake up."

Frog turned his head to the wall and felt the burning tears cascading from his bulging eyes, felt them scald his puffy cheeks, sear the whole wide gape of his lips, and tumble from him onto the disposable paper cover of the pillow on the couch.

"Yes," he croaked. "Always."

The Manuscript of Dr. Arness

Before I do what I must do, I suppose it would be a good idea to leave behind an explanation. I generally detest suicide notes. They tend to be pathetic, often mawkish monuments. But then, most suicides themselves are pathetic and mawkish—the puerile resolution to a neurotic stupidity.

I do love life. Perhaps not as passionately as some men do, or say they do, but I love it. I am not pleased at the idea of giving it up. If I could discover any reasonable alternative I would not, even now, give it up. But there is no alternative.

My main reason for writing this is to leave behind a warning. Because I am brilliant, what I have done is brilliant, and ordinary men are hardly likely to have the requisite ingenuity to blunder into anything like my present predicament; but there are many other brilliant men in this world and some of them, even now, may be engaged in an experiment similar to my own, unaware of where it is leading them. I address myself to this elite.

It is ironic that I have been pushed into suicide because of an attempt to prolong my life. Like most thinking individuals, I have always been galled by the tiny span allotted to us by a supposedly beneficent providence. A man has barely attained a state of mature efficiency before he finds himself advancing rapidly into his decline. It is infuriating to contemplate what a Newton or a Kepler, or a Beethoven or a Dante could have accomplished if his creative years had been extended. Imagine, to take an example, how much richer our artistic heritage would be had Cézanne been given a mere decade more of productive existence.

The stretching out of old age has my sympathy, but not much of my interest. If I had lived to be a tottering ancient, I suppose I would be as eager for a few more blurry years as they appear to be, but I do not see any particular value for the race as a whole in the prolongation of an individual long after he has passed anything that could be described as a fully operative condition. If the present triumphs of geriatrics continue, we shall probably find ourselves wandering among vast legions of the vague elderly. I would not for the world deny them their extra years, but I cannot see that it renders the rest of us any more than a sentimental service.

No, it is the extension of men at their working best that obsesses me. I use the word advisedly, for it is, with me, truly an obsession. Since childhood I have been consumed with this single ambition. It's quite possible that the germ of the concept first came to me wrapped in a nursery tale. In any case, it has been my driving motive for as long as I can remember.

I am, as I said, brilliant. I am not boasting, for it isn't something I've accomplished, but merely a quality with which I was born. I did, however, make full use of it and managed to crowd a sizable amount of learning into a very short period of time, establishing, in passing, a quantity of records in various educational establishments. I felt, you see, that I was working against the clock. I wanted to cheat the time trap as much as I possibly could.

So it was that I began the serious phase of my investigations while still a comparatively young man. Despite this initial advantage, I was in my mid-thirties before I had completed the fundamental structure of my theory, and well into my forties before I was in a position to bring it to the actual physical test.

My technique was a radical departure from the previous approaches to the problems of aging, all of which may be satisfactorily grouped under two rough headings: the propping-up school, which employs preventive medicines, vitamins, exercises, and so on; and the patching-up school, which makes use of reparative operations, stimulants, artificial supplements or replacements to damaged organs, and the rest. My aim was to bring about a fundamental reorientation of the body's molecular structure. I intended to alter its metabolic operations by manipulating the tiny components that control it. This I accomplished by means of an electrochemical process, the details of which are given in the notebook that I shall leave behind to accompany this brief note.

I proceeded in the classical manner, testing my theories on animals under controlled conditions, taking copious notes and records on their reactions. I began with mice, went on to guinea pigs, and worked the final experiments on a group of chimpanzees named, unromantically enough, One, Two, and Three.

The effect of my treatment is cumulative. It is a slow transformation, a gradual alteration of the body, working from the large to the small, so that the small can work on the large. There is no discernible change during the first phase, but after a period of time, depending on the eccentricities of the particular animal's construction, new elements become evident. Their mood becomes buoyant and their health is dramatically improved. One interesting, and unanticipated, bonus is that all congenital defects disappear. Chimpanzee Two, for example, had a slightly stunted arm that he could move only with some difficulty. After three weeks, that arm was fully grown and completely operative. One by one, the predictions of my theory checked out, all on schedule, all completely fulfilling or exceeding expectation.

To say that I was pleased with the results of these experiments is to profoundly understate the case. The dream of my life was proving itself before my eyes; I had achieved the power to work the miracle for which I had been born. I, myself, not some distant inheritor of theory, could become, for all intents and purposes, immortal.

It was at this point that I erred, and the error was precipitation. But can you blame me? The years were passing, each one, it seemed, faster than the year before. Freedom from time was in my grasp; I could not resist the temptation to reach out and take it. I was guilty of undue haste, but, even now, I cannot blame myself too much.

I began to apply my treatment to myself. As with my animals, there was no observable reaction at first, but then I became aware of a growing peace and contentment, and I saw, clearly, that I was much improved in every bodily function. I had worn thick glasses. In four weeks I dispensed with them altogether, having no further need of them. My digestion had been faulty. Now it was perfect. I could hardly believe the image in my mirror. It was like some incredible before-and-after ad in the back pages of a magazine. I positively radiated health.

By now the lack of aging had become evident in my animals. The mice, which would have died long ago under normal conditions, were all alive and thriving. Each of the creatures was totally unaltered since its first transformation. They could be killed, of course, by any normal means, but if they were only wounded, their rate of recovery was staggering. A scalpel cut that would ordinarily take weeks to mend would heal in a matter of days. My triumph was past all belief. These few glorious days are, still, worth all the rest. Not many men taste perfect victory.

Now I must proceed to the less happy events that followed.

It was my habit to occasionally run my mice through mazes to determine their reaction time. At the start of the experiment, when the initial alteration was effecting itself, their increased abilities had afforded me much joy. Now, to my growing apprehension, I observed that the period of time they took to complete their chore was unmistakably graphing up. I examined them carefully. I dissected a few to see if anything had gone wrong with their internal organs. They were all in flawless condition, but still, each day, they took a little longer to find their way through the maze. In a month I discovered, to my great discomfort, that they took twice as long to find their way from the beginning to the end.

By this time a similar phenomenon had begun to manifest

itself in my guinea pigs, and even in One, Two, and Three. There was nothing, not the slightest thing, wrong with any of them except that they needed more and more time to accomplish any task.

In another month, the condition of my mice had become positively grotesque. At their peak they had averaged about a minute and a half to complete their trek through the maze; now they all required approximately two hours. It was not that they had become sluggish, in the ordinary sense of the word. They did not lie down or take any periods of rest at all. They worked at their task steadily, even intelligently, but they lingered agonizingly over each and every move. It was the same with all their activities. They ate, they played, they fought and made love, but one's patience was worn thin watching them at any of it, because it took them such a damnably long time to move from one part of it to the next. I can only compare the effect to that of a slow-motion movie.

This slowness, if I may use a contradiction in terms, accelerated. Each of the various groups of animals proceeded in proportion to its own metabolism. By the time the guinea pigs had achieved the condition I have just described in regard to the mice, the mice were moving so slowly that it required an extended period of observation to determine whether they were moving at all. I attached an ink marker to the tail of one mouse so that the creature would leave a thin black line behind itself as it moved. After one full week, the tiny trail was only one and one quarter inches long. Yet all of my mice remained in the best of health. Their coats were still glossy, and their eyes sparkled with undimmed enthusiasm. The only trouble was that to a casual observer in my laboratory they would have appeared to be absolutely inert.

As the reader will have surmised, I was not exempt from this slowing process. Subjectively, I was not aware of it at all, but by timing my actions against an external check, such as the rotations of my watch's hands, I could see only too well that my movements had become increasingly slower. The alteration continued in the same snowballing fashion as with my pets, and now I no longer need anything as delicate as a clock to remind myself of my condition. I cannot strike a match fast enough to ignite it. By counting the sunrises and sunsets through the window, I determined that it took me nine days to arrange my typewriter so that I could type this note.

I determined to end my life after what might seem a trivial enough incident. I gave Three a banana and observed that it took him an entire afternoon to peel it. He looked so contented, so blissfully unaware of his snail-paced condition, that I began to laugh at him. My laughter became hysterical, and I ended by crying. I have no idea how long ago this happened, as I have lost all track of time, ordinary time. It has become a foreign thing to me.

I can see no point in becoming a comical object. One, Two, and Three now look like so many stuffed monkeys and I, without any doubt, would also come to resemble a particularly successful example of the taxidermist's art, were I to allow myself to survive. I have no intention of doing so. I shall now take the gun, which I have placed beside my typewriter, and blow out my brains with it. I wonder how long it will take me to do it? As I said, the situation is not without iron

Thus ends the manuscript of Doctor Arness. The last page remains, as you can see for yourself in the exhibit, rolled in the platen of his typewriter. The placement of the typewriter

in relation to the gun, the table, the chair, and to Doctor Arness himself is exactly the same as when he and the objects were discovered in his laboratory. Although Doctor Arness appears to be—to use his tragic description—"stuffed," he is not. He is alive, in good health, and he is moving. His index finger, even now, is actually approaching the final "y" in "irony," although at a speed that can be measured only with the most delicate of instruments. Doctor Arness is now 250 years old.

The animals referred to in his manuscript are also all alive and well, and may be seen in the Hall of Mammals. Attractive models of chimpanzees One, Two, and Three have been created, and they are available, in various sizes, at the Museum Curio Shop.

Hansel and Grettel

Once upon a time there was a simply adorable brother and sister who were so lovely that it is almost impossible to describe how really lovely they were, but I shall try, my dears, I shall do my very best.

Of course the one you would notice first would always be the sister, whose name was Grettel, my sweets. She was so very beautiful that when she entered a room all heads would turn in her direction—absolutely all of them without exception—and their eyes would follow her as she made her way to the very best table in the restaurant or the finest seat in the theater, and the men would do their best to try and hide it from the women they were with how furious they were to be with those women instead of being with Grettel. And the women would try to hide it from the men they were with that they knew their men felt that way and would wish deep down in the darkest depths of their hearts—oh my God how they would wish!—that they were as beautiful as Grettel and that the men they were with were dead and buried and out of the way so that they could enter a room as *she* did and have all the new, the fresh men, gaze at them with that much yearning and desire.

But then the women would notice Hansel.

My darlings, it was a quiet thing that Hansel did, getting this second notice, but oh what a noticing it was, for when they saw Hansel the women forgot all about Grettel and the men they were with, and all that was in their pretty little heads were dreams of themselves running far away with Hansel, to Hawaii, perhaps, to any place where the men they were with would be distant, forgotten creatures, someplace where they and Hansel could and would spend twenty-four hours a day, day after day, making love to one another.

And the men they were with would shift in their chairs and glance sidewise with squinting eyes at their women from behind their menus or their theater programs and when they saw the rapt expression on their faces as they gazed, dreaming, at Hansel, they would glare unseeing at their menus or theater programs while they plotted how to kill the women they were with very slowly so that they would suffer excruciating agonies before they finally died.

But the sad thing about it was, you know, the real pity was that Hansel and Grettel never did a thing about it. All those hopeful, yearning men and women, and they never did a thing about a single one of them. Not ever. Not once.

They seemed totally unaware of all those yearning looks, did handsome Hansel and lovely Grettel, as they entered those rooms or restaurants or theaters. They smiled and glowed and shone and sparkled and flowed gracefully before all those adoring gazes without appearing to notice a single aching glance or hear a solitary heartfelt sigh.

But of course they did notice them, my dears, they noticed every one of them. They lapped them up. They would have died without them.

Still one must have sympathy for Hansel and Grettel as the story behind them was rather tragic, rather sad. Their parents had cast them out, you see. Not once, but twice. The first time is still quite a well kept secret, my dears, a very well kept secret. The very, very few who know the real truth about the first time never ever speak of it in pubic where reporters and people like that might overhear, and of course you darlings won't say a word about it, now, will you? Of course you won't because you know that would make me very sad and very angry. Very angry. And you wouldn't want me angry at you, would you, my dears? No, of course you wouldn't.

There, there, did I frighten you? Now don't fret so or I won't go on with the story. That's better. That's my good little darlings, my bitsy snookumses.

Well, anyhow, when they were very young, just as young as you are, there was a great financial depression going on and all those funny people you see when you're out in the streets were losing their jobs in amazing numbers and looking more ragged and dirty by the day. Of course that was nothing near so bad as what was happening to people like ourselves, darlings, people who had *real* money to lose.

Hansel and Grettel's parents were starting to notice that there wasn't quite as much to spend as there used to be, and less all the time, and they realized they'd have to do something really serious about it if they wanted to avoid dipping into their capital, so, just like that, they decided to kill their children.

Now, now, don't look at me that way, my dears. It's only that sometimes grownups have to do things they'd really rather not. It's just the way it is, so stop fretting.

As it happened their plan didn't work out and the children lived because Hansel was very clever and left a little trail of stones which led them back to safety, you see. Grettel was most impressed, and of course their parents were fit to be tied.

There was quite a to-do about it at the time—headlines in the tabloids and things like that—but of course they got it all wrong and thought it was a kidnapping or something like that because, of course, they were *supposed* to, darlings, and fortunately Hansel and Grettel's mother and father still did have quite a bit of money in spite of the depression, **and** considerable influence, and after they'd spent a year or two in Europe the whole thing had blown over and their lawyers told them they could come back home.

But it did something to Hansel and Grettel, it really did; it seriously affected their attitude toward their parents and perhaps embittered them just a little toward the world in general. Things never really did work out emotionally in the family after the episode, and it was finally arranged that when Hansel and Grettel finished with their education they would receive an enormous amount of money—for you see, darlings, that nasty depression thing had run its course and everyone was rich again—and go off on their own and nobody would ever again mention the unfortunate business about the attempted murder.

So they permanently left their parents and just traveled and traveled and traveled to their hearts' content, my darlings, and bought everything they wanted, and at first they rented things, chateaux in Switzerland and Mas in the south of France and golden palaces in Thailand and so on and so on, but then they settled on the grand hotels, darlings, because it seemed so much simpler that way. No permanent servants, you see, no fussing about with gardens and all that, and it was such a delightful game finding the very best suites and getting more service and attention from the management than anyone else in the place.

Of course the hoteliers loved them, simply adored them, couldn't get enough of them. They knew their season was made if Hansel and Grettel decided to spend it with them and they were very careful to see to it that they did have the best accommodations since they were of course aware that Hansel and Grettel always knew at once if they *didn't* have the very best accommodations, and they tried to anticipate their every wish, giving them all the little treats and extras they could possibly desire, and to dream up and arrange a few delightful surprises if it was at all possible.

But as time went by Hansel and Grettel began to realize they were staying at the same places again and again because, my darlings, the awful truth is there simply aren't that many really good grand hotels, some of them are not even all that grand if the truth be told, so eventually they very understandably began to fret at the lack of novelty.

They were brooding about it in the salon of the very best suite in the very best grand hotel in all of Belgium when Grettel suddenly brightened, gave the most exquisite little cry of joy, and sat up in her chaise longue.

"I know what," she cried happily, turning to her brother. "Let's discover little places no one tells anyone else about because they want to keep them for themselves—people will be ever so deliciously *furious* when they've found out that we've found them!"

"Oh, what fun!" said Hansel, gazing dreamily into space and imagining all those hilariously angry people as he neatly popped a new Astrakhan cigarette into his holder.

So they started a whole new game and what a perfectly delightful one it turned out to be, darlings; what a marvelous time they had tracking down lovely, tucked-away resorts which people had spent fortunes trying to keep hidden and ferreting out exquisite auberges whose very existences had been jealously kept secret by their wealthy clientele for generations.

And what a highly satisfactory sensation was always reliably caused when the regulars of these establishments arrived at their previously exclusive hideaways and not only discovered Hansel and Grettel there before them, but occupying the very best suites or cabins in the whole place! Oh, they **were** furious, my darlings, you can be sure of that. Wildly, uncontrollably furious. Though, of course, they did their very best not to show it.

Naturally locating these marvelous spots wasn't at all easy because, of course, considerable ingenuity had gone into keeping them secret, but Hansel and Grettel were both not only very clever, they were also, as I've told you, very beautiful and charming and they knew how to use these things to worm secrets out of positively anyone. And it goes without saying they had the money and the common sense to hire a number of highly efficient agents to help them in their continuing quest.

Well, it did turn out to be absolutely marvelous fun, my dears, just as Hansel had guessed it might—uncovering the most fabulous places and spoiling them for everybody else; finding more and more deeply concealed retreats as they and their agents grew increasingly skillful in sniffing them out, but never, not in their greediest, gaudiest dreams, did they imagine what a strange and magical place all of this would eventually lead them to!

They first learnt of it while staying at a tiny spa attractively blended into a Romanian hill village, in full possession of a sumptuous but amusingly peasanty cottage which had up to then always been occupied during the season by an industrialist and his fat wife, who were presently sulking in a definitely inferior sort of hut down the glen.

Hansel and Grettel's cottage had its very own mineral bath built into the rock grotto of its terrace and the two of them were gaily splashing about in it, enjoying a little soak, when the steward came by with a particularly interesting report which had been wired to them by one of their very best agents, a wealthy young American woman, Bobsie, who had taken the job as a kind of hobby. You can imagine their excitement, darlings, when they read that Bobsie had managed to track down a spectacularly thrilling new find and the more they read, the more their excitement grew.

Her first clue came, Bobsie told them, when she remembered hearing marvelous rumors as a little rich girl in Philadelphia about a wonderful secret castle somewhere in Europe to which only the very, very wealthy could go on account of its being so expensive, you see, and because none but the very best people were allowed.

Once she recalled this charming childhood tale she couldn't resist looking into it to see if there might be some truth to the story, after all. At first she could find absolutely no hard information to back it up and she began to suspect the whole thing might only have been a girlish fantasy her little friends had made up to amuse themselves on rainy afternoons, but then she started coming across tiny bits of really solid, *grownup* gossip about it here and there, and in the end her persistence and her connections won out—she was, after all, the daughter of a prominent senator and the heiress to several large newspapers from her mother's previous marriage—and the truth finally tumbled into her lap.

The place was located deep within the Black Forest and was without doubt the oldest and most distinguished retreat any of Hansel and Grettel's agents had come across so far. No one knew when it had actually been built—the report by no means dispelled the charming air of mystery which enshrouded all of the establishment's history—but its tall towers with their conical roofs and its surrounding moat appeared to mark it as medieval, and since its general grandiosity left no doubt that some unknown regal hand had been involved in its construction, it had come to be known as King's Retreat, only in German of course, my darlings.

Royals of various nations were always associated with the place, the Hapsburgs primarily, but Bobsie had discovered that it was a favorite hideaway of many foreign blue bloods such as Queen Victoria's Duke of Clarence when he felt like being especially naughty on the Continent, and scads and scads of other sorts of famous people went there, darlings, whom you may learn about when you get a little older and interested in such things. Zelda and Scott Fitzgerald just loved the wine list, for example, and Hermann Goering simply adored the hunting.

Of course you can see that nothing would do but that Hansel and Grettel must go to King's Retreat as soon as possible, so Bobsie—and an *awful* lot of money—saw to it that the absolute best suite in the whole place would be ready and waiting for them the very next day. Off they went, darlings, leaving the rich industrialist and his fat wife to take over the Romanian cottage which, of course, would never again give them anywhere near as much pleasure as it had before.

Grettel fell in love with King's Retreat at her first sighting of it from their Rolls' window. It was perched proudly atop a mountain with bright white, bannered turrets and spotless, gracefully curving walls which had an interestingly irregular glitter of gold running along the rims of their high upper edges. It seemed in every way to be just like a castle in a fairy story, darlings, which of course is why I'm telling you about it now at bedtime. Of course Grettel was thrown into a perfect transport of delight.

"It's so sparkly and bright," she cried happily, tightly grasping one of her little pink hands with the other. "It looks like a candy castle!"

"Why so it does!" said Hansel, pouring them both another glass of champagne without spilling so much as one single solitary drop.

It shows you both what a grand job Bobsie had done and what an impressive reputation Hansel and Grettel had gotten among hoteliers when I tell you that when their Rolls pulled up to the graceful bank of steps leading to the main entrance of King's Retreat, they observed not only the Major Domo himself in all his regalia awaiting them, but to the total astonishment of them both, they saw, standing regally by his side, none other than the formidable, the nothing short of spectacular person of Opal Driscoll herself: the legendary and years-missing queen of all the society hostesses of Washington, New York, and Palm Beach.

Flashing her famously toothy smile, she reached out one diamond-ringed hand each to Hansel and Grettel as they emerged from their Rolls, frankly gaping up at her.

"Now you have the answer to the first question everyone's been asking since I left them flat," she said in her grand, full voice, leading them up the steps like two children. "I am here."

She paused at the entrance as its huge golden doors were swung gently open by minions and her smile grew even broader.

"The answer to the second question?" she asked, giving both their hands an affectionate little squeeze. "The answer is that once I found King's Retreat I simply could not *stand* the thought of hanging around those silly people in those silly places, desperately trying to force a little sparkle into their dreary parties. I knew from the day of my arrival here that my final fulfillment was to be its hostess. King's Retreat is my Shangri-la."

And then she studied Hansel and Grettel with such a long and thoughtful look that they both grew just a little intimidated, which was very unusual for them, my dears.

"I think you two will fit in very well," she said finally, giving them both a little nod and a pat each on their rosy cheeks. "As a matter of fact, I think you're *made* for the place."

And the more Hansel and Grettel saw of King's Retreat, the

more they began to suspect that what Opal Driscoll had said was true as true could be, darlings. Everything was just right for them, every last little detail was absolutely perfect. Grettel rather summed it up for both of them one morning while they were having breakfast on the spacious balcony which curved along the wall outside her bedroom.

"I just love this balcony," she said. "I love this table and this chair. I love the way the egg has been cooked for exactly three minutes, and I love that it's been brought to me while it's still nice and hot. I love the air, I love the view, I love absolutely everything I can see and feel and taste and smell and hear."

"It is really grand, isn't it?" said Hansel, adding just enough cream to his coffee to make it perfect.

There was one aspect to the castle, however, which stuck out from its unobtrusive, universal perfection in a way that both Hansel and Grettel had to admit was distinctly odd. It was not in the slightest way irritating; actually it was quite lovely; actually it would be fair to say that it was even extraordinarily beautiful, but it *was* undeniably odd.

I told you that when they first drove up to King's Retreat Hansel and Grettel had noticed a golden glittering along its upper ramparts. A day or so later, after they had both got themselves comfortably settled in, the Major Domo—everyone called him Herr Oskar—took them on a delightfully complete tour of the castle starting from its deepest basements and dungeons and bringing them all the way up to its tallest roofs and spires.

As a climax to this tour, after going around and around and higher and higher on the almost comically interminable spiraling of a stone staircase, Oskar led them out into the brisk, fresh breeze blowing onto a high rampart's walkway and proudly spread both his arms wide with a great sweep like some gold-buttoned eagle. Following the pointings of his fingertips, Hansel and Grettel looked first one way, then the other, and they discovered that the glittering they had seen came from seemingly endless rows of golden statues which stood upon those ramparts.

Standing almost elbow to elbow, the statues gazed up at the sky, or peered far off toward the blue Alps lining the distant horizon, or stared with varyingly thoughtful expressions down the great drop into to the green and peaceful valley far below. They were exactly life size, all dressed in the costumes of Imperial Rome, and their togas and sandals and occasional spears and shields put the cultured viewer—you will be sent to schools and become cultured in time I am sure, my dears—in mind of the figures painted on antique vases or carved into friezes running round the tops of ancient temples.

"It was begun, they tell me, as a whim of our original royal founder," Herr Oskar told them in his deep, carrying voice, and then he raised a large, white-gloved hand and pointed its forefinger to a tall golden figure standing where the highest end of the topmost rampart connected smoothly with the tallest tower.

"That statue was the first, and is the oldest," he informed them, indicating a dignified figure wearing the costume and regalia of a Caesar, "but you will see that every leaf on his laurel crown shines as bright as new. They never need polishing nor any kind of maintenance, these marvelous likenesses. They are pure gold, all of them, and every bit as perfect as when first they were made."

Then Oskar told them a strange thing about the statues, something that was actually a little spooky, my darlings, though you mustn't let it frighten you and give you nightmares when I turn off the light and leave you all alone in the dark—it seemed that every one of them, without exception, looked exactly like an honored guest who had stayed at King's Retreat at some point in its long and interesting history.

They followed the Major Domo on a tour of the castle's high and windy walks, halting behind him as he now and then paused before a particular golden image, and listened with increasing interest as he proudly spoke the name of the famous or infamous person which it so perfectly resembled. Occasionally he would smile and tell a little story concerning why some guest had been chosen for so notable an honor. Sometimes the stories were solemn and sometimes they were quite amusing, but he told them all with the utmost dignity and respect.

It is not easy to visibly impress people like Hansel and Grettel—you will find that out as you grow older, darlings—but the statues and Oskar's stories concerning them managed to do the job quite nicely. Their eyes grew wider and wider as they heard of the great statesmen and scientists and artists and captains of industry who had spent every moment they could possibly spare from their busy and highly important lives at King's Retreat and who, at the end, had eagerly accepted, had sometimes even fought over, the great distinction of having their exact likeness added to the long, gleaming, golden line which wound its way along the crenellated heights of their beloved hideaway.

Inwardly delighted at how thoroughly his little tour was impressing his guests, and seeing how each further revelation increased the effect, Oskar became, perhaps, just a trifle too pleased with himself, just a little too eager to bedazzle his charges.

"There *is* another group of them, you know," he said in a portentous tone, ignoring a cautionary voice which had begun to whisper warnings with mounting alarm deep down inside him, "a *secret* group. A much more important group than even *these!*"

The sudden, sharp interest which flared in the faces of both Hansel and Grettel, the abrupt increase somehow in the *shine* of them, both these things abruptly warned Oskar that he had gone too far and said too much. He stood with one gloved hand barely touching the burly golden arm of a statue perfectly resembling Germany's greatest writer of operas and warily observed his guests edging ever closer to him like a couple of foxes closing in on a cornered hen.

"Indeed?" said Hansel, smiling up at Oskar with an intense attention which gleamed brighter by the second in his already bright blue eyes. "And who, pray, is in this so very special group, Oskar?"

"Yes, Oskar," chimed in Grettel, "And where are they hidden?"

"We must definitely see them," said Hansel, employing a tone of quiet firmness Oskar had learned to recognize, respect and dread in his most important guests. "We must hear all about them."

"You must take us to them at once," finished Grettel.

They stood silently while the poor fellow studied their raised brows, their cold little smiles, and their unwaveringly steady gazes. It is greatly to his credit that he weathered all this for almost a full minute before he buckled and—without another word—turned and led them where they'd asked to go.

He took them on a complicated and devious route which traversed territories in the castle completely unexplored by their previous tour. It involved secret panels and hidden staircases and cobwebby hallways and dark chambers, which were made hideous by the flappings and billowings of dusty, ragged tapestries tossed by mysterious and clammy drafts.

Eventually they passed through an opening provided by the smooth sliding aside of an enormous oil portrait of a family whose faces had all been macabrely distorted by centuries of smudgy soot and found themselves stepping into what seemed to be the transept of an enormous cathedral whose high arches could only be dimly made out in the darkness far above them.

Grimly, Oskar led them past the choir toward the cathedral's sanctuary and a dim gleaming ahead slowly resolved itself into a bright, curving row of golden statues surrounding and staring at a large raised platform made of dark wood upon which stood a sort of hollow altar which was built of the same somber material. The Major Domo bowed slightly and indicated the statues with a dignified sweep of one gloved hand.

"Here, before you in this holy place," he intoned with the greatest possible solemnity, "commencing with no less than His Original Majesty, stand all the past hosts of King's Retreat!"

Hansel and Grettel studied the golden statues carefully and in silence, beginning with the King—who was, indeed, crowned and who bore a royal scepter and wore an ermine-edged cape—and going on through at least two dozen statues until they'd reached the last one, a distinguished-looking man in modern evening dress who sported a monocle.

It was immediately clear to both brother and sister that there was something about these statues, something disturbing, something sinister, which set them entirely apart from those which stood so proudly in the clean fresh air and sunlight so high above this dim, dark place, but full minutes passed before Grettel managed to put that difference into words.

"They're afraid," she breathed. "They're all simply terrified!"

The Major Domo cleared his throat, looked at her nervously, then cast a hesitant glance over his shoulder at the statues ranged somehow ominously behind him.

"I have noticed that seeming effect, myself, Miss," he began, "but I have always put it down to—"

"*OSKAR!!!*"

The Major Domo's lips snapped shut and his head cringed as far back down as it could into his high collar as that terrific, terrible shout rung and echoed all about them, then mingled with the sound of determined footsteps marching up the transept.

"What have you *done,* you foolish man?" cried Opal Driscoll as she neared her unfortunate flunky. "What *foolishness* have you been up to?"

Only then did Hansel and Grettel notice another figure lagging somewhat behind their hostess. It was none other than General Brigham S. Parker, a fellow guest at King's Retreat, the hero of the battle of Bestokia, and lately the Supreme High Commander of the Allied European Forces, looking more than a little uncomfortable and perhaps even a tiny touch ridiculous in the leather kilt and feathered helmet of a Roman soldier.

Opal Driscoll noticed the direction of their gaze and immediately tempered her mood—albeit with a shudder which shook her from head to foot—from total fury to a kind of philosophical annoyance.

"Ah well, ah well," she said, glaring at Oskar, but then smiling on Hansel and Grettel and upon General Parker as he managed to catch up with her in spite of his cumbersome sandals.

"I suppose it can't be helped," she said with a sigh and a shrug. "I suppose it's the sort of thing that's simply bound to happen, now and then."

And then she graciously explained that she had brought the General to this secret place to pose for a sculptor who was to model a statue of him as a Roman soldier which would then be cast in gold and set up on the ramparts.

"Of course you must not tell anyone any of this," she said, smiling at Hansel and Grettel benignly, "nor about this place, which is the very heart of King's Retreat."

She paused and looked at them with great significance.

"You understand that if Oskar had committed this breach of security with ordinary guests we would have had a very serious problem," she said. "But since he committed his indiscretion with you most especial people, the situation is manageable since . . ."

She paused again, then reached out and put her hands on Hansel and Grettel's shoulders with the air of a high priestess conferring initiation.

". . . since it has already been decided that both of you, in time, will be chosen to pose for statues of gold."

Of course, darlings, you can see that Hansel and Grettel were initially delighted to learn that they were to receive this remarkable honor, but as Oskar began to lead them away from the hidden cathedral, leaving Opal Driscoll and General Brigham S. Parker to await the arrival of the sculptor, a thoughtful look began to grow upon Hansel's face.

The trip back from the cathedral was, if anything, even more arcane than the approach had been. It was almost as if Oskar was carefully selecting the most involved and confusing pathways he could devise, and it even seemed that sometimes he was carefully improvising additional complications as he led them along. Secret panels opened upon trap doors which exposed twisting stairways leading to hidden tunnels which wormed unexpectedly up to perilously high catwalks that blended into mysterious labyrinths occasionally interrupted by underground waterways which had to be negotiated by means of gondolas and led to bat-infested caves requiring smoking torches for traversement.

In the end they found themselves exiting into a lovely salon with which they were perfectly familiar and there Oskar left them after much bowing and scraping and multitudes of apologies for any inconveniences his lack of judgment might have caused.

Only when the Major Domo's footsteps had faded entirely away did Hansel grin slyly at his sister, wink, and hold up a small appointment book which he always kept on his person. He opened it and slowly turned its pages to show her that only three or four of them remained.

"I just *knew* you were doing that!" she said proudly, smiling and patting him affectionately on his arm, for what Hansel had done, darlings, was a variation on what he had done before to thwart the murderous plans his father and mother had set in motion against himself and his sister when they were helpless little children such as yourselves—he had left a trail so that they could retrace their steps, only this time he had used little bits of torn paper instead of stones.

Wasn't that extremely clever of him, darlings?

Without a moment's hesitation on either one of their parts they both smartly turned around and—going from one bit of torn paper to the next—easily retraced the complicated route Oskar had created in order to confuse them. In almost no time at all the two of them had once more made their way through the involved innards of King's Retreat and were tiptoeing as quietly as they could back into its hidden cathedral.

Opal Driscoll was standing before the dark platform and staring thoughtfully at General Brigham S. Parker, who was looking rather lost in the center of the hollow altar as he held a wide Roman sword out awkwardly before him. There was no sign at all of any sculptor.

"Grip the sword as if you were about to kill someone with it, General dear," said Opal Driscoll firmly. "And please do try to look a little fiercer."

The General attempted both of these things, and when she saw he was not being particularly successful with either one of them she sighed and shrugged.

"Well, I suppose it will have to do," she said. "But you must promise not to move!"

The General nodded obediently.

And then, darlings, Opal Driscoll carried out the most extraordinary, the most absolutely peculiar actions you could possibly imagine, one right after the other.

First she stuck both her arms straight up into the air and began to revolve them round and round with her fingers spread out like the ribs in bats' wings, and somehow this made nasty little sparks leap out from the sides of the altar to attack the General like a horde of glowing wasps whose massive stingings instantly and firmly paralyzed the poor fellow into his heroic posture; though, if you looked very closely, you could see his eyes were bulging slightly from their sockets.

Then she stamped her left foot and then her right foot as

hard and flat as she could on what Hansel and Grettel now perceived to be strange cabalistic patterns worked into the marble floor, and this made the altar glow with a throbbing yellow light that began to spread insidiously forward into the body of the General, who now began a muffled screaming, which was made considerably more horrible by the soldierly calm into which his face had been frozen.

Then she opened her large, toothy mouth very, very wide and howled out a series of perfectly ghastly words, darlings, which I absolutely will not repeat to you at this time—even though I *do* know them, every one of them—because they are terribly dangerous and I don't want any harm to come to my darlings, no I don't, because I love them, because they do everything I say.

Anyhow, the General's screaming chopped right off at the sound of the very first ghastly word and the yellow light began to crawl in funny, twisty ways through his stiffened body like so many glowing worms, and the next thing you knew he had turned into solid gold and Opal Driscoll was laughing and laughing like a crazy mad thing, fit to beat the band.

After a while she calmed down a bit and when she'd got her breath back she began to study the General and it was obvious she was highly pleased with the overall effect. She stepped onto the platform and paused before the altar to get a closer look at what she'd done.

It was at that point that Grettel noticed that Hansel was very carefully studying something she had seen him copying down on the pages remaining in his notebook just a moment or so ago.

Then Opal Driscoll stepped forward and the moment Hansel saw for sure that she was standing *inside* the hollow in the dark altar, next to her brand-new golden statue, he stuck both his arms straight up into the air and began to revolve them round and round with his fingers spread like the ribs in bats' wings, and he kept on going through all the magical steps exactly as he had seen Opal Driscoll do them, stamping on the floor and howling the ghastly words—which I'm sure you've guessed, darlings, is what he had copied into his notebook—and Opal Driscoll went through all the eye-popping and screaming and turning into solid gold the General had suffered, but she did it much more visibly and gruesomely because she knew what was happening to her, having done it so many times to others, so that by the time she was transformed entirely into a statue she was crouched low with her fingers clawed out viciously before her snarling face, looking for all the world like a rat trapped by a farmer about to smash it flat with his hoe.

Following Hansel and Grettel's instructions, the Major Domo installed Opal Driscoll at the end of the line of statues curving round the altar, and then he stood the General up on the ramparts so that the old soldier might forever hold his golden sword menacingly before him as though he was about to kill someone with it, and even now his somewhat bulging eyes still glare fiercely into the void from that high perch. Once I saw an eagle land on his golden shoulder, darlings, and I confess the effect was really quite magnificent.

Of course Hansel and Grettel then became the host and hostess—for that is the ancient tradition—and they are to this day, and it's not likely anyone will come along who'll know how to find their way into the secret cathedral and say the ghastly words and turn *them* into golden statues and thus take their place as the *new* host and hostess of King's Retreat.

Not unless they're as well informed as *you*, my darlings!

The Sea Was Wet as Wet Could Be

I felt we made an embarrassing contrast to the open serenity of the scene around us. The pure blue of the sky was unmarked by a single cloud or bird, and nothing stirred on the vast stretch of beach except ourselves. The sea, sparkling under the freshness of the early morning sun, looked invitingly clean. I wanted to wade into it and wash myself, but I was afraid I would contaminate it.

We are a contamination here, I thought. We're like a group of sticky bugs crawling in an ugly little crowd over polished marble. If I were God and looked down and saw us, lugging our baskets and our silly, bright blankets, I would step on us and squash us with my foot.

We should have been lovers or monks in such a place, but we were only a crowd of bored and boring drunks. You were always drunk when you were with Carl. Good old, mean old Carl was the greatest little drink pourer in the world. He used drinks like other types of sadists use whips. He kept beating you with them until you dropped or sobbed or went mad, and he enjoyed every step of the process.

We'd been drinking all night, and when the morning came, somebody, I think it was Mandie, got the great idea that we should all go out on a picnic. Naturally, we thought it was an inspiration; we were nothing if not real sports, and so we'd packed some goodies, not forgetting the liquor, and we'd piled into the car, and there we were, weaving across the beach, looking for a place to spread our tacky banquet.

We located a broad, low rock, decided it would serve for our table, and loaded it with the latest in plastic chinaware, a haphazard collection of food and a quantity of bottles.

Someone had packed a tin of Spam among the other offerings, and when I saw it, I was suddenly overwhelmed with an absurd feeling of nostalgia. It reminded me of the war and of myself soldierboying up through Italy. It also reminded me of how long ago the whole thing had been and how little I'd done of what I'd dreamed I'd do back then.

I opened the Spam and sat down to be alone with it and my memories, but it wasn't to be for long. The kind of people who run with people like Carl don't like to be alone, ever, especially with their memories, and they can't imagine anyone else might, at least now and then, have a taste for it.

My rescuer was Irene. Irene was particularly sensitive about seeing people alone because being alone had several times nearly produced fatal results for her. Being alone and taking pills to end the being alone.

"What's wrong, Phil?" she asked.

"Nothing's wrong," I said, holding up a forkful of the pink

Spam in the sunlight. "It tastes just like it always did. They haven't lost their touch."

She sat down on the sand beside me, very carefully, so as to avoid spilling the least drop of what must have been her millionth Scotch.

"Phil," she said, "I'm worried about Mandie. I really am. She looks so unhappy!"

I glanced over at Mandie. She had her head thrown back and she was laughing uproariously at some joke Carl had just made. Carl was smiling at her with his teeth glistening and his eyes deep down dead as ever.

"Why should Mandie be happy?" I asked. "What, in God's name, has she got to be happy about?"

"Oh, Phil," said Irene. "You pretend to be such an awful cynic. She's *alive*, isn't she?"

I looked at her and wondered what such a statement meant, coming from someone who'd tried to do herself in as earnestly and as frequently as Irene. I decided that I did not know and that I would probably never know. I also decided I didn't want any more of the Spam. I turned to throw it away, doing my bit to litter up the beach, and then I saw them.

They were far away, barely bigger than two dots, but you could tell there was something odd about them even then.

"We've got company," I said.

Irene peered in the direction of my point.

"Look, everybody," she cried. "We've got company!"

Everybody looked, just as she had asked them to.

"What the hell is this?" asked Carl. "Don't they know this is my private property?" And then he laughed.

Carl had fantasies about owning things and having power.

Now and then he got drunk enough to have little flashes of be-
lieving he was king of the world.

"You tell 'em, Carl!" said Horace.

Horace had sparkling quips like that for almost every occasion. He was tall and bald and he had a huge Adam's apple
and, like myself, he worked for Carl. I would have felt sorrier
for Horace than I did if I hadn't had a sneaky suspicion that he
was really happier when groveling. He lifted one scrawny fist
and shook it in the direction of the distant pair.

"You guys better beat it," he shouted. "This is private
property!"

"Will you shut up and stop being such an ass?" Mandie
asked him. "It's not polite to yell at strangers, dear, and this
may damn well be *their* beach for all you know."

Mandie happens to be Horace's wife. Horace's children
treat him about the same way. He busied himself with zipping
up his windbreaker because it was getting cold and because he
had received an order to be quiet.

I watched the two approaching figures. The one was tall
and bulky, and he moved with a peculiar, swaying gait. The
other was short and hunched into himself, and he walked in a
fretful, zigzag line beside his towering companion.

"They're heading straight for us," I said.

The combination of the cool wind that had come up, and
the approach of the two strangers, had put a damper on our
little group. We sat quietly and watched them coming closer.
The nearer they got, the odder they looked.

"For heaven's sake!" said Irene. "The little one's wearing a
square hat!"

"I think it's made of paper," said Mandie, squinting. "Folded
newspaper."

"Will you look at the mustache on the big bastard?" asked Carl. "I don't think I've ever seen a bigger bush in my life."

"They remind me of something," I said.

The others turned to look at me.

The Walrus and the Carpenter . . .

"They remind me of the Walrus and the Carpenter," I said.

"The who?" asked Mandie.

"Don't tell me you never heard of the Walrus and the Carpenter?" asked Carl.

"Never once," said Mandie.

"Disgusting," said Carl. "You're an uncultured bitch. The Walrus and the Carpenter are probably two of the most famous characters in literature. They're in a poem by Lewis Carroll in one of the Alice books."

"In *Through the Looking Glass,*" I said, and then I recited their introduction:

The Walrus and the Carpenter
Were walking close at hand:
They wept like anything to see
Such quantities of sand . . .

Mandie shrugged. "Well, you'll just have to excuse my ignorance and concentrate on my charm," she said.

"I don't know how to break this to you all," said Irene, "but the little one *does* have a handkerchief."

We stared at them. The little one did indeed have a handkerchief, a huge handkerchief, and he was using it to dab at his eyes.

"Is the little one supposed to be the Carpenter?" asked Mandie.

"Yes," I said.

"Then it's all right," she said, "because he's the one that's carrying the saw."

"He is, so help me, God," said Carl. "And, to make the whole thing perfect, he's even wearing an apron."

"So the Carpenter in the poem has to wear an apron, right?" asked Mandie.

"Carroll doesn't say whether he does or not," I said, "but the illustrations by Tenniel show him wearing one. They also show him with the same square jaw and the same big nose this guy's got."

"They're goddamn doubles," said Carl. "The only thing wrong is that the Walrus isn't a walrus; he just looks like one."

"You watch," said Mandie. "Any minute now he's going to sprout fur all over and grow long fangs."

Then, for the first time, the approaching pair noticed us. It seemed to give them quite a start. They stood and gaped at us and the little one furtively stuffed his handkerchief out of sight.

"We can't be as surprising as all that!" whispered Irene.

The big one began moving forward, then, in a hesitant, tentative kind of shuffle. The little one edged ahead, too, but he was careful to keep the bulk of his companion between himself and us.

"First contact with the aliens," said Mandie, and Irene and Horace giggled nervously. I didn't respond. I had come to the decision that I was going to quit working for Carl, that I didn't like any of these people about me, except, maybe, Irene, and that these two strangers gave me the honest creeps.

Then the big one smiled, and everything was changed.

I've worked in the entertainment field, in advertising, and in public relations. This means I have come in contact with some of the prime charm boys and girls in our proud land. I have become, therefore, not only a connoisseur of smiles, I am a being equipped with numerous automatic safeguards against them. When a talcumed smoothie comes at me with his brilliant ivories exposed, it only shows he's got something he can bite me with, that's all.

But the smile of the Walrus was something else.

The smile of the Walrus did what a smile hasn't done for me in years—it melted my heart. I use the corn-ball phrase very much on purpose. When I saw his smile, I knew I could trust him; I felt in my marrow that he was gentle and sweet and had nothing but the best intentions. His resemblance to the Walrus in the poem ceased being vaguely chilling and became warmly comical. I loved him as I had loved the teddy bear of my childhood.

"Oh, I *say*," he said, and his voice was an embarrassed boom, "I *do* hope we're not intruding!"

"I daresay we are," squeaked the Carpenter, peeping out from behind his companion.

"The, uhm, fact is," boomed the Walrus, "we didn't even notice you until just back then, you see."

"We were talking, is what," said the Carpenter.

They wept like anything to see
Such quantities of sand . . .

"About sand?" I asked.

The Walrus looked at me with a startled air.

"We *were,* actually, now you come to mention it."

He lifted one huge foot and shook it so that a little trickle of sand spilled out of his shoe.

"The stuff's impossible," he said. "Gets in your clothes, tracks up the carpet."

"Ought to be swept away, it ought," said the Carpenter.

"If seven maids with seven mops
Swept it for half a year,
Do you suppose," the Walrus said,
"That they could get it clear?"

"It's too much!" said Carl.

"Yes, indeed," said the Walrus, eyeing the sand around him with vague disapproval. "Altogether too much."

Then he turned to us again and we all basked in that smile.

"Permit me to introduce my companion and myself," he said.

"You'll have to excuse George," said the Carpenter, "as he's a bit of a stuffed shirt, don't you know?"

"Be that as it may," said the Walrus, patting the Carpenter on the flat top of his paper hat. "This is Edward Farr, and I am George Tweedy, both at your service. We are, uhm, both a trifle drunk, I'm afraid."

"We are, indeed. We are that."

"As we have just come from a really delightful party, to which we shall soon return."

"Once we've found the fuel, that is," said Farr, waving his saw in the air. By now he had found the courage to come out and face us directly.

"Which brings me to the question," said Tweedy. "Have you

seen any **driftwood** lying about the premises? We've been
looking high and low and we can't seem to find **any** of the
blasted stuff."

"Thought there'd be piles of it," said Farr, "but all there is is
sand, don't you see?"

"I would have sworn you were looking for oysters," said Carl.
Again, Tweedy appeared startled.

"O oysters come and walk with us!"
The Walrus did beseech . . .

"Oysters?" he asked. "Oh, no, we've **got** the oysters. All we
lack is the means to cook 'em."

"Course we could always use a few more," said Farr, looking
at his companion.

"I suppose we **could,** at that," said Tweedy thoughtfully.

"I'm afraid we can't help you fellows with the driftwood
problem," said Carl, "but you're more than welcome to a
drink."

There was something unfamiliar about the tone of Carl's
voice that made my ears perk up. I turned to look at him, and
then had difficulty covering up my astonishment.

It was his eyes. For once, for the first time, they were really
friendly.

I'm not saying Carl had fishy eyes, blank eyes—not at all.
On the surface, that is. On the surface, with his eyes, with
his face, with the handling of his entire body, Carl was a master of animation and expression. From sympathetic, heart-felt
warmth, all the way to icy rage, and on every stop in-between,
Carl was completely convincing.

But only on the surface. Once you got to know Carl, and it took a while, you realized that none of it was really happening. That was because Carl had died, or been killed, long ago. Possibly in childhood. Possibly he had been born dead. So, under the actor's warmth and rage, the eyes were always the eyes of a corpse.

But now it was different. The friendliness here was genuine, I was sure of it. The smile of Tweedy, of the Walrus, had performed a miracle. Carl had risen from his tomb. I was in honest awe.

"*Delighted,* old chap!" said Tweedy.

They accepted their drinks with obvious pleasure, and we completed the introductions as they sat down to join us. I detected a strong smell of fish when Tweedy sat down beside me but, oddly, I didn't find it offensive in the least. I was glad he'd chosen me to sit by. He turned and smiled at me, and my heart melted a little more.

It soon turned out that the drinking we'd done before had only scratched the surface. Tweedy and Farr were magnificent boozers, and their gusto encouraged us all to follow suit.

We drank absurd toasts and were delighted to discover that Tweedy was an incredible raconteur. His speciality was outrageous fantasy: wild tales involving incongruous objects, events, and characters. His invention was endless.

> *"The time has come," the Walrus said,*
>> *"To talk of many things:*
> *Of shoes—and ships—and sealing wax—*
>> *Of cabbages—and kings—*
> *And why the sea is boiling hot—*
>> *And whether pigs have wings."*

We laughed and drank, and drank and laughed, and I began to wonder why in hell I'd spent my life being such a gloomy, moody sonofabitch, been such a distrustful and suspicious bastard, when the whole secret of everything, the whole core secret, was simply to enjoy it, to take it as it came.

I looked around and grinned, and I didn't care if it was a foolish grin. Everybody looked all right, everybody looked swell, everybody looked better than I'd ever seen them look before.

Irene looked happy, honestly and truly happy. She, too, had found the secret. No more pills for Irene, I thought. Now that she knows the secret, now that she's met Tweedy who's given her the secret, she'll have no more need of those goddamn pills.

And I couldn't believe Horace and Mandie. They had their arms around each other, and their bodies were pressed close together, and they rocked as one being when they laughed at Tweedy's wonderful stories. No more nagging for Mandie. I thought, and no more cringing for Horace, now they've learned the secret.

And then I looked at Carl, laughing and relaxed, and absolutely free of care, absolutely unchilled, finally, at last, after years of——

And then I looked at Carl again.

And then I looked down at my drink, and then I looked at my knees, and then I looked out at the sea, sparkling, clean, remote, and impersonal.

And then I realized it had grown cold, quite cold, and that there wasn't a bird or a cloud in the sky.

The sea was wet as wet could be,
  The sands were dry as dry.

You could not see a cloud, because
  No cloud was in the sky:
No birds were flying overhead—
  There were no birds to fly.

That part of the poem was, after all, a perfect description of a lifeless earth. It sounded beautiful at first, it sounded benign. But then you read it again and you realized that Carroll was describing barrenness and desolation.

Suddenly Carl's voice broke through and I heard him say:

"Hey, that's a hell of an idea, Tweedy! By God, we'd love to! Wouldn't we, gang?"

The others broke out in an affirmative chorus and they all started scrambling to their feet around me. I looked up at them, like someone who's been awakened from sleep in a strange place, and they grinned down at me like loons.

"Come on, Phil!" cried Irene.

Her eyes were bright and shining, but it wasn't with happiness. I could see that now.

"It seems a shame," the Walrus said,
  "To play them such a trick . . ."

I blinked my eyes and stared at them, one after the other.

"Old Phil's had a little too much to drink!" cried Mandie, laughing. "Come on, old Phil! Come on and join the party!"

"What party?" I asked.

I couldn't seem to get located. Everything seemed disorientated and grotesque.

"For Christ's sake, Phil," said Carl, "Tweedy and Farr, here, have invited us to join their party. There're no more drinks left, and they've got plenty!"

I set my plastic cup down carefully on the sand. If they would just shut up for a moment, I thought, I might be able to get the fuzz out of my head.

"Come *along,* sir!" boomed Tweedy jovially. "It's only a pleasant walk!"

> "O oysters come and walk with us,"
>> The walrus did beseech.
> "A pleasant walk, a pleasant talk,
>> Along the briny beach . . ."

He was smiling at me, but the smile didn't work anymore.

"You cannot do with more than four," I told him.

"*Uhm?* What's that?"

> ". . . we cannot do with more than four,
>> And give a hand to each."

"I said, 'You cannot do with more than four.' "

"He's right, you know," said Farr, the Carpenter.

"Well, uhm, then," said the Walrus, "if you feel you really *can't* come, old chap . . ."

"What, in Christ's name, are you all talking about?" asked Mandie.

"He's hung up on that goddamn poem," said Carl. "Lewis Carroll's got the yellow bastard scared."

"Don't be such a party pooper, Phil!" said Mandie.

"To hell with him," said Carl. And he started off, and all the others followed him. Except Irene.

"Are you sure you really don't want to come, Phil?" she asked.

She looked frail and thin against the sunlight. I realized there really wasn't much of her, and that what there was had taken a terrible beating.

"No," I said. "I don't. Are you sure you want to go?"

"Of course I do, Phil."

I thought of the pills.

"I suppose you do," I said. "I suppose there's really no stopping you."

"No, Phil, there isn't."

And then she stooped and kissed me. Kissed me very gently, and I could feel the dry, chapped surface of her lips and the faint warmth of her breath.

I stood.

"I wish you'd stay," I said.

"I can't," she said.

And then she turned and ran after the others.

I watched them growing smaller and smaller on the beach, following the Walrus and the Carpenter. I watched them come to where the beach curved around the bluff, and watched them disappear behind the bluff.

I looked up at the sky. Pure blue. Impersonal.

"What do you think of this?" I asked it.

Nothing. It hadn't even noticed.

"Now, if you're ready, oysters dear,
    We can begin to feed."
"But not on us!" the oysters cried,
    Turning a little blue,

"After such kindness, that would be
   A dismal thing to do!"

A dismal thing to do.

I began to run up the beach, toward the bluff. I stumbled now and then because I had had too much to drink. Far too much to drink. I heard small shells crack under my shoes, and the sand made whipping noises.

I fell, heavily, and lay there gasping on the beach. My heart pounded in my chest. I was too old for this sort of footwork. I hadn't had any real exercise in years. I smoked too much and I drank too much. I did all the wrong things. I didn't do any of the right things.

I pushed myself up a little and then I let myself down again. My heart was pounding hard enough to frighten me. I could feel it in my chest, frantically pumping, squeezing blood in and spurting blood out.

Like an oyster pulsing in the sea.

"Shall we be trotting home again?"

My heart was like an oyster.

I got up, fell up, and began to run again, weaving widely, my mouth open and the air burning my throat. I was coated with sweat, streaming with it, and it felt icy in the cold wind.

"Shall we be trotting home again?"

I rounded the bluff, and then I stopped and stood swaying, and then I dropped to my knees.

The pure blue of the sky was unmarked by a single bird or cloud, and nothing stirred on the whole vast stretch of the beach.

But answer there came none—
And this was scarcely odd, because . . .

Nothing stirred, but they were there. Irene and Mandie and Carl and Horace were there, and four others, too. Just around the bluff.

"We cannot do with more than four . . ."

But the Walrus and the Carpenter had taken two trips.

I began to crawl toward them on my knees. My heart, my oyster heart, was pounding too hard to allow me to stand.

The other four had had a picnic, too, very like our own. They, too, had plastic cups and plates, and they, too, had brought bottles. They had sat and waited for the return of the Walrus and the Carpenter.

Irene was right in front of me. Her eyes were open and stared at, but did not see, the sky. The pure blue uncluttered sky. There were a few grains of sand in her left eye. Her face was almost clear of blood. There were only a few flecks of it on her lower chin. The spray from the huge wound in her chest seemed to have traveled mainly downward and to the right. I stretched out my arm and touched her hand.

"Irene," I said.

But answer there came none—
And this was scarcely odd, because
They'd eaten every one.

I looked up at the others. Like Irene, they were, all of them, dead. The Walrus and the Carpenter had eaten the oysters and left the shells.

The Carpenter never had found any firewood, and so they'd eaten them raw. You can eat oysters raw if you want to.

I said her name once more, just for the record, and then I stood and turned from them and walked to the bluff. I rounded the bluff and the beach stretched before me, vast, smooth, empty, and remote.

Even as I ran upon it, away from them, it was remote.

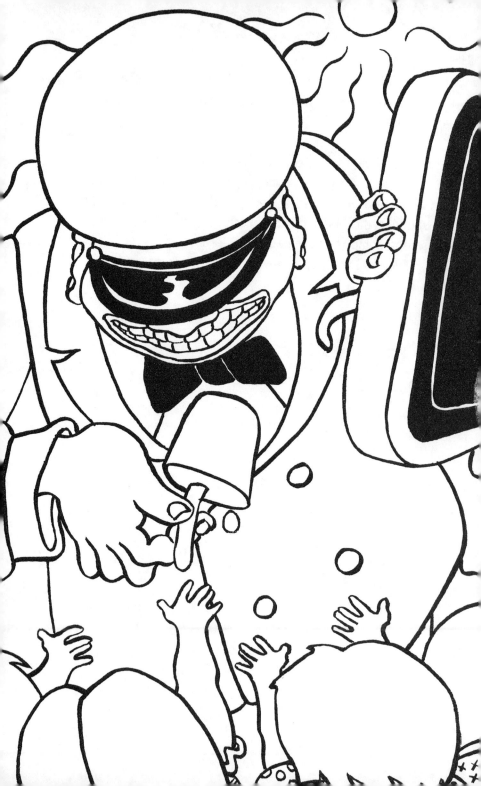

Mister Ice Cold

Listen, children! Hear the music? Hear its bright and cheerful chiming coming down the street? Hear it playing its pretty little tune—*dingy di-ding, dingy di-ding*—as it sings softly through the green trees, through the blue sky overhead, as it sings through the thick, still, sultry summer heat?

It's Mister Ice Cold coming in his truck! Mister Ice Cold and his nice ice cream! Fat, round, cool balls of it plopped into cones! Thick, juicy slabs of it covered in frozen chocolate frosting and stuck on sticks! Soft, pink, chilly twirls of it oozed into cups!

The music's coming closer through the heat—*dingy di-ding, dingy di-ding*—and excitement starts stirring where all was lazy and drowsy just a sweaty blink before!

Bobby Martin's no longer lying flat on the grass, staring up at a slow moving summer cloud without seeing it at all; he's scrambled to his feet and is running over the thick summer grass to ask his mother—nodding on the porch over a limp magazine almost slipped from her fingers—if he can have enough money to buy a frozen lime frog.

And Suzy Brenner's left off dreamily trying to tie her doll's bonnet over her cat's head (much to the cat's relief) and is desperately digging into her plastic, polka-dot purse to see if there's enough change in there to buy her a cup of banana ice cream with chocolate sprinkles. Oh, she can taste the sweetness of it! Oh, her throat can feel its coolness going down!

And you, you've forgotten all about blowing through a leaf to see if you can make it squeak the way you saw Arnold Carter's older brother do it; now you're clawing feverishly with your small hands in both pockets, feeling your way past that sandy shell you found yesterday on the beach, and that little ball chewed bounceless by your dog, and that funny rock you came across in the vacant lot which may, with luck, be full of uranium and highly radioactive, and so far you have come up with two pennies and a quarter and you think you've just touched a nickel.

Meantime Mister Ice Cold's truck is rolling ever closer—*dingy di-ding, dingy di-ding*—and Martin Walpole, always a show-off, wipes his brow, points, and calls out proudly: "I see it! There it is!"

And, sure enough, *there it is,* rolling smoothly around the corner of Main and Lincoln, and you can see the shiny, fat fullness of its white roof gleaming in the bright sun through the thick, juicy-green foliage of the trees which have, in the peak of their summer swelling, achieved a tropical density and richness more appropriate to some Amazonian jungle than to midwestern Lakeside, and you push aside one last, forgotten tangle of knotted string in your pocket and your heart swells for joy because you've come across another quarter and that means you've got enough for an orange icicle on a stick which will freeze your fillings and chill your gut and stain your tongue that gorgeous, glowing copper color which never fails to terrify your sister!

Now Mister Ice Cold's truck has swept into full view and its *dingy di-ding* sounds out loud and clear and sprightly enough, even in this steaming, muggy air, to startle a sparrow and make it swerve in its flight.

Rusty Taylor's dog barks for a signal and all of you come running quick as you can from every direction, coins clutched in your sweaty fingers and squeezed tightly as possible in your damp, small palms, and every one of you is licking your lips and staring at the bright blue lettering painted in frozen ice cubes and spelling out MISTER ICE COLD over the truck's sides and front and back, and Mister Ice Cold himself gives a sweeping wave of his big, pale hand to everyone from behind his wheel and brings his vehicle and all the wonders it contains to a slow, majestic halt with the skill and style of a commodore docking an ocean liner.

"A strawberry rocket!" cries fat Harold Smith, who has got there way ahead of everyone as usual, and Mister Ice Cold flips open one of the six small doors set into the left side of the truck with a *click* and plucks out Harold's rocket and gives it to him and takes the money, and before you know it he has smoothly glided to the right top door of the four doors at the truck's back and opened it, *click,* and Mandy Carter's holding her frozen maple tree and licking it and handing her money over all at the same time, and now Mister Ice Cold is opening one of the six small doors on the right side of the truck, *click,* and Eddy Morse has bitten the point off the top of his bright red cinnamon crunchy munch and is completely happy.

Then your heart's desire is plucked with a neat *click* from the top middle drawer on the truck's right side, which has always been its place for as long as you can remember, and you've put your money into Mister Ice Cold's large, pale, always cool palm, and as you step back to lick your orange icicle and to feel its coolness trickle down your throat, once again you find yourself admiring the sheer athletic smoothness of Mister Ice Cold's movements as he glides and dips, spins and turns, bows and rises, going from one small door, *click,* to another, *click,* with never a stumble, *click,* never a pause, *click,* his huge body leaving a coolness in the wake of his passing, and you wish you moved that smoothly when you ran back over the gravel of the playground with your hands stretched up, hoping for a catch, but you know you don't.

Everything's so familiar and comforting: the slow quieting of the other children getting what they want, your tongue growing ever more chill as you reduce yet another orange icicle, lick by lick, down to its flat stick, and the heavy, hot, summer air pressing down on top of it all.

But this time it's just a little different than it ever was before because, without meaning to, without having the slightest intention of doing it, you've noticed something you never noticed before.

Mister Ice Cold never opens the bottom right door in the back of the truck.

He opens all the rest of them, absolutely every one, and

you see him doing it now as new children arrive and call out what they want. *Click, click, click,* he opens them one after the other, producing frozen banana bars and cherry twirls and all the other special favorites, each one always from its particular, predictable door.

But his big, cool hand always glides past that *one door* set into the truck's back, the one on the bottom row, the one to the far right. And you realize now, with a funny little thrill, that you have never—not in all the years since your big brother Fred first took you by the hand and gave Mister Ice Cold the money for your orange icicle because you were so small you couldn't even count—you have never *ever* seen that door open.

And now you've licked the whole orange icicle away, and your tongue's moving over and over the rough wood of the stick without feeling it at all, and you can't stop staring at that door, and you know, deep in the pit of your stomach, that you have to open it.

You watch Mister Ice Cold carefully now, counting out to yourself how long it takes him to move from the doors farthest forward back to the rear of the truck, and because your mind is racing very, very quickly, you soon see that two orders in a row will keep him up front just long enough for you to open the door which is never opened, the door which you are now standing close enough to touch, just enough time to take a quick peek and close it shut before he knows.

Then Betty Deane calls out for a snow maiden right on top of Mike Howard's asking for a pecan pot, and you know those are both far up front on the right-hand side.

Mister Ice Cold glides by you close enough for the cool

breeze coming from his passing to raise little goose bumps on your arms. Without pausing, without giving yourself a chance for any more thought, you reach out.

Click!

Your heart freezes hard as anything inside the truck. There, inside the square opening, cold and bleached and glistening, are two tidy stacks of small hands, small as yours, their fingertips reaching out toward you and the sunlight, their thin, dead young arms reaching out behind them, back into the darkness. Poking over the top two hands, growing out of something round and shiny and far back and horribly still, are two stiff golden braids of hair with pretty frozen bows tied onto their ends.

But you have stared too long in horror and the door is closed, *click,* and almost entirely covered by Mister Ice Cold's hand, which now seems enormous, and he's bent down over you with his huge, smiling face so near to yours you can feel the coolness of it in the summer heat.

"Not that door," he says, very softly, and his small, neat, even teeth shine like chips from an iceberg, and because of his closeness now you know that even his breath is icy cold. "Those in there are not for you. Those in there are for me."

Then he's standing up again and moving smoothly from door to door, *click, click, click,* and none of the other children saw inside, and none of them will really believe you when you tell them, though their eyes will go wide and they'll love the story, and not a one of them saw the promise for you in Mister Ice Cold's eyes.

But you did, didn't you? And some night, after the end of summer, when it's cool and you don't want it any cooler, you'll be lying in your bed all alone and you'll hear Mister Ice Cold's pretty little song coming closer and closer through the night, through the dead, withered autumn leaves.

Dingy di-ding, dingy di-ding . . .

Then, later on, you just may hear the first *click.*

But you'll never hear the second *click.*

None of them ever do.

Traps

Lester adjusted his brand new cap with ROSE BROTHERS EX-
TERMINATORS stitched in bright scarlet on its front and
stared gloomily down at the last of the traps and poisons he had set the week before.

"It's just like I told you it would be, Lester Bailey," hissed
Miss Dinwittie. "They're too smart for you is what it is!"

Lester winced away from Miss Dinwittie's fierce, wrinkled
frown and considered the trap the Rose Brothers Exterminators people had given him to lay on the floor of her basement.

It was a very impressive machine. When you touched the
bait it slapped shut sharp serrated jaws, which not only pre-
vented your going elsewhere but insured your bleeding to
death as you lingered. If you were a rat, that is. A man would
probably only lose a finger.

This time, in spite of the bait being removed, the trap remained unsprung. Impossibly, its shiny teeth continued to

gape wide around the tiny platform which they were supposed to have infallibly guarded. Lester shook his large, rather square head, in mortification.

It was not bad enough that the trap had been gulled. The bait, which had been carefully poisoned, was uneaten. It lay demurely five inches from the trap. Outside of one light tooth-mark, evidence of the gentlest and most tentative of tastes, it was spurned and virginal.

"I ain't never seen nothing like it, Miss Dinwittie," admitted Lester with a sign.

"That's quite obvious from the expression on your face," she piped. "All this folderol you've put around hasn't done a thing except stir them up!"

She snorted and kicked at the trap with one high-button shoe. The mechanism described a small parabola, snapped in-effectually at the apogee, and fell with a tinny clatter.

Lester was not surprised by this contemptuous action of Miss Dinwittie. Miss Dinwittie was customarily contemptuous for the simple reason that she felt she had every right to be. Her father had been a remarkably greedy man, and by the time he'd died had managed to pretty well own the small town he'd settled in, and Miss Dinwittie had not let go a foot of it. The children believed she was a witch.

"They get brighter every day," she snapped. "And now you've gone and got them really mad!"

She looked around the gloom of the basement, moving her small, gray head in quick, darting movements.

"Listen!"

Lester stood beside her in the musty air and did as he was told. After a time he could make out nasty little noises all around. Shufflings and scratchings and tiny draggings. He peered at the ancient tubes and pipes running along the walls and snaking under the beams and flooring.

"They're just snickering at you, Lester Bailey," said Miss Dinwittie.

She sniffed and marched up the basement steps with Lester dutifully following, looking up at her thin, sexless behind. When they reached the kitchen she made him sit on one of the rickety chairs, which were arranged around the oilcloth-covered table, and poured him some bitter coffee. He drank it without complaint. He had no wish to further offend Miss Dinwittie.

She prowled briefly around the room and then surprised him by suddenly sitting by his side and leaning closely toward him in a conspiratorial manner. She smelled dry and sour.

"*They've got together!*" she whispered.

She clutched her bony hands on the shiny white oilcloth. Lester could hear the air rustling in the passages of her nose. She frowned and her eyes shone with a dark revelation.

"They've got together," she said again. "It used to be you could pick them off, one by one. It was each rat for himself. But now it's not the same."

She leaned even closer to him. She actually poked a thin finger into his chest.

"Now they've *organized!*"

Lester studied her carefully. The people at Rose Brothers Exterminators had in no way prepared him for this sort of thing. Miss Dinwittie sat back and crossed her arms in a satisfied way. She smiled grimly and nodded to herself.

"Organized," she said again, quietly.

Lester fumbled uncertainly over the limited information he had at his disposal concerning the handling of the violently insane. There was not much, but he did recall it was very important to humor them. You've got to humor them or they'll go for the ax or the bread knife.

"They're like an army," said Miss Dinwittie, leaning forward again, too self-absorbed to notice Lester's reflex leaning away. "I believe they have officers and everything. I *know* they've got scouts!"

She looked at him expectantly. Lester's reaction, a blank, wide-eyed look, irritated her.

"Well?" she snapped. "Aren't you going to ask me *how* I know?"

"About what, Miss Dinwittie?"

"Ask me *how I know* they've got scouts, you silly boob!"

"How do you come to know that, Miss Dinwittie?"

She stood and, beckoning Lester to follow, crossed the cold linoleum floor. When he reached her side at a particularly dark corner of the kitchen, she pointed to the base of the wall. Lester squinted. He believed he could make out something on the molding. He squatted down to have a better look at it. Scrawled clumsily on the cracked paint with what seemed to be a grease pencil was a tiny arrow and a cross and a squiggle that looked like it came from a miniature alphabet.

"It's some kind of *instruction,* isn't it?" hissed Miss Dinwittie. "It's put there to *guide the others!*"

Lester stood, unobtrusively. It had suddenly occurred to him that the old woman could have crowned him easily with a pan as he'd hunkered down at her feet. She glared at the weird little marks and snarled faintly.

"They're all over the house," she said. "In the closets, on the stairs, inside cabinets—everywhere!"

Suddenly her mood changed and, giving a small, vindictive laugh, she once again poked Lester in the chest.

"Gives them clean away, doesn't it?" she asked. "And there's *something else*! I'll go up and bring it down and you take it over to those silly fools who hired you, so they'll see what they're dealing with and give me some *service* for my money!"

Putting a thin finger to her lips, she backed out of the room. Smiling, she closed the door.

Lester stared after her and then a sudden hissing behind him made him wheel to see coffee boiling from its pot onto the stove. He turned off the burner, frightened at the way his heart was thumping in his chest. He wished to God he could have a cigarette, but he knew Miss Dinwittie didn't hold with smoking or anything else along those lines.

He could hear the rats. He decided he had never seen such a house for rats in all his life. One of them was making scuttling noises in the wall before him so he thumped the wall, but the rat just scuttled right along, behind the dead flowers printed on the paper, paying him no mind. Lester sighed and sat down in one of the inhospitable chairs.

Another rat started scratching over at the wall where those funny marks were, and then another in some other part, and then a third and then a fourth. Lester began to estimate how many rats there might be in the old house and then decided maybe that wasn't such a good idea, his being alone in this gloomy kitchen and all.

He wiped the back of his hand against his lips and wished again for a cigarette. He stood and went to the hall door and opened it, looking up at the narrow staircase leading to the second floor. The carpeting on the stairs and floor was a smudgy brown.

He went back into the kitchen and took out his cigarettes and lit one. To hell with Miss Dinwittie, anyways. Besides, he'd hear her coming and snuff it out. He bet those steps creaked something awful.

If you could hear them over the sound of the rats, that is. They'd gotten louder, he could swear to it. He let the smoke drift out of his mouth and listened carefully. They said you could hear better if your mouth was open. He pressed his ear to the ugly floral paper and then drew back in fright when the sound of them instantly spread away from where he'd touched the wall. He ground the cigarette out on the sole of his shoe and dropped it in a box of garbage by the sink. He went to the hall again and called out, "Miss Dinwittie?"

He gaped up into the darkness of the second floor. Had something moved up there?

"Miss Dinwittie? You all right?"

He shuffled his feet on the dusty carpet. It looked a little like rat skin itself, come to think of it. Was something rustling up there?

"Miss Dinwittie? I'm coming up!"

That would get a rise out of the old bitch if anything would. She wouldn't tolerate folks like him coming where they hadn't been asked.

But there was no objection of any kind, so he rubbed his nose and began, slowly, to climb the stairs. The bannister was repulsively smooth and slick. Like a rat's tail, he thought.

"Miss Dinwittie?"

It was dark as hell up here. He took the flashlight from his belt and turned it this way and that, continuing to call as he peered through old doorways. When he came to her bedroom he was careful to call her name three times before he went in.

On the dresser, between a silver comb and brush, lying right in the center of a dainty antimacassar doily, was the desiccated body of a rat in the convulsions of a violent rigor mortis. Its dried fingers clawed the air and its withered lips pulled back from dully gleaming teeth. It looked furious.

"Shit!" said Lester.

The top of its head had been flattened, perhaps by the heel of one of Miss Dinwittie's shoes. Around its waist was tied a bit of gray string, and fixed to one side of this crude belt, by means of a tiny loop, was a small sliver of glass tapered on one end to a vicious point and wrapped about the other with a fragment of electrician's tape so as to form a kind of handle. It was an efficient-looking miniature sword.

Why that goddam old bitch's gone right out of her goddamn head, thought Lester; she's dressed that goddamn dead rat up just like a little girl dresses up a doll!

He heard a faint noise in the hall and turned, sweating in the clammy chill of the room. Was she out there waiting for him with a sword of her own? You read all the time in the papers about the awful things crazy people do!

He tiptoed out of the room and peered down the hall and his breath stopped. The beam of his flashlight pointed at the bottom of the door leading to the attic and revealed Miss Dinwittie's high-button shoes with their toes up in the air. Even as he gaped at them they edged out of sight in uneven little starts to the sounds of a faint bumping and an even fainter scrabbling.

Oh my God, thought Lester, oh my Jesus God, oh please don't let none of this happen to me, please, God!

Still on tiptoe, even more on tiptoe, he worked his way to the stairs. He wanted to sob but he told himself he mustn't do it because he'd never be able to hear the rats if he was sobbing. He started down the stairs and was halfway when a dim instinct made him look back up to the top.

There, peering down at him, was a lone rat holding a discarded plastic knitting needle proudly upright. Fixed to the needle's top was a tiny rectangle of foul, tattered cloth. It took Lester several horrible seconds to realize he was looking at the flag of the rats.

"I didn't mean nothing!" he whispered, groping his way backward down the stairs. He plucked the cap with ROSE BROTHERS EXTERMINATORS from his head and flung it from him, crying: *"It was just a goddam way to make a living!"*

But the time for all that was long since past, and the rat army, in perfect ranks and files on the floor below, watched its enemy approaching, step by step, and eagerly awaited its general's command.

Yesterday's Witch

er house is gone now. Someone tore it down and bull-
dozed away her trees and set up an ugly apartment
building made of cheap bricks and cracking concrete
on the flattened place they'd built. I drove by there a few
nights ago; I'd come back to town for the first time in years to
give a lecture at the university, and I saw blue TV flickers
glowing in the building's living rooms.

Her house sat on a small rise, I remember, with a wide
stretch of scraggly lawn between it and the ironwork fence
which walled off her property from the sidewalk and the rest
of the outside world. The windows of her house peered down
at you through a thick tangle of oak tree branches, and I can
remember walking by and knowing she was peering out at me,
and hunching up my shoulders because I couldn't help it, but
never, ever, giving her the satisfaction of seeing me hurry because of fear.

To the adults she was Miss Marble, but we children knew better. We knew she had another name, though none of us knew just what it was, and we knew she was a witch. I don't know who it was told me first about Miss Marble's being a witch; it might have been Billy Drew. I think it was, but I had already guessed in spite of being less than six. I grew up, all of us grew up, sure and certain of Miss Marble's being a witch.

You never managed to get a clear view of Miss Marble, or I don't ever remember doing so, except that once. You just got peeks and hints. A quick glimpse of her wide, short body as she scuttled up the front porch steps; a brief hint of her brown-wrapped form behind a thick clump of bushes by the garage where, it was said, an electric runabout sat rusting away; a sudden flash of her fantastically wrinkled face in the narrowing slot of a closing door, and that was all.

Fred Pulley claimed he had gotten a good long look at her one afternoon. She had been weeding, or something, absorbed at digging in the ground, and off guard and careless even though she stood a mere few feet from the fence. Fred had fought down his impulse to keep on going by, and he had stood and studied her for as much as two or three minutes before she looked up and saw him and snarled and turned away.

We never tired of asking Fred about what he had seen.

"Her teeth, Fred," one of us would whisper—you almost always talked about Miss Marble in whispers—"did you see her teeth?"

"They're long and yellow," Fred would say. "And they come to points at the ends. And I think I saw blood on them."

None of us really believed Fred had seen Miss Marble, understand, and we certainly didn't believe that part about the blood, but we were so very curious about her, and when you're really curious about something, especially if you're a bunch of kids, you want to get all the information on the subject even if you're sure it's lies.

So we didn't believe what Fred Pulley said about Miss Marble's having blood on her teeth, nor about the bones he'd seen her pulling out of the ground, but we remembered it all the same, just in case, and it entered into any calculations we made about Miss Marble.

Halloween was the time she figured most prominently in our thoughts. First because she was a witch, of course, and second because of a time-honored ritual among the neighborhood children concerning her and ourselves and that evening of the year. It was a kind of test by fire that every male child had to go through when he reached the age of thirteen, or be shamed forever after. I have no idea when it originated; I only know that when I attained my thirteenth year and was thereby qualified and doomed for the ordeal, the rite was established beyond question.

I can remember putting on my costume for that memorable Halloween, an old Prince Albert coat and a papier-mâché mask which bore a satisfying likeness to a decayed cadaver, with the feeling I was girding myself for a great battle. I studied my reflection in a mirror affixed by swivels to my bedroom bureau and wondered gravely if I would be able to meet the challenge this night would bring. Unsure, but determined, I picked up my brown paper shopping bag, which was very large so as to accommodate as much candy as possible, said goodbye to my mother and father and dog, and went out. I had not gone a block before I met George Watson and Billy Drew.

"Have you got anything yet?" asked Billy.

"No." I indicated the emptiness of my bag. "I just started."

"The same with us," said George. And then he looked at me carefully. "Are you ready?"

"Yes," I said, realizing I had not been ready until that very moment, and feeling an encouraging glow at knowing I was. "I can do it all right."

Mary Taylor and her little sister Betty came up, and so did Eddy Baker and Phil Myers and the Arthur brothers. I couldn't see where they all had come from, but it seemed as if every kid in the neighborhood was suddenly there, crowding around under the streetlamp, costumes flapping in the wind, holding bags and boxes and staring at me with glistening, curious eyes.

"Do you want to do it now," asked George, "or do you want to wait?"

George had done it the year before and he had waited.

"I'll do it now," I said.

I began walking along the sidewalk, the others following after me. We crossed Garfield Street and Peabody Street and that brought us to Baline Avenue where we turned left. I could see Miss Marble's iron fence half a block ahead, but I was careful not to slow my pace. When we arrived at the fence I walked to the gate with as firm a tread as I could muster and put my hand upon its latch. The metal was cold and made me think of coffin handles and graveyard diggers' picks. I pushed it down and the gate swung open with a low, rusty groaning.

Now it was up to me alone. I was face to face with the ordeal. The basic terms of it were simple enough: walk down the crumbling path which led through the tall, dry grass to Miss Marble's porch, cross the porch, ring Miss Marble's bell, and escape. I had seen George Watson do it last year and I had seen other brave souls do it before him. I knew it was not an impossible task.

It was a chilly night with a strong, persistent wind and clouds scudding overhead. The moon was three-fourths full and it looked remarkably round and solid in the sky. I became suddenly aware, for the first time in my life, that it was a real *thing* up there. I wondered how many Halloweens it had looked down on and what it had seen.

I pulled the lapels of my Prince Albert coat close about me and started walking down Miss Marble's path. I walked because all the others had run or skulked, and I was resolved to bring new dignity to the test if I possibly could.

From afar the house looked bleak and abandoned, a thing of cold blues and grays and greens, but as I drew nearer, a peculiar phenomenon began to assert itself. The windows, which from the sidewalk had seemed only to reflect the moon's glisten, now began to take on a warmer glow; the walls and porch, which had seemed all shriveled, peeling paint, and leprous patches of rotting wood, now began to appear well kept. I swallowed and strained my eyes. I had been prepared for a growing feeling of menace, for ever darker shadows, and this increasing evidence of warmth and tidiness absolutely baffled me.

By the time I reached the porch steps the place had taken on a positively cozy feel. I now saw that the building was in excellent repair and that it was well painted with a smooth coat of reassuring cream. The light from the windows was now unmistakably cheerful, a ruddy, friendly pumpkin kind of orange suggesting crackling fireplaces all set and ready for toasting marshmallows. There was a very unwitchlike clump of

Indian corn fixed to the front door, and I was almost certain I detected an odor of sugar and cinnamon wafting into the cold night air.

I stepped onto the porch, gaping. I had anticipated many awful possibilities during this past year. Never far from my mind had been the horrible pet Miss Marble was said to own, a something-or-other, which was all claws and scales and flew on wings with transparent webbing. Perhaps, I had thought, this thing would swoop down from the bare oak limbs and carry me off while my friends on the sidewalk screamed and screamed. Again, I had not dismissed the notion Miss Marble might turn me into a frog with a little motion of her fingers and then step on me with her foot and squish me.

But here I was feeling foolish, very young, crossing this friendly porch and smelling—I was sure of it now—sugar and cinnamon and cider and, what's more, butterscotch on top of that. I raised my hand to ring the bell and was astonished at myself for not being the least bit afraid when the door softly opened and there stood Miss Marble herself.

I looked at her and she smiled at me. She was short and plump, and she wore an apron with a thick ruffle all along its edges, and her face was smooth and red and shiny as an autumn apple. She wore bifocals on the tip of her tiny nose and she had her white hair fixed in a perfectly round bun in the exact center of the top of her head. Delicious odors wafted round her through the open door and I peered greedily past her.

"Well," she said in a mild, old voice, "I am so glad that someone has at last come to have a treat. I've waited so many years, and each year I've been ready, but nobody's come."

She stood to one side and I could see a table in the hall

piled with candy and nuts and bowls of fruit and plateful of
pies and muffins and cake, all of it shining and glittering in the
warm, golden glow which seemed everywhere. I heard Miss
Marble chuckle warmly.

"Why don't you call your friends in? I'm sure there will be
plenty for all."

I turned and looked down the path and saw them, huddled
in the moonlight by the gate, hunched wide-eyed over their
boxes and bags. I felt a sort of generous pity for them. I
walked to the steps and waved.

"Come on! It's all right!"

They would not budge.

"May I show them something?"

She nodded yes and I went into the house and got an enormous orange-frosted cake with numbers of golden sugar
pumpkins on its sides.

"Look," I cried, lifting the cake into the moonlight, "look at
this! And she's got lots more! She always had, but we never
asked for it!"

George was the first through the gate, as I knew he would
be. Billy came next, and then Eddy, then the rest. They came
slowly, at first, timid as mice, but then the smells of chocolate
and tangerines and brown sugar got to their noses and they
came faster. By the time they had arrived at the porch they
had lost their fear, the same as I, but their astonished faces
showed me how I must have looked to Miss Marble when she'd
opened the door.

"Come in, children. I'm so glad you've all come at last!"

None of us had ever seen such candy or dared to dream of
such cookies and cakes. We circled the table in the hall, awed
by its contents, clutching at our bags.

"Take all you want, children. It's all for you."

Little Betty was the first to reach out. She got a gumdrop as big as a plum and was about to pop it into her mouth when Miss Marble said:

"Oh, no, dear, don't eat it now. That's not the way you do with tricks or treats. You wait till you get out on the sidewalk and then you go ahead and gobble it up. Just put it in your bag for now, sweetie."

Betty was not all that pleased with the idea of putting off eating her gumdrop, but she did as Miss Marble asked and plopped it into her bag and quickly followed it with other items such as licorice cats and apples dipped in caramel and pecans lumped together with some lovely-looking brown stuff, and soon all the other children, myself very much included, were doing the same, filling our bags and boxes industriously, giving the task of clearing the table as rapidly as possible our entire attention.

Soon, amazingly soon, we had done it. True, there was the occasional peanut, now and then a largish crumb survived, but by and large, the job was done. What was left was fit only for rats and roaches, I thought, and then was puzzled by the thought. Where had such an unpleasant idea come from?

How our bags bulged! How they strained to hold what we had stuffed into them! How wonderfully heavy they were to hold!

Miss Marble was at the door now, holding it open and smiling at us.

"You must come back next year, sweeties, and I will give you more of the same."

We trooped out, some of us giving the table one last glance just to make sure, and then we headed down the path, Miss Marble waving us good-bye. The long, dead grass at the sides of the path brushed stiffly against our bags, making strange hissing sounds. I felt as cold as if I had been standing in the chill night air all along, and not comforted by the cozy warmth inside Miss Marble's house. The moon was higher now and seemed—I didn't know how or why—to be mocking us.

I heard Mary Taylor scolding her little sister: "She said not to eat any till we got to the sidewalk!"

"I don't care. I want some!"

The wind had gotten stronger and I could hear the stiff tree branches growl high over our heads. The fence seemed far away and I wondered why it was taking us so long to get to it. I looked back at the house and my mouth went dry when I saw that it was gray and old and dark, once more, and that the only light from its windows was reflections of the pale moon.

Suddenly little Betty Taylor began to cry, first in small, choking sobs, and then in loud wails, George Watson said: "What's wrong?" and then there was a pause, and then George cursed and threw Betty's bag over the lawn toward the house and his own box after it. They landed with a queer rustling slither that made the small hairs on the back of my neck stand up. I let go of my own bag and it flopped, bulging, into the grass by my feet. It looked like a huge, pale toad with a gaping, grinning mouth.

One by one the others rid themselves of what they carried. Some of the younger ones, whimpering, would not let go, but the older children gently separated them from the things they clutched.

I opened the gate and held it while the rest filed out onto the sidewalk. I followed them and closed the gate firmly. We stood and looked into the darkness beyond the fence. Here and there one of our abandoned boxes or bags seemed to glimmer faintly, some of them moved—I'll swear it—though others claimed it was just an illusion produced by the waving grass. All of us heard the high, thin laughter of the witch.

Them Bleaks

Sheriff Olson had no sooner emerged from Mae's Cafe and tilted the big, gold-starred car toward the driver's side by heaving his considerable bulk down behind its wheel when he heard the voice of Wilbur, his chief deputy, fighting its way through the speaker of the two-way radio along with a tangle of static.

"It's them Bleaks, Sheriff." Wilbur's voice was muffled in what seemed to be a fearsome cold. "It's that Mr. Bleak, the writer fellah. He just called in and says you're so hurry over to his place right away on account of what he found."

Olson leaned forward and snatched the microphone from its dashboard hammock as the frown line between his tufty orange eyebrows extended slightly. There had been no frown line on the Sheriff's broad, smooth forehead before the Bleaks moved into Commonplace, but now there was, and every week it seemed to grow just a little longer and dig in just a little deeper.

"What's he got to show me, Wilbur?" the Sheriff asked, speaking very calmly.

"He says he's gone and found somebody what's been murdered."

The crease in the Sheriff's forehead climbed like the red line in a thermometer nearly halfway up to the edge of his close-cropped, copper hair. Wilbur's words had struck him like a snake. He turned, quietly and gently like a fragile man, and then suddenly pounded the cushions violently enough to bounce himself in the seat.

"Damn!" he shouted, raising muffled echoes from the car's padded insides. "Damn and double goddam damn!"

He took three deep breaths in a row, holding the microphone helpless in a strangler's grip before his blotching, swelling face. Now he could no longer even pretend to doubt. Now he knew for certain sure he'd been wrong all along about the Bleaks.

"I'll take care of that call, Wilbur." He growled it out in a soft, confidential whisper through grinding teeth. "Don't you let nobody else take that call, you hear me? Don't you let nobody else get *near* it!"

The second he heard Wilbur's awed "Yezzur," he started up the engine with a roar, gripped the wheel with both his big, freckly hands, and spat gravel as he spun out of Mae's parking lot and down the road with the car's sparklers and sirens on full tilt.

They'd seemed to be so nice, he thought grimly to himself, giving his square head a fierce, bulldog shake as two of Willy Orville's chickens died all unnoticed underneath his wheels.

He'd checked the whole family over carefully, or thought he had, and they'd looked to be just as nice and friendly a bunch as you could hope for.

Of course he'd been downright pleased when they'd come house hunting here in Commonplace half a year ago, bringing their two kids and their big, black, toothy old mastiff. He had to admit he was awed by the very idea a famous and successful writer like Robert Bleak, a man who could live wherever he chose, would even consider living in Le Piege county. Most outsiders who had any choice at all steered clear of this whole part of the state and were unkind enough to call it the armpit of America when they didn't call it worse.

It seemed difficult for strangers to get by the endless flatness of the landscape, not to mention the unusual and persistent gloominess of its climate, and he supposed that the gray, twisty scrub growth together with the withered, gnarly trees didn't help too much, nor did those bogs and swamps and hollows full of all that spooky, clammy mist. You had to make the best of things in Le Piege county, truth be told.

Then people would keep on spreading the worst rumors they could get hold of, going all the way back to those foolish tales the early settlers spread about every local Indian they came across being a cannibal down to the last brave and squaw, and if the newspapers or the television anchormen ever spoke of the area they were always sure to insert some witty reference to those old-time legends about the scruffy, spooky Hawker family and the weird and deadly hotel they operated during the gold rush days where the guests were killed and robbed and then served up as stew dinners to any following pioneers who'd paused to take advantage of the Hawker hospitality.

Of course what really got the place's reputation permanently into trouble was the Worper child, Wendell, who'd killed his bullying mother and then stitched her up and stuffed her because he'd felt guilty about hacking her into small, gory pieces with his ax, and because he didn't like messes. When Wendell saw that she'd come out of the process looking rather well it seemed to have stirred up some sort of peculiar creative spark in the boy and inspired him to go on to produce further artistic sculptures using the corpses of other ladies he'd acquired from various local graveyards rather than killing a variety of old women who'd been unlucky enough to remind him of his mother.

Naturally all that might have gone unnoticed and no one the wiser, but Wendell hadn't been content with confining his new hobby to interior decoration; no, he'd felt the need to continue by suspending a quantity of new dead females from the outside corners of his house like gargoyles and to beautify the roof with others, including rigging up one of them so that she held out a black lace umbrella and then mounting her onto a swivel atop the peak over the widow's walk to serve as a weather vane.

Even that wasn't enough for Wendell now he'd hit his full creative stride, and he was soon happily absorbed in the process of posing and arranging more than a dozen more stuffed dead women as lawn ornaments on the property overlooking the road. It may be significant that he was working on the thirteenth one, seating her on a planter made from a truck tire painted white, when a gentleman from the Museum of Folk Art in the city who was passing through had to stop his car in the middle of the road at the sight of all that beauty, and in no time at all Wendell found himself having a one-man retrospective show filling two floors of the museum, but when the big city police read the rave reviews in the papers and started pondering his sources of supply, Wendell soon commenced his long unhappy slide into trouble and the State Asylum for the Criminally Insane.

However none of all that seemed to bother the Bleaks the tiniest little bit. They even surprised Dorry Phipps, the realtor who showed them the place, by falling in love with the Worper place on first sight—which she had to admit to herself was a decidedly gloomy old pile, especially now that it had been cleared of the brightening effect which Wendell's funereally gaudy art works had lent it—and when she finally got her nerve up enough to tell Mr. Bleak about who had lived there she was amazed and delighted to find the author was so pleased about the revelation that he clapped his hands and chuckled!

The rest of the family seemed just as nice, Dorry said, and she told about Mrs. Bleak lighting up when she spotted some pumpkins growing in a corner of a field and making a homely little joke about having a jack-o'-lantern patch, and Dorry and old Ned Whalen at the garage had to smile at one another when they saw the Bleak children enthusiastically pretending to bring a plastic toy Frankenstein monster to life in the back seat of the car when the family stopped for a little gas. The Sheriff listened to all that along with a good many other encouraging reports, and when he read a few of the horror stories Mr. Bleak wrote for a living on top of that, every doubt fled and it seemed to him that they were just the sort of people who'd blend right into the admittedly eccentric ways of Commonplace without giving the town any problems at all. Now, speeding faster and faster down Route 46 until the fence posts blended, he knew with a sickening certainty that he had aided and abetted the establishment of a vipers' nest in the very heart of the community he'd solemnly sworn to protect.

The first hints he might have guessed wrong on the Bleaks came in fairly early, but though they did sound a little odd, he didn't find it all that hard to brush them off, and he never even so much as noticed the first little dent between his eyes which marked the commencement of his brand-new frown line.

The postman, Harry Billings, started it all by informing the Sheriff about the time he came by with his mail truck and found Mrs. Bleak pulling weeds alongside the fence as he drove up. He had barely managed to get in a good morning before she stood, wringing her hands, and proceeded to go on about how worried she was about their neighbors on the opposite hill, the Whitbys, and she asked him in a whisper did he know if there'd been some tragedy? When Harry said as how he didn't know of one Mrs. Bleak anxiously told him about the Whitbys' lights going off and on at "odd hours" during the night, and how she and Mr. Bleak had been awakened time after time by "strange noises." Harry asked her what kind of noises and she paused and swallowed and then suddenly blurted out that they were sometimes "like the horrible screams of people being killed!" When Harry gave her a grin and shrugged and tried to reassure her by pointing out that since it was warm and folks' windows weren't shut like they would be in colder times you had to expect to hear private doings every now and again, this reassurance didn't seem to calm Mrs. Bleak in the least. She silently opened and closed her mouth a couple of times as though she were trying to speak but only succeeded in making a couple of soft little squawks, and Harry said she watched after him as he drove off, and kept doing it till he was all the way out of sight, and he recalled clearly that she had a very odd look on her face.

Then one day Ed Pierce at the hardware store started to chuckle and told the Sheriff about the time Mr. Bleak had been in to buy a shotgun because he and Mrs. Bleak were terribly concerned about "all the people" they'd heard lately sneaking about in the grounds outside the house in the dark of night, and how once they thought they'd caught a glimpse of someone dragging someone else wrapped in what looked to be a bloody sheet. Harry said when he tried to calm him down by telling him you "just naturally got to expect folks to take advantage of these nice summer nights," Bleak went still and then, after staring at him very intently and quietly for a moment or two, told him to add on five more boxes of ammo to his order. Sheriff Olson looked in the mirror while he was shaving the very next morning after he heard that and for the first time noticed a tiny frown line had blossomed on his forehead

But though he didn't like the sound of what he'd heard, the Sheriff assumed it was all only a case of city people being understandably jumpy because they were new to the country life style, to all that quiet at night, to the way the local inhabitants tended to keep their private business private. He would listen to the stories, and then he would smile and scratch his big jaw and try to paper it over by telling anybody who had brought him another depressing story to be patient, that it wouldn't be any time at all before the Bleaks got used to things, that soon you wouldn't hear of any more complaining. He would assure them all the Bleaks would fit in fine.

But the stories kept coming in and they kept adding up. Ben Frazier at the butcher shop said he saw Mrs. Bleak studying

the specialty meats in the separate case at the back with extreme care one day when she was waiting for the rain to ease
off when suddenly she gave a little cry and began to peer
harder and harder until she started to actually tremble. When
Ben walked over to her she pointed at an arm and asked him
"What's that?" in a kind of a hiss, and there was something in
her tone of voice that made him decide not to tell her just
then what it was, so he said it was a leg of veal though he
knew she didn't believe him. After she left he looked at the
meat carefully and was more than a little irritated to realize
that the tourist lady's watch had left an easily recognizable in-
dentation on her wrist.

And Doc Huggins at the pharmacy said he cut Mr. Bleak
short with a friendly smile once when he'd started going on
and on about how he was killing some rats in order to explain
why he needed a tin of cyanide he'd come to buy. Doc did his
best to assure him that no excuses at all were needed when it
came to buying poison in Commonplace; he told his that as a
matter of fact the store took special pride in the quality and
wide variety of the poisons which they stocked. He was in the
process of proving the point by bending down and fishing
around in a lower drawer in order to get a jar of the new nerve
gas the Ryan boy had brought in on his last leave from the
Marines, but when he straightened up with the jar in his hand
he realized Mr. Bleak had left and that he'd scuttled right out
of the establishment in such a rush that he'd left his package
of cyanide behind all wrapped up neatly and tidily as you
please on the counter.

There was all of that and a lot more and it just would not
stop and the frown line got so deep and long that the Sheriff's

wife had taken to fretting over it audibly, but somehow he'd managed to fend all these tales off, to keep pushing them away, to make excuses.

Then, just before he'd left the cafe and gotten that call from Wilbur which had proven to be the final straw, Mae had to go and tell him her funny little story.

It would never have seemed anywhere near so ominous by itself since it wasn't more than a tiny thing, but landing as it did atop of all those other accumulated accounts which had been steadily heaping up through the days and weeks and months, it somehow managed to strike Sheriff Olson as being particularly discouraging.

He remembered he'd paused after turning off the engine when he'd parked in Mae's lot to stand and listen to the early morning birds chirping in the soft, fresh air, and it had put him into such a pleasant, peaceful mood that he'd walked into the cafe whistling, something he' never done before, but he stopped that on a dime when he saw Mae studying him side-wise and slyly with her tiny, cold little eyes and noticed she was wearing that twisty, snaky smile she only let show when she knew she'd snagged onto something that would really hurt.

She didn't say anything much in particular while he worked his way through his chili burger, she just hovered over her grill, picking at little raised bits of carbon with the sharp tip of a long, red fingernail. He ate as quietly as he could, then snuck his money under the side of his plate and was nearly beginning to believe he'd manage to sneak out of there without her noticing when she was on him with the suddeness of a shark, full of simpers and coy cooings and giving his cup an extra, un-wanted pour of coffee.

"You hear about what little Harold Bentley told his maw and paw about the Bleak kids, Sheriff, honey?" she asked in an almost motherly manner.

"Can't say as I have, Mae," he murmured

"Well it's quite a shock and that's the truth," she said, shaking her head in a slow, sad righteous manner, "Particularly seeing as how it all come up in a schoolyard where you wouldn't expect anything of that nature to take place."

"In a schoolyard," he repeated.

"All the poor, dear children was trying to do was teach them Bleak kids an innocent playground game when the girl begun to cry and holler something awful and her brother got so darn fool mad things almost ended in a fist fight!"

"What game was that, Mae?" Sheriff Olson asked, standing and carefully adjusting his belt so that his belly would pop over it comfortably.

"Why good old 'Rob the Coffin,'" said Mae, her eyes widening with astonishment. "The same game as you and I and every boy and girl that's grown up around hereabouts has played since lord knows when. The sweet little dears explained them all the rules, such as how each member of the one team plays a body part—choosing the head or the heart or the bowels and such—while the other team plays the ghouls. That cute little Finley girl was showing them how you draw the blood pump in the funeral parlor diagram with a stick on the playground dirt, and Harold Billins was explaining how if you shout 'I'm embalmed!' three times before the ghouls grab you they can't eat you, when out of the blue and all of a sudden the Bleak girl began screaming and carrying on fit to beat the band and her brother got all mad and uppity and like to pop poor Harold Perkins right on the nose and maybe broke it if the teacher hadn't heard all the caterwauling and come rushing out to calm things down."

Mae paused in order to give the counter a little swipe with a paper towel before she twisted her knife.

"I hate to mention it because I know you vouched for them Bleaks, Sheriff, honey, and are more responsible than anybody else for them presently living in our little community," she purred, "but I feel it's my civic duty, painful though it may be, and besides, we're all sure you'll put things right again once you've gone and realized your mistake."

When Sheriff Olson saw the shiny new stainless steel mailbox with BLEAK glued on it in bright red, reflective letters he extinguished his car's flashing lights and siren, slowed to a civilian speed, and turned off Route 46 onto a dirt road winding up a craggy hill. He cringed a little when, in the process of doing all this, he caught a peek at his reflection in the rearview mirror and hoped he hadn't looked that dismally gloomy when he'd been leaving Mae's Cafe as it would have pleased her far too much. The frown line, which was now the most noticeable feature of his face, presently traversed the entire length of his forehead and he feared if it cut any deeper it might expose his very skull.

He chewed a corner of his moustache as he bumped up the road, watching the gray spot on the mountain top grow into a big, old, drearily menacing house with tall, thin, secretive windows peering over and under a quantity of crouching roofs, and he didn't even try to fight off wishing little Wendell Worper still lived there. Peaceful Wendell, with never a complaint from him or about him, content to play shyly and quietly with his mother and all the rest of those stuffed dead women, always careful never to bother a soul, save for his victims.

But that brief, nostalgic revery was exploded by the sight of Robert Bleak leaning his scrawny frame over the fence and flapping his long arms at him like an agitated blue jay. Olson sighed, smoothed the frown line from his forehead with a great effort, and arranged his face into what he hoped would seem a relaxed, convincingly official smile as he pulled to the side of the road.

"Well now, Mr. Bleak," he said, easing his big body out of the car, "what seems to be the trouble?"

"That," said Bleak, waving frantically at the ground, and the Sheriff saw a pale object jammed onto the end of a short board stuck into the ground. It was a hand with its index finger pointed in Bleak's general direction and its other fingers and thumb tightly clenched. It was a macabre object, without doubt, but it undeniably had a peculiar kind of charm. It looked very much like an antique direction indicator in some old-fashioned place of business except, perhaps, for its gory stump.

Sheriff Olson studied it for a moment with his eyes narrowed slightly and his head tilted to one side. There seemed to be something oddly familiar about that hand; those chubby, spatulate fingers definitely rang a muffled bell.

"Well now," said Olson after a pause, "so this here is why you called me? This is what the fuss is all about?"

"All the fuss?" gritted Bleak, leaning even farther over his fence and firmly fixing his visitor with an incredulous glare. "All the *fuss*? I should think the discovery of an item as horrible and gruesome as this would be a perfectly appropriate occasion for a fuss! I should indeed!"

"Well now," Olson said again, visibly disconcerted at the sight of Bleak actually wringing his hands, "I want you please to understand I meant no offense when I said that, Mr. Bleak, sir, none at all. The truth be told, I'd really hoped you'd take it as a kind of compliment!"

Bleak blinked, obviously puzzled. His jaw moved slightly as if he were chewing over what he'd just heard.

"Compliment?" he said at length. "I'm afraid I don't follow you at all on that, Sheriff Olson."

Extending both his palms before him in a double-barreled gesture of peace, Olson made his way to the fence, speaking as he went.

"What I was trying to say, sir, is that I wouldn't think a person such as yourself would bother to call the police about some little bitty thing like this," he said, indicating the severed hand with an almost dismissive wave. "I'd expect a lot of folks might be spooked by it, sure, but not you, sir, not *you!*"

Now the Sheriff was directly across the fence from Bleak. He was trying to keep his easy, friendly, Sheriff's smile in place but it persisted in slipping away whereas his frown line kept treacherously popping into view in spite of all his efforts. The author studied him warily as the Sheriff continued speaking more and more in a rush.

"Heck, sir, if anything, I'd have thought you'd be able to manage something like this little old hand here a whole lot better than me. Oh, sure, I've seen a bunch of bodies and stuff like that what with one thing and another, but, hell, I'm just a country cop, Mr. Bleak, I'm just a hayseed, and you're worldwide known as a *master of the macabre,* dammit, sir, just like it says on the covers of your books, and I know you really *are,* sir, because I've read those books and what it says is the plain truth, so I just can't see how come a bitty piece of corpse meat has got you so riled up!"

Bleak stared at him with bug-eyed incredulity for a moment and then pointed back at the pointing hand.

"That thing stuck on that little post in the ground between your feet and mine is real, Sheriff Olson," he said, speaking slowly and grimly. "It is part of a genuine dead body. In my stories amputated hands are only made-up things which I create both because I enjoy doing it and because it makes me a feasible living. They are works of fiction and therefore they won't slowly turn into green slime or mummify into cracklings or attract worms or do any of the other things a real dead hand such as that one there can do. My dead hands are just pretend dead hands."

Olson took hold of the top rail of the fence as a man will when he clutches something at the edge of a high precipice to keep from falling.

"But those godawful stories you write, sir," he said, an audible desperation creeping into his voice, "like that *La Traviata* where you dreamt up the dead Italian opera star stuffed full of singing worms, or that yarn of yours which still gives me the jimjams every time I think of it, the one where you show that Jack the Ripper was actually Queen Victoria all along, how can anybody who's thought up such stuff as that be put off by a dinky, no-account, bitty old hand?"

"Since you persist in missing my point, Sheriff Olson," said Bleak exasperatedly, "I suggest we abandon it and move on to a far more important aspect of this situation. It is not *only* that hand which concerns me. There is more."

"More?" the Sheriff asked in a dazed tone of voice, clearly floundering. "More?"

"More," said Bleak. "See where the hand is pointing."

Sheriff Olson's gape obediently followed the direction indicated by the dead finger as the author had asked him until he saw, lying in the tall grass a little closer to the house, a pale, misshapen lump.

He climbed over the fence without the least awareness he was doing it and followed Bleak as he walked over to the lump. It was the naked left half of a male corpse, minus its hands and head. Its wrist stump was pointing up the slope toward the house as the hand had done. The Sheriff peered at the thing thoughtfully for a moment and then jumped and wheeled to his rear at the sound of a soft rustle behind him.

It was Mrs. Bleak, looking pale and distracted. She edged closer to him, wringing her hands almost exactly as Mr. Bleak had done.

"I'm so glad you've come, Sheriff Olson!" she said, speaking with a kind of anxious calm and staring at him with her wide, frightened-looking eyes. "I do so hope you can do something about all these terrible, awful things!"

Olson opened his mouth to reply but Bleak cut him off.

"All he has done so far is to advise me not to take them all that seriously," said the author. "Maybe you can convince him we hold a dim view of this sort of thing. He seems altogether very unimpressed with our corpse so far."

"Then you're just like all the rest of the people here in Commonplace!" she cried, stepping hurriedly back from the Sheriff, a sudden expression of horror on her face.

"Now, please, Mrs. Bleak, just hear me out—" he began, but Bleak cut him off again.

"Being an investigator of crime, you might be at least vaguely interested in looking where this part of the body's pointing," he said.

The Sheriff did and there was yet another pale lump in the

grass farther on ahead, and standing by it, hand in hand, were both of the Bleak children, staring at the lawman accusingly.

"Is he like the others, Mommy?" asked the little girl in a tearful voice which made the Sheriff wince. "Is he going to tease us about killing people? Is he, Mommy?"

The new lump was the right-hand half of the corpse, and now the Sheriff knew for certain he'd been acquainted with it in life. Like the left half, it had come from a chubby man, probably somewhere in his mid-thirties. Its wrist, too, pointed ahead and this time Olson needed no prompting to look in the direction specified. There, on the top step of the open storm door leading into the basement, pointing downward, was the other hand, and seated next to it, looking at him in an accusatory fashion, just like every other member of the family, was the Bleaks' big, black mastiff.

"I suppose there's more of it down there," said the Sheriff.

"There is," said Bleak. "One thing more. Shall we go look at it, or do you think it's not all that important and that we should walk off and forget all about it?"

"Now just hold on," said the Sheriff angrily, and then paused to heave a deep sigh, "Let's all just hold on. There's been a misunderstanding here and I admit it's all my fault. I got you folks wrong. It was my business to figure if you would or would not fit in around these parts and I figured wrong. I don't know what I'm going to do about you all, I truly don't, but please understand, no matter what happens, I didn't never mean no harm."

Bleak stared at him for a long moment, then slowly shook his head.

"Perhaps, someday, I'll have at least a vague idea what you meant just then, Sheriff," he said at last. "But for now, just as a matter of form, let's go look at what's down there in the basement."

It was awkward descending the steps in the dark, but the Sheriff had gone down them before, on the last occasion, to supervise the investigation and photography of the place when it had been Wendell's Worper's little embalming room. Here is where the boy had neatly gutted his prey and soaked them in vats of nitron before patting them dry and sewing them up with a stitch he'd learned from studying leather baseball skins. Here is where he dressed them up again in their graveyard clothes, which he'd cleaned and pressed for them, or arrayed them in pretty dresses which he'd bought from department stores in the city for just that purpose.

The Sheriff paused when he felt the concrete of the basement's floor scuff under his shoes, and at that moment he heard a click behind him as Robert Bleak turned on the lights. There, a yard or two before him, Olson saw a human head sitting on the center of a sterling silver serving platter, resting just where the turkey would ordinarily go. It stared at him open-mouthed and stupidly with its round, blue eyes as it often had in life, but this time it didn't see him, being dead.

"It's Wilbur," gasped Olson, in astonishment. "It's my deputy, Wilbur! But that can't be because he's the one that called me about this on the damn car radio just a bitty while ago!"

"That wasn't Wilbur," whispered a voice directly behind him which sounded for all the world like Wilbur himself, only with a bad cold, just like he'd had on the radio. "That was me!"

The Sheriff turned and his jaw dropped in astonishment both at the sight of the remarkably sinister, bulge-eyed expression playing on Robert Bleak's face and at the enormous

chef's knife which he both saw and felt being driven quickly
and skillfully through the flesh between his shoulder blades.

The Sheriff had only fallen halfway to the ground when
Mrs. Bleak, wearing an expression as surprisingly diabolic as
her husband's, drove a somewhat smaller, but no less effective, knife firmly into the side of his thick neck as she gave a
cachinnating laugh.

The Sheriff had barely thumped onto the concrete when he
felt simultaneous sharp pains on either side of his torso as his
fading vision dimly made out both the Bleak children eagerly
and adroitly inserting even smaller knives between his ribs,
and just before sight and all other physical sensations departed him altogether, he became aware that the mastiff had
enthusiastically begun to tear at his legs.

"I was right, goddammit, I was right!" his voice echoed, tri-
umphantly, if only in his skull: "*I was right all along about
them Bleaks!*"

And the frown line faded completely and entirely and forever from his forehead.

The Marble Boy

I t was like a huge hole cut into our ordinary world, a great, aching gap sawed right out of the middle of everything that made us and our world seem to make sense, a fatal hollow dug into the very center of the simple, optimistic philosophies our parents were trying to make us live by.

I did by no means realize at the time that I thought of it in those terms, but I know now that is what all of us, all the children, knew the Lakeside Cemetery to be. It wasn't just a weird place isolated permanently from the day-to-day pretend reality of the grownups; it was an accessible and explorable proof to us, to their young, that even our adults—so huge and powerful, so full of rights and wrongs from the newspapers—were just as fragile and afraid as we were, after all.

The graveyard spread itself out northward from just this side of the city border for five blocks where it ran into the alley in back of Mulberry Street, and living people in houses, and was temporarily stopped. To the east, it crowded all the way up to the beach drive so that its gray fence and ominous, high gates could remind us of the eventual certainty of our mortality just when we had bobbed up wet and blinking into the summer air after momentarily convincing ourselves otherwise by holding our breath for a full minute underwater. To the west it was bordered firmly by the train tracks which were the extension of the city's elevated line, now turned suburban and ground bound. If you were up there on the track in order to put pennies on them so that the copper would be squished flat and spread bigger than a half dollar by the wheels of passing trains, you had a fine, panoramic view of the graveyard spread out beneath you like a verdigris carpet splotched with fuzzy brown stains and sprinkled with a multitude of tiny little stones and statues and tombs.

It was, and is, a fine graveyard, thanks to the prosperity and grief of many Lakesidians from the far and near past, and it boasts as excellent and varied a collection of midwestern funerary art as you could hope to come across. There are any number of elaborate and diverting memorials; rows and rows of mausoleums vie with one another in sustained contests of marble pomposity, and the number of flamboyantly sculptured mourning angels is past counting.

Of course we, like kids of any generation, were perpetually fascinated with death, and of course we had long since learned that grownups were useless in any consultations on the subject since they seriously disliked talking with their children about even the possibility of dying, and, astonishingly, they never seemed to bring the subject up even among themselves unless one or another of them had recently expired, so we had to satisfy ourselves by quizzing one another on the subject in alleys and other dark places where adults wouldn't hear and disapprove and stop us.

Why, we earnestly asked one another, do pets expire even when we love them so much? How come the universe permits birds to be flattened into gory, smelly messes by cars, one wing still pointing prettily skyward like a sail? Is it fair that a friend as young as ourselves can sicken and die because he or she caught a bug drinking from a public fountain, or from inhaling the wrong stranger's breath in a movie theater? Does everybody rot the same, or do we all do it differently, and are we in the body when it happens or have we already left it when the eyes melt and fall into the hollow space where the brain was before it shriveled down to the size of a nut? *Why* does death happen? How *can* it happen? *Must* it happen?

So, if we were in the mood for a particularly adventurous and daring sort of day, a visit to the graveyard was always likely to be suggested, if only to widen everybody's eyes a little, and now and then we actually went ahead and did it.

Naturally, any expedition to the cemetery was always very heavily draped in secrecy, unannounced and unrecounted to any parent, and we made a great business of carefully avoiding the men who gardened its grounds and dug its graves and patched up its tombs because we had a highly detailed, horrifying body of superstition about what these men would do to us if they caught us, most of it involving, one way or another, fiendish misuse of formaldehyde.

When we made our plans we never even considered going in either one of the two huge, lacy iron gates because they each had an attached gatehouse with dark little windows for watchmen smelling of embalming fluid to hide behind and peer out of. Our preferred means of entry was a certain part of the graveyard's heavy, chain-link fence which faced the alley to its north and was satisfactorily lined with the backs of grimy garages and intriguingly decorated with tilting garbage cans full of spoiled, smelly things.

At some time in the ancient past, no one knew when or by what means, this section of the fence had become detached at its base so that it could be lifted up and crawled under and then carefully replaced so that no patrolling gardener or digger or patcher would ever know a child had snuck into their domain and was available for formaldehyde experiments.

This secret and ancient means of entrance was the one chosen by Andy Hoyle and George Dulane one mild November day when they decided the time had come for another tour of the graveyard with all its tests.

Andy and George were friends of long standing, and they had visited the graveyard once before that year in a group of five and enjoyed it very much. Today was Andy's twelfth birthday—George had been twelve for three months—and the two of them, after a long and serious discussion, had come to the conclusion that since George had used up sneaking into the school building at night without the superintendent knowing, a graveyard exploration would be a properly scary and solemn way for Andy to mark the occasion.

They looked carefully up and down the alley and when they were sure that the only living thing in sight was a small dog who was totally preoccupied in trying to tug an interesting bone covered with dried blood out of a box, they pulled firmly at the chain links. Of course the fence held firmly for a moment, as it always held, and Andy and George went through the usual, breath-holding moment before it let go and the two of them knew for certain that the fence's bottom still remained unattached.

They scuttled under it, pressing their fronts against the cold, leafy ground and, once inside, followed the time-honored tradition of pushing its base back down and burying it under the leaves so that no one would know. Then they scuttled a yard or two into the cemetery and paused by the gnarled, mossy side of a concrete log molded into the corner of a sooty rustic tomb.

They brushed chilled, damp bits of sod from the knees of their pants, pretended their hearts were not pounding in their chests, and looked at each other and the tall, bare trees and the endless ranks and files of stones and statues and tombs with an almost convincing casualness, and once they'd managed to get their breathing under control they savored the oldness and moldiness in the air and the way the menace of death all around them ran through their veins and arteries.

Afar off to the east they heard the metal dither of a lawn mower of the old timey, nonpowered variety and began wandering, taking paths which veered from the sound.

Old friends loomed before them as they walked: the tomb with the stone clock fixed forever at three-thirty over its door, which prompted them once again to speculate whether this signified the exact hour of the occupant's death; the eight-foot-high angel with one missing ear and carved tears running down its pitted, gray cheeks, and, one of their particular favorites, the oddly cheerful skull whose jolly grin still beamed out from under the tilting urn pressed against the back of its cranium.

The sound of the mower faded and stopped and they

angled back to the east, taking the path pointed toward one of the goals especially selected for this day: a particularly sinister-looking mausoleum which you knew contained dead members of a family named Baker, because they had carved that name boldly and deeply across its ornate pediment. The Bakers, or at least the Baker who had commissioned the tomb, had been deeply enamored of rococo ornamentation and the little house of death was so heavily burdened with scrollings and floral fantasies that it looked like the rump of a Spanish galleon turned to stone.

But it wasn't the gorgeous architectural detail of the Bakers' tomb which drew Andy and George to it; it was the delicious almost-openness of its heavy, rusting, iron door. Thick chains and a huge padlock insured that the door would go no more than ajar, but ajar it was, and you could peer through the opening at the cobwebby dimness beyond and, even better, you could whisper hoarsely into the tomb and hear the sibilant echoes which your voice had raised.

They glanced at each other and then, because he was the bravest, Andy pressed his body against the door, enjoyed a quick shiver when it gave ever so slightly, and hissed softly into the spooky dark.

"Hello?" he whispered. "Bakers?"

George, standing just behind, felt goosebumps popping out all over his arms.

"Bakers?" Andy persisted relentlessly. "Are there any Bakers lying in there?"

After a fair pause, Andy turned to George and whispered: "I guess there aren't any Bakers."

To which George replied on cue: "Or, if there *are* any Bakers . . ."

Then together, in a ghastly wail: ". . . then they must be *dead!*"

And that, as usual, was their signal to turn as one and run off at a full gallop as if pursued by generations of moldering Bakers and not to stop running until they were both satisfactorily winded.

That had been the high point in their last adventure in the graveyard, and in their planning, they had assumed it would be the high point in this one as well, but it turned out not to be so, because thanks to an odd break in the clouds and the sudden appearance of a bold shaft of sunlight, both boys simultaneously spotted a bright glinting among the stones off to their left. Something, they had no idea what, was shining like a huge diamond.

Without saying a word the two began walking together toward the spot of brilliance. The closer they got to it, the less it became pure radiance and the more it took on solid shape until they saw it was a case of glass mounted on a raised marble casket, and as they came even closer they could make out, through the shining of the glass, a small, standing figure.

There was a pale marble boy carved full size in the glass case. He had only been eight, you could figure that out by subtracting the dates, and he had been alive a long time ago. His marble clothes were very old-fashioned with many marble buttons on the jacket and knickers, and a fluffy marble bow was tied at his throat.

The case was sealed with some black substance at the joinings of the glass, but the closure was now far from perfect; the passing of all those years had made the black stuff shrivel, and there were many tiny droplets of water shining on the inside of all its panes.

The boy's marble hair was curly, and his carved marble eyes stared out with colorless irises and pupils and gave the odd illusion of seeming to be looking directly at the viewer no matter where he stood.

Andy and George remained silent for a good long while, staring at the marble boy, wondering about him and speculating, each one secretly to himself, about his own mortality.

At length Andy stirred and pointed to the small sarcophagus the statue and its case stood upon. The case, like the statue, was carved from pale, unveined stone and was waxy smooth.

"Do you suppose he's in that thing or buried underground?" Andy asked.

George stared and pursed his lips in thought.

"I think he's in there," he said at last. "It's just about the right size, isn't it?"

Andy nodded and then he stiffened and pointed.

"Look at that!" he said.

There was a crack running wavelike through the lid of the sarcophagus from one side to the other of its middle. It was clearly not only a surface crack. The lid was split.

"I'll bet you could open that if you wanted to," said Andy.

He crouched down and bent close to the crack in the lid. He reached out his right hand and traced the crack with his forefinger.

"Hey!" said George. "What're you *doing*?"

Andy looked up at him thoughtfully, then back at the crack, then he placed both hands, timidly at first, palms down on the lower half of the lid.

"Hey!" said George again.

"Shut up," said Andy softly, and he pressed down on the lid and felt it wobble. "It's loose," he said, still in the same soft tone.

"Come on now, Andy," said George. "Stop that! You aren't supposed to do things like that!"

Andy ignored him, pushing the lid carefully in the direction of the foot of the little marble coffin. The cement which had held the lid in place had crumbled from more than a hundred years of rain and frost and rot, and with a grating sound which sent chills up both their backs, Andy got the lid moving until the crack was a little over two inches wide. Then Andy withdrew his hands and the two boys stared quietly at the opening.

"I can't see anything," George said in a muffled voice. "Can you see anything?"

Andy bent down until his nose poked just through the crack, and squinted.

"No," he said.

He cupped his hands around his eyes to block out sidewise rays of sunlight and continued to peer until George could hardly stand it anymore and then he finally spoke.

"It's just dark," he said.

George couldn't figure out whether he was relieved or disappointed when his eyes widened in horror as he saw Andy lean back on his knees and begin pulling back the right sleeve of his jacket until he had bared his whole forearm.

"Oh, *no*, Andy!" said George.

"I'm going to do it," Andy said, and slowly but steadily, he put his hand through the crack and reached in and down, and farther down, and only when his arm was in the little marble casket all the way to the elbow did he stop. He looked up at George with a thoughtful expression.

"I'm touching something," he said.

"Oh, gee!" said George. "Oh, gee, Andy, whyn't you stop this? Whyn't you just *stop* it?"

"It's him," said Andy, and suddenly there were little drops of perspiration all over his forehead. "I'm touching him."

He looked up, staring blankly ahead, and began searching with his unseen hand in the darkness of the marble box. He paused, took a deep breath, and made a decisive movement.

"I've got something," he said, pulling his hand out into the light and staring wide-eyed at something small and green held between his thumb and forefinger.

George backed up and almost tripped over a gravestone.

"Put it back!" he cried. "For Peter's sake, Andy!"

But Andy stood, still holding his prize. He looked over at George with mixed triumph and confusion.

"I never thought I could ever do anything like this," he said, in an exultant whisper. "Jeez, I really didn't think I could *do* it!"

George opened his mouth to speak but stopped with an abrupt, startled jerk of his whole body at a sudden rustling coming, unmistakably, absolutely unmistakably, from the interior of the little marble casket.

"What's *that*?" he hissed.

Then they both ran, this time really ran, hard as they could, banging their feet onto the graveyard earth. Andy fell once, heavily, with a loud thud, but he scrambled up almost as quickly as a ball bounces.

Somehow or other, with no idea at all how they did it or any memory whatsoever of doing it, they made their way to the fence and through it, and only when they were clear of the alley and more than half a block up Mercer Avenue to the east did they become aware of what they were doing or where they were. Still moving, they shot quick glances to their rear and began reviewing what had happened.

First it was only gabble, but then, with a little more distance between them and the graveyard and that small, marble box, they began to make a little sense. Eventually they were only walking very rapidly.

"Was it him?" George gasped, staring sidewise at his friend. "Was it the marble boy made that noise in there?"

But they had to walk on another full half block before Andy got his answer ready.

"Yes," he said. " 'Cause he was rotting. The air got at him and he fell apart."

He looked over at George and George looked back at him and they went on a little more in silence.

"I think he was just kind of caving in," Andy continued. "It wasn't that he was really moving."

"It wasn't?" George asked.

"No."

By the time they had reached Maple Street and Main Street they were walking at a reasonable pace. This was the corner where Andy would turn east and George continue on north. George reached out and touched Andy's arm.

"Let me see," he said.

They both looked around, making sure no one was near, and then Andy opened his hand.

The green thing rested on Andy's palm as the two of them studied it in awe. It was a tiny, withered business, like a broken-off stick.

"What's that?" George asked, pointing at a sort of curved flake growing out of one end of the thing.

"I don't know," said Andy, frowning and squinting his eyes. "I can't figure it out."

"Oh," said George in a hushed voice, after a pause, "I think I know what it is."

"What?"

"Can't you see?" asked George, reaching out to touch the edge of the flake, but then shying away from it. "It's his fingernail!"

"Wow!" said Andy, his eyes shining brighter and brighter. "Wow!"

That evening, at dinner, Andy's parents asked him a few carefully casual questions as it was obvious that something more or less serious was preoccupying their child, but when all they learned was that he had been nowhere in particular where nothing much had happened, they gave up on it, as they usually did, on the theory that whatever it was would eventually come out if it was really important enough to **have** to come out.

After dinner Andy unconvincingly pretended to do his homework, then he bid his mother and father good night a full half hour before the usual time, and quietly made his way to his room.

In bed, with his pajamas on, after listening carefully to make sure no one was in the hall outside, he leaned over and carefully slid the drawer of his bedside table open, noticing for the first time in his life that it moved with a slightly sinister *shushing* noise.

He licked his lips, for they had become suddenly very dry, and bent to look inside the drawer, doing it slowly so as not to rush the moment. It was still there, just where he had placed it, in the exact center of the bottom of the drawer. The two top joints of the left index finger of the marble boy. He knew exactly which finger it was because he had felt the rest of the marble boy's dry, tiny hand in the darkness in that casket when he had pulled the finger loose.

Andy stared at it with a kind of solemn joy and shook his head in wonder. He had never had such a thing. He had never heard of any other kid having had such a thing.

Wait until Chris Tyler had a look at it! Or Johnny Marsh! Or, *yes*, Elton Weaver! Andy could hardly wait to see the sick, envious expression on Elton Weaver's usually smug face when he got a look at it!

He smiled at the finger affectionately, then gently closed the drawer, *shush,* then turned off the lamp and settled into his bed with a sigh of deep contentment. He pulled the covers up until they were just under his chin, and with a clear, shining vision of Elton Weaver's tortured face floating before him, he drifted contentedly off to sleep.

When he awoke, some hours later, he had no idea why. He stirred, blinked, and then looked up with a growing sense of wrongness to observe that the bedroom door was open. He could see the pale paint of its outer surface gleaming faintly in the dim light coming from the bathroom down the hall.

He sat up, puzzled. He was sure that the door had been closed. He *knew* that it had been closed. He had been particularly careful that evening about closing it because of the finger. Had his father or mother peeked in and then gone off and left the door open by mistake? It didn't seem like them.

But then he realized that something was happening to the door even as he looked at it. It was changing shape, growing narrower. He couldn't understand how that could possibly be happening until he realized, with a sharp, hurtful pang in his chest, that he was watching the door being slowly and deliberately closed.

He had just cowered back to the headboard in a kind of half sitting position when he heard the faint, crisp click of the latch announce that the door's shutting was complete. He peered into the gloom at the foot of his bed but he could see nothing. Absolutely nothing.

He swallowed and opened his mouth in order to speak, but found he couldn't. He swallowed again and this time managed to whisper: *"Who's there?"*

Had he heard a noise? Had there been a brittle grating? An odd, grotesquely unsuccessful effort to reply from somewhere in the darkness over there?

He tried again: "Who's *there?*"

This time he knew he'd heard a noise, a different sort of noise than the last one, but definitely a noise. What had it been? A sort of dry rustle, that was it. There'd been a faint sort of rustle at the foot of his bed in the darkness over there.

He pulled more of himself nearer to the headboard until he was crouching against it as far away as possible from the bed's foot. He gathered the sheets and blankets, bunching them in front of him like a soft cloth wall. He strained his eyes, peering into the darkness as hard as he could.

Was there something there in the dark? It almost seemed so. It almost seemed he could barely make out a small something only barely higher than the top of the bed. Something moving.

Andy squeezed his knees against his chest and lifted the edge of the sheets and blankets so that only his eyes looked over the top edge. He was sure, now, absolutely certain that he was seeing something in the dark, even though he could only make it out as a faint silhouette.

It was working its way along the side of the bed. Very slowly. Very, very carefully. Awkwardly. Now Andy was able to see just a little something of the shape of the silhouette. It was round at the top.

Then he realized that he was breathing so hard that it was impossible to listen to anything else, particularly to the sort of soft sounds he'd heard before when he'd seen the bedroom door close, so he held his breath completely, and sure enough! he could hear the rustling which he'd heard before. And it was much closer.

Andy let himself breathe again because he realized he didn't want to hear the rustling after all, because he'd heard it before, and not just tonight but earlier that day! He'd told himself and George a lie about the rustling, saying it was probably only the falling in of old bones and rotting fabric, but he'd known better. He'd known it hadn't been any such thing at all. He'd known, deep down inside of him, standing by the cracked casket back there in the graveyard, that he and George were listening to the stirrings of the marble boy!

There was something else in the bedroom which he remembered from the graveyard: the sour, bitter smell which had oozed out of the casket when he'd opened up its lid, only this time it came from next to his bedside table where the silhouette now stood.

But, being this close to Andy, it was no longer just a silhouette. There was a lace collar, the sunken shoulders of the jacket were moldering velvet, and the brass buttons had all turned to lumps of verdigris. There was quite a bit of straight blond hair left on the skull and though someone had long ago carefully parted it in the middle, it stood up at all sorts of horrible angles. He could make out nothing of its face.

"Your finger's in the drawer!" Andy whispered with a great effort and hardly any breath at all to do it with. "I'm sorry I took it! Honest I am!"

It wavered and half turned to the bedside table. It even reached out to it, and a black little spider of a hand hooked its fingers over the knob, but then it slowly rotated its head on its thin little log of a neck until it was staring directly at Andy and Andy could just make out the stirring of leathery wrinklings deep inside its sockets. It made a small forward lurch and reached out spastically toward the bed with both of its shriveled, stumpy arms. A great gust of foul air puffed out from it.

"I'm sorry," said Andy in a voice so weak and faint he could barely hear himself. "I'm sorry!"

It clutched the blanket and pulled itself up onto the bed, and as it dragged its stiff little body over the covers, closer and closer to Andy, he could see its rigid smile widen terribly.

He opened his mouth to plead again and had just discovered that he lacked the breath to even whimper when it suddenly grabbed both his wrists with an unyielding, merciless grip and bent its round, sour head over Andy's left hand and bit the edges of its sharp little teeth deeper and deeper into the skin of Andy's forefinger.

It wasn't going to settle for what was in the drawer.

End Game

Balden's mouth worked, chewing sidewise like a parrot, or a turtle, or some other hard-beaked creature, and he moved his bishop to his queen's knight four with a sparse, economical shove of the hand. I leaned back in an ostentatiously casual fashion and lit my pipe. Balden's eyes remained fixed stonily on the board, I wafted forth a tiny plume of smoke and watched it drift slowly over Balden's head like a small cloud working its way past Abraham Lincoln's portrait on Mount Rushmore.

"Did I ever tell you about the circumstances surrounding Mannering's death?" I asked.

"No," said Balden shortly, his voice, as always, muffled and remote.

"I speak not of the circumstances before, nor those during. It is the circumstances that came after of which I speak."

I gazed at the ceiling, ignoring Balden's obvious disinterest, and continued.

"The instructions in Mannering's will concerning his post-mortem treatment were peculiar, to say the least. As his lawyer, however, it was my duty to see that they were properly carried out, no matter how bizarre they might seem."

"Your move," said Balden.

I lazily advanced a pawn and went on with my narration, seemingly all unaware of Balden's glaring indifference.

"He had always been a great traveler, as you doubtless know, and thanks to the family money, was able to indulge his predilection to the full. Reports of his activities came in from the most exotic places. Amazonian explorations, dizzying mountain climbs in Tibet, deep African probes—he seemed always to be investigating some new corner of the Earth."

Balden's eyes glittered coldly as he moved a knight to one side, exposing a thrusting rook.

"He died in a fitting room at Abercrombie and Fitch while preparing for a polar journey. He was being measured for an insulated parka when he suddenly keeled over and died."

"A pity," said Balden, tapping meaningfully at the edge of the board.

"The strange conditions of his will were a direct outgrowth of his lifelong passion for travel." I moved my hand vaguely this way and that over my pieces. "I shall never forget the growing expressions of stunned incredulity on the faces of the beneficiaries as I read the terms out, one by one."

I absentmindedly interposed a bishop between Balden's rook and my threatened queen. He sighed.

"The body was to be dressed in a specified wool suit, placed in a natural-looking position, and coated with a clear, nonreflecting plastic. The general effect to be strived for was that of an elderly gentleman, comfortably seated, with his eyes alertly open. The slightest suggestion of the macabre was to be studiously avoided."

Emitting a rasping cackle, Balden captured my queen knight with a rook. I let him study my expression of benign serenity for a moment and then picked up my tale.

"Thus prepared, the body was to be sent perpetually from one part of the world to another on an eternal global tour. Always first class, of course, and always accompanied by someone familiar with the area so that the corpse would not miss any local points of interest."

Balden had taken to clearing his throat rather noisily and I was forced to raise my voice.

"The family put the whole business into the hands of a carefully chosen undertaker and travel agent, who to this day remain in their employ. Both did their jobs well, and for a period of several months, everything went beautifully."

A slight but unmistakably convulsive movement on the part of Balden pulled me temporarily back to the business of the game. I moved my queen one square to unpin my bishop, doing it with the air of one who is only dimly aware of his surroundings, and continued my account.

"Then, in Hong Kong, the whole plan went dreadfully awry. In an ill-advised attempt to show Mannering's cadaver an interesting quarter of the city, his guide had installed the body in one rickshaw while he took another. They had barely reached their destination, an unbelievably crowded sector, when a street riot broke out. Horrified, Mannering's guide saw his dead client's vehicle vanish into the swarm. The desperate fellow struggled frantically to follow after, but he was hopelessly pinned by the howling multitude to the wall of a bean curd factory. There was nothing he could do to alter the ghastly course of events. Mannering was gone."

Some time since, Balden had made his next move. He brought the fact home to me now by repeatedly indicating the piece's change in position with jabs of his index finger. It was a bishop, and I captured it quietly and unobtrusively with one of my knights.

"A search was initiated instantly, of course. At first it was thought that the task would be a fairly easy one. We broadcast a description of Mannering and, considering his unique condition, had the firmest expectation it would quickly bring results. It did not."

"Check," said Balden. With some force.

"Nor did any of our other efforts meet with the slightest success. We tracked down every rumor and followed up each clue, but all to no avail."

Abstaining from giving it so much as a glance, I moved my king one square to the right.

"After two full years of fruitless search, the police of a dozen nations were ready to admit defeat. The small army of private investigators which we had hired fared no better. The corpse of Arthur Mannering was conceded lost."

"Check," said Balden, again.

"It was at this gloomy moment that I received a midnight telephone call from Mannering's nephew, Charles Addison Vaughn." I blocked Balden's attack with a move of my bishop. "He had a remarkable tale to tell. It seemed that he had wandered into a Forty-second Street sideshow emporium, drawn by a poster advertising an attraction billed as Oscar, the Romanian Robot. Oscar, so the poster claimed, could do lightning calculations, play chess and checkers, recite poetry, and execute pastel portraits of surpassing charm."

"Check," said Balden, yet again.

"Imagine Vaughn's astonishment when the curtains of Oscar the Romanian Robot's booth parted to reveal nothing less than the corpse of his uncle, clothed in mandarin attire, seated on a large wooden throne, a chessboard before it and a blackboard at its side. While Vaughn gazed on, appalled, the corpse did indeed do lightning calculations, play chess and checkers, recite several atrocious poems, and essay a number of rather muddy drawings. The jerky movements of the jaw, arms, and torso which accompanied all this were accomplished by means of an intricate system of wires and pulleys connected to an involved, cog-wheeled machine built into the body of the throne."

My next move, which I made with my eyes fixed on Balden's, simultaneously captured his attacking piece and placed his king in jeopardy.

"Check. I joined Vaughn and we both went at once to the Forty-second Street place of entertainment, but we arrived too late. Oscar, the Romanian Robot, had severed his connections with that establishment. The boards of his accustomed booth were bare."

For the first time, Balden seemed undecided as to his next move. His hand went here and there over the board, then retreated to scratch nervously at his thick beard.

"We traced the history of Oscar and found the trail led straight back to Hong Kong. His first appearance had been in an alley theater, an unsavory den presided over by an Arabian midget, Salaman Ruknuddin."

Balden pushed a piece several squares to the right, then

attempted to take the play back. I forestalled him with an up-raised palm.

"No fair changing the move after you let go."

I captured the piece, smiling thinly.

"Ruknuddin closed his theater shortly thereafter, and he and Oscar began a meteoric rise in show business. First in the Far East, then in Australia, on to England and Europe, and finally to America. Everywhere they went the audiences flocked to see Oscar's marvelous performance. Then the fatal flaw in the robot was uncovered, and overnight, Oscar turned from a wonder into a laughingstock."

"Check," said Balden, a little shakily.

"Stonewosk, the Polish master, discovered that Oscar was a patsy for the Ethiopian end game." I took Balden's piece. "An absolute sucker for it. No matter how many times you pulled it on him, he'd tumble right into the trap. Shaken badly, his confidence gone, Oscar's other talents coarsened or disintegrated altogether."

Balden's next move was done with a spastic gesture which very nearly knocked several men from the board.

"Check," he said, in a voice so faint as to be hardly audible.

"Oscar's career, and Ruknuddin's, went into a speedy decline and then into total eclipse. The last that was heard of them was their pathetic final stand at the Forty-second Street dive. The Ethiopian end game had pursued them to the end."

My voice rose.

"It pursues them even now, Balden," I said, moving my king. "Checkmate!"

Suddenly the figure sitting opposite me began to twitch and shudder in a remarkable fashion. I stood, reached over the board, and plucked off the false beard worn by my opponent to reveal the face of a tired-looking, certainly dead Arthur Mannering.

"The game is up, Ruknuddin!" I cried.

Abruptly the figure stopped its struggling, and as if to compensate, the chair on which it sat began a series of violent movements. After a moment or so a cog-bedecked panel in its side flew open and a tiny figure dashed out, spun, and streaked for the door. The curtains behind me were pulled apart and a group of anxious men rushed into the room.

"We must stop him!" shouted Charles Vaughn, and he was seconded by the others, but I held them back with a gesture.

"Let him go," I said, watching the desperate fugitive scuttle out of the apartment. "He is finished. He can do no more harm."

I saw that the mortician had already begun to restore Mannering to his former seemliness. I was glad to observe that there was no serious damage. The travel agent was also present and he stepped forward, a quantity of folders and time-tables in his hand, to look at me expectantly. Mannering's journeyings were, of course, to continue. I suggested a quiet sea voyage for a restful start.

A Gift of the Gods

Spring always snuck up on the children in Lakeside. The winters were so convincing and so durable that we eventually forgot about other possibilities, about a chance of change.

Then, always without warning, there were tender new leaves on the bushes surrounding the apartment buildings; a fresh, clayey smell of earth everywhere; birds picking up broom and mop fragments for making nests; summer vacation becoming an actual possibility; the bravest new flies crawling out from their hiding places along the edges of windows and wandering on the sunny panes—and the children began taking ruminative walks, going places they wouldn't ordinarily go and observing things they would ordinarily ignore.

It was the time of exploration come again, and the taste and feel of new adventure were everywhere, infusing the world, and none of the implications of any of it was lost on Henry Laird.

He had been walking, for no conscious reason, along the broad quietness of Harmon Avenue, gazing at the fine old trees and the low hills of the lawns and the looming bulks of the old mansions that lined its sides, when he found he had come to the little park that sat at the end of Main Street and faced the great spread of the lake.

The park was a small jewel of design, with its gardens gracious even now, before their real blooming; and its budding trees, waiting for their new leaves, stood composed in smooth, stylish curves and clumpings.

In the center of the park, or, rather, just enough off its center to make its location more interesting, was a small Grecian temple of the open, pillared style. Henry climbed the western steps and stood on the porch like a lost prince come at last to his kingdom.

The air from the lake wafted as gently over his face as a deliberately loving stroke, so he pulled his wool cap from his head in order to let the breeze caress more of him. He closed his eyes for a long moment and after some time, let them flutter open. At first, he looked about dazedly, enjoying the faint, odd, golden gleam that everything about him had taken on; but then he began to observe his surroundings in some detail, looking around in the manner of one who has returned home after a long and hazardous voyage.

It was then, for the first time, that he saw the greasy paper sack.

A thing as ugly as that had no business being in such surroundings. It belonged in a dingy alley next to garbage cans. It was not proper that such an object be in such a place as this.

Henry advanced to the brown sack and, after a moment's hesitation over its really spectacular filthiness, bent down and picked the thing up with both his hands.

It was nowhere near as heavy as its bulk seemed to indicate. Although it was jammed full, almost to bursting, it could not weigh a full three pounds. A rich animal reek exuded from the sack, and Henry peeked down into its gaping mouth and saw that it seemed to be stuffed full of grayish-black hair. He would remove the disreputable, odious thing.

But just before he left the park—just before he stepped from its grass to the sidewalk that would lead him back into the twentieth-century maze of concrete and asphalt that made up the basic webbing of this modern world—he became aware of being observed.

Something, he knew it, something with shiny, dark eyes was watching him, was carefully taking his measure as a hunter does of a rabbit or a lion of a zebra colt; and it was thinking, he could feel it in his own mouth, how Henry Laird would taste if you sunk your teeth into his shoulder until the skin split and the muscles tore and the blood spurted into your maw. And it was enjoying the taste, enjoying it very much.

So Henry quit the little park with more speed than he ordinarily might have used, and he was very glad when he reached his apartment building with his shoulder still unsplit and whole, and he was even gladder when he had gained the safety of his bedroom, having gotten past his mother, who, thank God, was busy making Jell-O with fruit in it and so hadn't caught as much as a glimpse of him or what he bore.

In his room, on his desk, the sack looked even worse than it had before. Its splotchings were more numerous and varied now, it seemed, and the disreputable, furtive look of it, its sullen poverty, made it stand out starkly against its present comfortable surroundings.

Henry took hold of the long, dark hair that poked from the sack's mouth, and when he tugged, it slithered forth and cascaded smoothly to the floor almost like liquid, like thick blood or oil. Henry tossed the sack aside and went to his knees, smoothing the fur with his hands, spreading it out; and then, with a silent gasp and a widening of his eyes, he saw what he had got.

From its head (for it certainly had a head) to the sharp, curving claws of its hind feet (for it had them, too), it was a kind of nightmare costume made of, as far as Henry could see, one single pelt for all its six-foot length and the wide stretch of its arms or upper legs.

It was animalskin, no doubt of it, bestial for certain, and yet there was an extremely disquieting suggestion of the human about it, too. It seemed to have been scalped from something between species, something caught in the middle of an evolutionary leap or fall.

The ears were animal in shape, pointed and high-peaked, with the wide cupping given to wild things that they might better hear their prey or would-be killer padding in the dark, and yet the placement of them, their relation to the forehead, was entirely human. And was that a nose or a snout?

It was hard to say, too, whether the appendages at the ends of its arms or forelegs were claws or hands, since they had something of the qualities of both. The cruelty in their design strongly suggested an anatomy too brutal to be human, yet the thumbs and the forefingers were clearly opposable, and there was something about the formation of the palms that denied their being exclusively animal.

Of course, in their present condition, these last were neither hands nor claws; they were gloves. Large gloves—far too large for the hands of Henry Laird, for instance—but gloves all the same.

Henry held his left hand over the left glove of the costume. Yes, it was far, far too small to fill that hairy, clawed container. The fingers of them were inches too long. If he slipped his fingers into them—it was a strangely disquieting thought that made all of his own skin tingle and crawl—the gloves would dangle limply hollow from the first knuckle.

Still, Henry would try; and he moved his hand down in a kind of slow swoop to where the skin gaped in a slit just under the costume's palm and slid his hand in, noting how smoothly and effortlessly it seemed to glide; and when it was in, entirely in, the glove, with an odd noise something like a cat's hiss, shrank in against the fingers and back and palm of Henry's hand until it fit him like a second skin.

Henry gave a kind of muffled shriek, stifling it with his unclad hand, and then pulled frantically at the glove. He expected a horrible resistance, but no such thing; it slid off most cooperatively—shot off, really, since he had pulled it so hard—and when Henry saw that his hand seemed none the worse for having worn it, he slipped the glove on and off again a few more experimental times.

Now it seemed that Henry's wearing of the glove had permanently affected it, for it remained his exact size, whether he had it on or not, which meant it was now ludicrously small for its opposite partner; so Henry, after giving the matter a little thought, slipped his other hand into the other glove with identical effect and the end result that the two were now precisely the same size—which is to say Henry's size.

The implications of this singular phenomenon gave Henry a clear challenge that very few boys his age could have resisted, and certainly Henry did not; and so, after going very quietly to the door and peeking out of it and listening carefully to make sure that his mother was still immersed in making fruit Jell-O, Henry picked up the costume and, with just a slight grating of his teeth and squinching up of his face, slipped it on.

He started with the legs, slipping into them as he would into pants, and gasped slightly as they shrank instantly to accommodate his size, again with that catlike hissing sound; and then he hunched into the arms, and they, hissing, fitted to him; and then there was a very alarming moment when the torso of the costume curled round his own and shrank to coat him smoothly; this with the loudest hissing of all; and then, by far the worst, the whole thing sealed up, the openings withering down to slits and the slits healing to unbroken skin, until his whole body was covered and wrapped with the dark-gray pelt.

Except for his head, that is. Henry had left the head for the last, just as he would have done with a Halloween costume.

He walked over to the mirror set into the door and gazed at himself in wonder, his pink face staring above the dark, hairy body, a mad scientist's transplant. He moved his arms and legs, experimentally at first, and watched their reflections make little, cautious movements. He reached out with one hand to touch the mirror and thrilled when he realized that he was actually feeling the glass not through the skin, as one does when wearing a glove, but *with* the skin!

After a time of touching and moving and carefully watching, Henry reached up behind him, groping for the mask, which was dangling down his back like a hood, and took hold of it and, very slowly and cautiously, watching anxiously all the time, slipped it over the top of his head and then his forehead; and then, closing his eyes—somehow, he did not want them to be open when they would be blind and covered—he pulled the mask completely down until the fur of its neck met the fur of the costume's chest, and he shuddered violently when he felt, with his lids still firmly closed, the whole business squeeze gently in, molding itself to the flesh of his face; and only when the catlike hissing had faded away entirely did he dare open his eyes.

There, facing him from the mirror of his own bedroom, with his desk covered with homework and a hanging model airplane for its background, was a monster—a small monster, true, but no less frightening for that.

Henry crouched a little as he studied his reflection. It seemed more comfortable that way. He moved his face closer to the glass. The nostrils worked as he breathed.

He lifted his head slightly and inhaled deeply and found he could smell the Jell-O his mother was making way off in the kitchen more clearly than he would ordinarily be able to do if he put his nose close enough to the pot to feel the heat.

He looked back at his reflection and studied his eyes intently. They were his eyes, no doubt of that, though the blueness of them was strange in their present setting. Then he opened his mouth and nearly fainted.

It was in no way the mouth of Henry Laird. It had fangs, for one thing, for the most obvious thing, but the differences did not stop there. All its teeth were as sharp as needles, every single tooth; and moving in and around them and lapping over them, constantly on the move, was a long, lean, curling tongue. Not Henry Laird's tongue. Not even a human tongue.

Without giving any thought to it, Henry pulled the skin costume from his head, his arms, his whole body, and threw it to the floor.

Again he studied himself in the mirror, touching his forehead, feeling his arms, wiggling his fingers; and then, only after all those preliminary tests, he opened his mouth and nearly cried aloud in his relief in seeing nothing more formidable in it than the ordinary incisors and molars with the occasional filling put here and there by Dr. Mineke, the family dentist, because of Mounds bars and licorice.

The skin was returned to its filthy paper sack, the sack was stuffed into the rear of the bottom drawer of his bureau and Henry took the most meticulous shower of his life and scrubbed his mouth three times in a row with Stripe toothpaste.

About ten that night, when Henry was just about to go to bed and had almost convinced himself that there was nothing waiting in his room, the doorbell rang and his father got out of his easy chair with a grunt and pushed the button by the doorbell so that he could talk with whoever it was downstairs and said, "Yes? Yes? Who's there?"

At first, there was nothing but breathing from downstairs; then they all heard a voice, Henry and his father and his mother—a deep, growly sort of voice.

"I want it back," the voice said, muffled and distorted.

"What?" asked Henry's father. "What did you say?"

"You give it back," the voice said louder; and this time you could hear the saliva in it, the drool. "It's mine, you! They gave it to me, see?"

"Look here," said Henry's father, "I don't know who you are or what you're trying to say."

"Who is that, dear?" asked Henry's mother. "What does he want?"

Now there was only breathing, heavier than before and with the hiss of spittle.

"You're going to have to speak up," said Henry's father. "I can't make out a word you're saying."

But now the breathing was gone and there was only the sound of rain, near and insistent, as it battered and spattered against the windows of the apartment. Henry quietly gathered up his books from the table where he had been doing his homework.

"Hello? Hello?" said Henry's father, pressing impatiently on the LISTEN button. "I think he's some drunk."

Henry started down the hall, holding his schoolbooks to his chest.

"Whoever he was, he seems to have gone," said Henry's father, and the rain, which had suddenly grown much fiercer, began throwing itself against the window in alarming, angry-seeming gusts.

"Well, he certainly doesn't sound like anyone we know," said Henry's mother, and his father, chewing his lip a little, casting a glance or two at the front-hall door of the apartment, settled again into his easy chair.

Lying in his bed, staring up at a ceiling too dark to be seen, Henry listened to the roaring wind and considered the situation.

Outside, in the wet wildness of this awful night, prowled a being dangerous to Henry and his family. It would not do just to give back what was asked for. Wearing the skin had roused something in Henry that knew all that and relished what it now made necessary.

When it seemed from the stillness of the apartment that his parents were asleep, Henry rose, carefully and quietly, padded across the floor to his bureau, extracted the skin from its double confinement of sack and drawer, and slipped it on.

The cat hissings merged into one smooth, unbroken cry when he donned the costume all at once, going from a kind of throaty purr to a final yowl of triumph as the mask sealed on, but all blended into the sound of the rain. Henry was sure his parents had heard none of it.

His passage through the apartment to the kitchen was so near to silent that even his hearing, heightened astoundingly by its joining with the high-peaked ears of what he wore, was unable to detect any of it save for the tiniest clicking as he turned the back-door lock. He took a deep breath, opened and closed the door as quickly and softly as he could, and he was standing in the wind and pelting rain on the apartment's back porch.

He rested his claws—for they were claws, not hands—on the wooden railing of the porch and peered down and around three stories below at the apartment's huge backyard.

There were occasional lights mounted here and there, none too solidly from the wild way they swayed in the wind: some on posts, spewing their swaying beams on parked cars; some fixed to the brick walls of the building, making a dancing shine on dark, wet windows or creating ominous shiftings of shadows in the depths of basement entrances; but none of them did much to dispel the dank gloom all about.

Henry lifted his snout and inhaled deeply and questingly and got a wild medley of night odors: rain and cinders; something strong blown in from the lake; a nest hidden on a nearby roof whose smell of new eggs and bird flesh made his mouth, with its needle-sharp teeth and long, lolling tongue, water—but not a whiff of his enemy.

He began to trot quietly down the rain-slicked wooden steps, glancing sharply about with his incongruous blue eyes as he moved.

He did not stop at the foot of the steps—there was a revealing pool of light from a lamp—but ducked quickly into a sooty patch of shadow before he crouched and sucked in great pulls of air, analyzing each one carefully before turning an inch or so to sample again. Then, suddenly, he froze and blinked and inhaled again without moving, this time even deeper, and a snarling kind of chuckle came from his throat, and his teeth were bared in a human, if singularly cruel, grin.

Bent low, ducking craftily from shadow to shadow, Henry dodged his way nearer and nearer to the wide gap in the wooden fence that led to the alley in back of the building.

He pressed himself against the wall, listening with his animal ears and feeling the rain exactly as though it were falling on his own bare skin. He could make out the motor of a far-distant car; someone in an apartment was playing dance music on a radio and humming to it; there was a muffled mewing from a covered nest of kittens; and there was the harsh, slurred breathing of his enemy.

He was near. His smell was mixed with garbage smells:

moldering oranges and lamb bones gone bad mingled with a hot hate smell, a killing smell out there in the dark. He was very likely watching the opening in the fence. Henry slowly backed up along the fence away from the opening until it joined a porch. After a listening pause to make sure the enemy had not moved, he stealthily climbed the porch's side, which gave him a perch just overlooking the alley.

The tar of the alley gleamed like black enamel in the rain from the light of the bare bulb mounted over the rear door of the apartment building opposite. The first sweep of his glance seemed to indicate that the alley was innocent of anything save a tidy army of garbage cans beside the building's concrete landing and a less respectable accumulation of cans and rubbish just outside the backyard of a private house farther down, but a squinting second look showed an ominous bulk hunkered down between the second batch of garbage and a low wooden fence.

Silently, hurrying as fast as he could so as not to give the enemy time to mull things over and change position, Henry made his way through his building and around the block so that he could approach the alley fence of the private house from its rear. Once in the house's backyard, he dropped to all fours and inhaled deeply. He grinned again, and this time the grin was significantly less human than it had been before. His prey was still there.

The impulse to rush with all speed so that he might throw himself at once upon his enemy and rip his skin and drink his spurting blood was so devastatingly strong that the flesh of Henry's flanks rippled suppressing it. He hunched down, puffing from the effort of wresting control from the sudden killing urge. He could not let such a thing master him. A blind scurry forward might undo all his cleverness so far. He had done well as a neophyte; he must continue to do so.

But still the smell of the enemy, the rich meatiness of it, was maddening. It seemed he could even detect the pulsings in the veins and arteries!

He forced himself into calmness, hunching low into the wet grass. He took a deep snuff of the earth scent in an attempt to clear his head and then began to work his way slowly and silently forward toward where the pile of garbage and his victim were lumped together on the fence's other side.

But as he drew nearer, he became aware of some confusion. It seemed the garbage stench was growing stronger than his victim's. Then it crossed his mind that that might well have been the reason that place had been chosen. He was, after all, dealing with someone far more experienced than himse——

Then there was a terrific shock and a sidewise lurch, and Henry's head exploded in a searing blast of light followed by a great, black rushing that threw him into a confusion of motion, not himself moving but himself being moved, roughly, brutally, and he screamed because of the awful, horrible pain—someone was tearing the skin from his face, ripping it off him, roots and all, and now his scalp and now the flesh of his neck—and he screamed and screamed and cried out, "Please, please stop!" but the tearing of the flesh from his body did not stop, only went on and on; and with each violent ripping and rending of himself from himself, the raw agony burned over more and more of him, until he was nothing but a scorched, stripped leaving thrown aside.

He lay naked on the wet grass, confusing his tears with the rain running over his body, and was profoundly grateful for the tears and the rain, for they were cooling and healing the rawness of him so that he was becoming aware of something other than pain, aware of the night and of movement before him.

There was the enemy before him, the victor, not the victim, huge and smelling—even to Henry's human nose, the stench of him was clear enough—hunched down and pulling this way and that at something in his hands.

"You spoiled it, goddamn, you little bastard!" the enemy sobbed and, leaning over, huge and dark in the night, sent a pale fist lashing out and knocked Henry's head back painfully against the fence. "You fucked it up, you little prick!"

Henry curled closer into himself and for the first time realized that the thing the enemy was tugging at was the costume. He did it with such absorption and violence that at one point his hat fell from his head and the rain streaked his long, black hair in curling ribbons down his furrowed forehead without his noticing.

The enemy's eyes were shiny and black, as Henry had sensed they were back in the park with the Grecian temple, and his teeth, though human, seemed much more pointed than the norm, the canines longer and sharper. All were bared in alternate snarling and sobbing, for the enemy was desperate. At length, he threw the costume down in fury and then lunged at Henry, taking him by the shoulders and shaking him hard enough to make his teeth rattle.

"It's all gone small, you little son of a bitch!" he shouted into Henry's face, and the stink of his breath made Henry gag. "What did you do, hah, you fucker? How did you make it shrink, you shit?"

"I put it on!" Henry sobbed, his head bouncing crazily as the enemy continued to shake him. "I put it on!"

A crafty look sprang into the enemy's face. He held Henry still for a long second, staring closely at his face.

"Yeah," he said. "Yeah, I remember. It changed when they gave it to me!"

He threw Henry hard against the fence and clawed up the skin, holding it spread open before him like a huge, soggy bat.

"Yeah," said the foe to himself, his wet face gleaming, his long canines shining. "Yeah!"

Then, with a growling chuckle, he lifted the costume's arm, pushed his huge hand into the skin glove of it and grinned wider and wider until it seemed that all of his teeth, his not really human teeth, were showing. The glove had stretched easily, and that which had been a small claw when Henry wore it was now something like a grizzly's paw.

He held his hand wearing the glove high into the rain in savage triumph, the rest of the costume trailing from it like a shaggy banner, and then he thrust it in front of Henry, waving it as a fist under his nose.

"You wait, you little piece of shit!" he crowed. "You wait till you see what I do to your face with this!"

He pulled on the other glove with equal ease, then stood and stepped into the hairy costume with his long, powerful legs, roaring with laughter when they slid in smoothly. A great flash of lightning made Henry blink, and when he opened his eyes, it was to see the costume curling round his enemy's chest, fitting it with a loving closeness.

His foe looked down at him with a grin of hate that made Henry shudder, and then, as a sudden crash of thunder made the ground jump, the grizzly paws took hold of the costume's mask, pulling it over the brutal, laughing face, so that the following volley of crackling lightning showed the monster standing there complete, towering awesomely over Henry, striding toward him, bending down and picking him up with a paw clutching either side of his throat. "I got you now, you little fuck!" the monster said, and Henry felt his weight making the long claws dig into his neck as he was swung in a high arc close to the hairy face grinning with fangs of such a fearsome length and sharpness that he almost vomited at the sight of them.

Then the monster suddenly froze position, and as Henry watched, the ghastly maw's grin made a weird, rapid transition, faltering, twisting, and finally turning into a wide gape of dismay.

"Naw!" his enemy snarled. *"Naaaw!"*

And then came a shocking crash of thunder, loud enough to make the very ground of Lakeside shudder, and as it pealed and pealed, rolling round in the sky, Henry saw the monster's eyes bulge impossibly, and then the paws released him with a spastic gesture and he landed with a hard thump on the ground to stare up in astonishment.

Lit by endless lightning, all sound of him drowned out by the ceaseless, merciless, air-flung cacophony, the monster pranced wildly in a crazy dance, arms and legs swinging like a mad jumping jack's, and from the gape of his horrible jaws and the spewing of blood and saliva, his screams must have been bloodcurdlingly ghastly could they have been heard.

But they could not; thunder censored all—and so it was in a kind of earsplitting silence that Henry saw the monster's eyes bulge more and more until the roundness of them projected entirely outside the sockets of the mask, and then they were violently ejected in a double spray of blood, and Henry found himself staring unbelievingly at the extraordinary sight of his blinded enemy beginning to shrink before him!

At first, the process was uneven, one huge paw shriveling at a time, an arm bunching oddly and then shortening in a jerky telescopic fashion; but then, almost as if getting the feel of it, the whole creature began to reduce itself in step, so to speak; and as Henry watched in appalled fascination but with an undeniable undertone of profound satisfaction, he saw the being crushed down by stages, dancing and screaming all the while, kept alive and conscious by some horrendous magic until it was no larger than he had been while in the costume—until, that is, the costume had returned itself to a perfect fit for Henry Laird. Only then, and not before, was the suffering of his enemy terminated and the creature allowed to drop to the rain- and blood-soaked grass on which it had danced these last awful minutes.

Its murderous readjustments completed, the costume opened its various slits and slowly disgorged Henry's enemy, now only a shapeless, glistening redness, washing itself carefully in the pouring rain after it did so. When it was entirely free of all traces of its recent tenant, and not before, it slithered smoothly over to Henry's curled and shivering legs, very much as a cat will work its way to the side of a beloved master, and, snuggling close to him, waited to see what he wanted to do next.

It Twineth Round Thee in Thy Joy

Ehnk Nahk S'Tak'n softly settled down on the coiling of his legs, but his eye never left the diary as his smallest frontal tentacles gently turned its yellowed, fragile pages while his midbrain deciphered and his aftbrain recorded the words written in faded ink upon them.

The first part of the diary was the routine sort of record any tourist might have kept in order to refresh himself so that he could enrich the anecdotes and brags he intended to inflict upon his home folk once he'd returned from his wanderings.

It began by describing the delights and wonders of voyaging first class on an interstellar ship, including a lengthy account of a conversation he'd had with a celebrity while seated at the captain's table. This was followed by a brief description of his arrival on New Mars, some details of his stay in the best hotel in its capital, and a list of historic sights he'd seen there with the more impressive ones carefully underlined.

Then the first hint of the strange turn this heretofore pro-
saic journey was to take appeared in the account of the diary
writer's meeting with an ancient New Martian guide in the hotel's cafe, and S'Tak'n's found his interest quickening as he
read the guide's intriguingly vague description of a legendary,
deserted village, which climaxed with the following tantalizing
comment:

> *"Understand, sir visitor, that there is no specific statement as
> to what is there," the old guide told me as he leaned over his still-
> living meal, " 'Tis only said that it is all one could wish for in this
> life."*

The author, who S'Tak'n judged to be a rather prissy sort of
fellow, paused to express his disgust at the guide's meal stirring as he forked it, then went on to describe his arrival at his
decision to abandon his original plans and form an expedition
to the village. S'Tak'n's mouths worked themselves into a variety of ironic grins as the old script spelled out to him the story
of a desert trek very like the one he'd finished within the last
half hour. It was exactly the same geographically, but significantly different in most other respects from the one he had
just completed since it had occurred a full three hundred
years ago.

He paused, lowered the delicate document, and focused his
gaze on the New Martian bearers he had hired. They were, under the astute direction of the head guide, efficiently and
carefully cutting their way through the thick, complex tangle
of desiccated vines which completely filled the narrow street
leading from the city's gate to its interior.

Moving their tall, excrutiatingly thin bodies with the care-

ful economy of movement so typical of them, they were guid-
ing the tightly focused, scarlet rays of their beam guns cagily
since they did not wish to start a general conflagration, but
had already cleared the way to the street's first turning, and
the lead members of the party were disappearing under two
overhanging balconies of bright pink stone. It would not be all
that long before they had carved a tunnel all the way through
the twisting tangle of wood to the central square of the city
and S'Tak'n might make his way there with ease and see for
himself if the heart of the mystery lay there as the eons-old
rumors held it did.

The diary had been plucked from the vine, or rather from
the fingers of a mummy complicatedly entwined within it, by
Soonsoon, the guide of the expedition. He had presented it
to his employer at once, without opening it, but S'Tak'n had
not been unaware of Soonsoon's many covert glances full
of speculation as the New Martian watched him reading it.
S'Tak'n beckoned with a wormish wiggle of the tentacles atop
his head, and striding like a wading bird, the guide approached him.

"What was that in life?" S'Tak'n asked, gesturing delicately
in the direction of the mummy.

"A humanoid," Soonsoon said in the dry, whispering voice
typical of New Martians. "Perhaps an Earthling. He has the
most amazing death grin I have ever seen. It appears to stretch
even beyond the lobes of his ears. I do not know whether it is
due to joy or dehydration."

S'Tak'n nodded, waved the guide back to his clearing of the
vine, and resumed reading the diary with increased curiosity
since it had begun to describe the clearing of an identical vine
in this same identical street. Three hundred years had again

made a considerable difference, however, and the diarist's progress had been slow and laborious in the extreme:

It has taken us three full days to chop our way within the village's square. There is a large fountain at its center and from a distance it seemed as though the bright, curling green coiled round it might be the body of a gigantic serpent, but as we drew closer we saw that it was, in truth, the living beginnings of the vine whose dead branches filled the rest of the city with their frozen writhings.

I went to touch it, but the old guide took hold of my arm with his spidery fingers and whispered, even more softly than was usual with him, that it might be best if someone else risked the first contact. He beckoned and one of the carriers bravely stepped ahead of all the rest. We all leaned forward eagerly to watch as he reached out and laid both his palms upon the smooth, glistening swell of an uppermost coil.

I started and felt the old guide's fingers dig into my wrist as we saw the green vine stir beneath the volunteer's touch. The thing was not only alive in its origins, it was clearly sentient!

"Pull back!" commanded the old guide. "Leave it!"

The bearer looked over his shoulder at him, and there was something indescribably piteous in his expression, but otherwise he did not move. The vine continued to stir, and as the rest of us watched in horror, we saw fresh, almost luminescently green new tendrils, pop out from its shiny skin and writhe upward even as they thickened. More and more appeared and steadily, layer upon layer, wrapped themselves possessively, even quite caressingly, about the bearer.

That unfortunate's body had now begun to tremble most oddly in all its parts, and his long mouth opened as he started a steady, monotonous, high-pitched wailing which was far and away the loudest sound I had, up to that moment, ever heard a New Martian make.

I turned to the old guide and was astonished to observe that his eyes had lost the haughty squint so typical of his race and were now positively bulging from their sockets as he stared at his compatriot.

"This cannot be!" he cried, totally abandoning his customary whisper. "There is no woman! This cannot be!"

I stared at him a second longer, then turned my attention back to the bearer and saw that a most remarkable transformation was beginning to take place.

I had, in the several weeks of my stay on the planet, found very little difficulty in becoming entirely accustomed to the structure of the New Martians. It was highly visible since their clothing consisted merely of short, diaphanous togas whose main purpose seemed not to be modest concealment or protection from the elements, but to carry and display their insignia of rank.

Though they were extremely tall and thin to the point of emaciation, and the glittering red polish of their featureless, poreless skin was at times a little disconcerting, they were, by interstellar standards, constructed along lines very similar to my own species, having four limbs and a head attached to a central torso in the same general fashion as were my own.

Now I saw that there were very important aspects of the New Martian anatomy which were ordinarily concealed from view. Under the stroking—I can think of no other word which would apply—of the constantly increasing number of tendrils enwrapping his form, dripping slits were opening between his ribs and along a line running from his groin to the base of his throat. From each and every one of those slits, with a languid, almost graceful turning, delicate pink spirals were beginning to emerge.

I had no doubt, no doubt at all, that I was observing a sexual arousal.

"How awful!" I exclaimed, and was surprised to realize that I had said it aloud.

The head guide turned and looked at me with interest.

"I am not surprised to hear you say that," he said, after a pause, his voice returned to its usual whisper. "The sexual functionings of species other than one's own often do seem revolting."

He paused again, and I observed considerable concern and puzzlement in his expression.

"But I must admit that this particular manifestation is," he continued, "highly disturbing even to myself, who reproduces in a like manner, since it is markedly unusual in two important respects: it is ordinarily quite impossible for us to become sexually activated in the absence of a female, and I have never heard of the emergence of more than four wanoon simultaneously, not even in the most erotic legends. Here we have all fourteen functioning at once. His state of arousal must be incredible."

The wailing of the bearer—who was now totally encaged in the ever-increasing accumulation of new green vines—reached an extraordinarily high, trilling note and then abruptly cut off.

For a long moment the head guide and I stood and watched as the bearer's thrashings diminished. Then, very slowly and carefully, we approached and peered down at him, only to pull back in horror when his body suddenly twisted in several enormous final spasms, then sagged inside its vegetable cocoon with the complete and unmistakable stillness of death.

"Is this the way it is with your kind, then?" I asked. "Is the sexual act fatal for the male?"

"No," said the head guide, his whisper grown so quiet I could hardly make it out at all, "It is not. This is a third, and by far the most depressing, variation from the norm."

A few hesitant steps nearer, and we saw that a new, different sort of tendril had begun to grow from the constantly extending vine. These differed from the previous forms by terminating with a sort of bulb which, even as we watched, opened and showed itself to be a dark, deep purple flower with a ring of what I took to be pointed pistils and stamens around the deep interior of its cup.

Something about the flowers had given me the dim but unmistakable sensation that they were oddly sinister, and when I leaned closer I saw clearly what before had frightened me only vaguely—that the pointed things in the central cavity were not pistils and stamens at all, but a ringed multitude of sharp, tiny teeth. I had barely managed to assimilate that grim new aspect of the vine before the flowers began, first one by one and then in nodding waves, to attach themselves systematically to the dead bearer's flesh.

I felt a soft, insistent, increasing pushing and turned my head to see that all the New Martians in the party had gathered close behind us and were steadily pressing against our backs in order to peer over our shoulders at their dead comrade.

When I looked again before me I felt a cold chill run through my body as I saw that the petals of all the flowers had spread and flattened and were now squeezing and kneading the dead bearer's skin. They looked like evil, purple stars as they began to pulse together as regularly and smoothly as a baby sucks, and I observed that every one of the vines leading from their bases had now become swollen and veined with red.

"Observe," whispered the old guide, almost dreamily, "they are drinking him dry. See how he shrinks."

What he said was true. First only the skin reaching to the points of the petals sank like little craters in a moon, but these depressions spread and joined and soon the whole form of the bearer began to steadily decrease and shrivel before our fascinated gaze. The eyes sank into their sockets even as they withered; the lips dried and wrinkled back to reveal the teeth they had heretofore concealed; the very joinings of the bones beneath the skin became more and more clearly defined.

As the body of the bearer slowly collapsed, new tendrils of the vine, doubtless encouraged by the end of their long drought, groped eagerly out beyond him in search of new nourishment. I stared transfixed and observed one of the revolting things pawing in my direction.

A coiling green branch of it paused just before me and I gaped stupidly as one of its leaves gently touched my fingers, then slid forward and flattened itself on the back of my hand. The leaf was warm and faintly throbbing and I felt a loathsome but seductive glowing spread insidiously out from its touch.

I found myself swaying and sagging where I stood as an extraordinary languor spread through my body like some interior version of the vine, but then I saw my hand—all on its own, with no command from my conscious mind—begin to stretch out longingly toward the nearest green swaying of the damned thing and a thrill of total disgust woke me suddenly from my trance. I cried aloud and pulled my hand quickly back and the spell was broken.

"We must leave this awful place!" I shouted.

I do not think that any one of the New Martians so much as heard me, so deep was their fascination with the growing plant. Their breathing was now clearly audible and was not coming in unison, each one like one great, hissing inhalation; their bodies exuded a thick, strong odor which was at the same time both bitter and sweet.

There was a terrible moment when I found I could not retreat because of the steady forward pressure exerted by the crowd of blankly staring creatures behind me, but then I discovered it was possible to edge sidewise, and I began a crablike scramble along the front of the mob, carefully arching my body back from the constantly exploring, greedy tendrils which, nevertheless, managed to flick at my flesh and clothing as their reach from the expanding vine grew longer and longer.

I had hardly left my space when a bearer who had been directly behind me shuffled forward. His mouth flopped open and he began a keening, monotonous moaning which was instantly taken up by all the others save for the head guide who reached out toward him vaguely, half trying to stop him.

The bearer evaded him easily and his moaning changed to a wavering howl, an awful sort of singing, as several dripping slits opened in his chest and I observed the pink corkscrews, which I now knew were called wanoon, begin to rotate, dripping, into view. As they continued to emerge and spiral and were joined by others besides, the New Martian, shuddering and jerking in ever more violent spasms, began to lower his body clumsily into a squirming tangle of juicy new vinelets even as they reached up to gather him into their writhings. The guide let his hands fall slowly back to his sides, continued to stare ahead with increasing fascination, and—softly at first, but then more and more loudly—began to join the others in their endless moronic keening.

In spite of all my efforts, I was totally unable to quell an increasing trembling as I worked my way past these hypnotized creatures. They were now, to the last one, starting to shamble forward, and though I greatly feared their mindless shoving would push me into one mass or another of the monstrous purple flowers, my struggles succeeded. I finally managed to force my way clear of them all and stagger some yards down the path which had been chopped through the old, withered growth of vine before I collapsed entirely, flopping like a rag doll onto a desiccated tangle of wood.

After my breathing became less than a painful gasping and the pounding in my chest receded to a tolerable level, I was able to gather myself together enough to look back.

I was appalled to see that so many of the New Martians had thrown their bodies into the fresh green sproutings of the vine that they had filled its first shoots altogether and their companions had been forced to shuffle slowly along the sides of the noxious plant so that they could eagerly follow the unfoldments of its steady growing.

As soon as those who had shouldered themselves into the lead judged that a sufficient tangle of new vines had sprouted to absorb them, they would throw themselves into the fresh green mass with its sprinkling of gaping flowers and leave those behind them in the shuffling line to wait for the next enthusiastic budding which the absorption of their bodies would produce.

For a short time I was so exhausted that I could only lie back on my complex hammock of dry twigs and watch this grotesque parade of New Martians and growing vine steadily work its way in my direction, but as the gap between us grew smaller and smaller I finally managed to summon the strength to pull myself up, stagger to my feet, and somehow lurch down the entire length of the tunnel we had all foolishly carved through the ancient growth of this fiendish vegetation during the last few days, before I completely lost consciousness.

When I woke I found that this diary had tumbled out of my pocket as I fell and was lying in the chill New Martian sun, spread open to my last entry, and I confess it struck me as looking more than a little pathetic on the ancient paving of the street. After staring at it vaguely for a while, I pulled it to me and began to put down this account of the vine for no particular reason.

It occurs to me only now, as I reach the end of this record, that I may have been writing a warning for the next visitors unfortunate enough to find their way to this accursed place and its hideous inhabitant.

If there is to be some reader of these pages, some traveler following after me, I beg you to leave now, while you are still in the outskirts where you will have found whatever husk remains of my body. In particular I implore you: do not go to the center of the village, to its well. Do not look on the living vine!

Some time ago it grew around the first bending of the road leading from the arched entrance of the village wall. I have watched its slow creeping under the twin pink balconies as I have lain here patiently on the cobbles. I have been writing and watching it near.

It moves a good deal slower now that it is not being constantly fed, but that is not what intrigues me most about its new mode of progress. What interests me most is that it did not come straight for me, as I expected, but rather circled round me in a graceful coil which was as large and spacious as the confines of the street would admit.

Even then it was leisurely in closing the gap, in sealing me in. I calculate I may have watched for as long as half an hour before it grew the last few inches and twined itself together.

Then, in a manner so slow as to be almost unobservable, the encirclement has thickened, the space about me gradually lessened.

Now, at last, the vine is all about me, touching my curled body gently on all sides. I am at the very center of a bower of purple flowers.

> *I could have left at any point heretofore. I've tried to tell myself*
> *that I stayed because I knew I could never make the journey through*
> *the desert on my own, but I'm well aware that's a lie.*
>
> *I stayed because I wished to.*
>
> *I want the damned plant as much as it wants me.*

Sighing very softly, licking his many lips, Ehnk Nahk S'Tak'n gently closed the diary and looked up to see the venerable guide, Soonsoon, looking curiously back at him.

"We have cut our way to the center of the village, sir visitor," Soonsoon reported with a tiny bow.

S'Tak'n flowed erect. He looked briefly at the arched entrance of the village and through it to the coral desert which stretched endlessly open beyond; then he looked back the other way to where the village road curved under the twin pink balconies on its way to the well.

"What do you wish to do, sir?" asked Soonsoon, after a respectful pause.

"Why, go to the center, of course," exclaimed S'Tak'n. "And find the root. And hope it's still alive!"

The Book

Doren's fingers found the black book before the rest of
him. They had cruised, almost independently, hopping,
groping, from book to book after the manner of the
fingers of collectors the world over, touching each book tenta-
tively, but with skill, and when they felt the odd, almost furry
spine of the black book they had stopped as quickly as an
owl's gaze halts on a mouse. He looked down at the book his
fingers had discovered for him and carefully concealed any
outward signs of the electric thrill which ran through him. Casually, studiously so, he took the black book from its place and
languidly began to turn its pages.

His eyes and fingers worked together now, taking in the peculiar softness of the skin pages, noting the heavy black type
deeply indented into its sienna-splotched, ocher background,
touching and seeing the barbaric woodcuts of astrological
signs and magic circles and imps and dark angels.

Doren's heart began to beat with a thudding intensity which frightened him. He almost believed it might be audible to others. He could imagine its thumping carrying across the empty shop where the ears of old Steiner would perk and listen. But Steiner's back remained solidly turned and Doren gave a strained smile at the fantasy.

He closed the book and carefully slipped it back where he had found it. His head buzzed with schemes and confusion. A large black cat jumped soundlessly onto the stall and Doren stroked it, thankful for the interruption. He felt the cat's back arch under his hand and he attempted to consider his situation coolly.

It was the sort of situation which never happened. People who didn't collect books, or who collected them only a little, always felt that they really might come across a Shakespearean folio, or a Gutenberg Bible, or, Doren swallowed, a black book such as this. But it never happened. Old Steiner and his fellow bookdealers saw to that.

He glanced down at the book again, tore his eyes from it, and selected another one at random. The cat mewed pettishly and he stroked it again to silence it.

It wouldn't take a Steiner to spot the black book, thought Doren. This was no subtlety, no delicately flawed wonder, no first edition panted after only by certain esoterics. There was nothing obscure about this treasure. Its feel, its look, even the smell of it broadcast its singularity. The most ignorant clerk would have been sophisticated enough to at least strongly suspect the black book's value.

He put down the book he'd been toying with, he couldn't even remember its title, and risked another inspection of his find. Its absurd, its altogether ridiculous price was lightly penciled on its end page: one dollar and seventy-five cents. He almost gasped when he recognized Steiner's European seven with its crossbar. That eliminated the idea of a blunder by a part-time assistant. The old man had priced it himself.

Had he been drunk? It wasn't in character. But how on earth could the old man have come to make such a gigantic error? How could he have given the black book its grotesque price and condemned it to a common stall?

Would he give challenge when Doren went over to buy the book? It seemed likely. The hideous mistake would be seen at once, a plausible explanation would be hastily presented, and the book would be out of Doren's hands forever. Forever—because Doren knew he would never be able to afford anything like its true cost. It was an item only for richly endowed libraries and millionaire collectors. The thing must be practically priceless.

Doren turned to a carefully cut magic circle. Each minute detail was sharp and clear. It was important, he reflected wryly, not to make mistakes when you drew a magic circle. He had seen plenty of them before, of course. Every *grimoire*, every warlock's spell book, contained at least one of them. The idea of the circle was central to the diabolist's art. But this one was, in some tingling way, different from any of the others. This one looked as if it might actually *work.*

He closed his eyes and opened them again, like a man with a bad headache, and the shop seemed to rush in at him. It was as if he had been away in some far-off place for an immeasurable time and only just returned. He looked down dazedly at the cat and it looked up at him with green expectation in its eyes.

Doren felt suddenly tired. He could not cope with the plots

and plans which flashed through his mind. He saw himself gathering an armful of books and taking them up to Steiner, shuffling them before the old man's eyes like a magician with a pack of cards, burying the black book in a flurry of unimportant others. He imagined himself waiting until a rush of customers were at the dealer's desk, and then shoving the book hurriedly into view, giving him money and going before the old man could properly take in what had happened. He seriously considered just slipping the book into his pocket and leaving without paying.

He sighed. He could do any of these things, but in his present peculiar state of exhaustion he felt he wouldn't be up to the simplest of them. For the first time in his life he found himself a convinced fatalist. If it was to happen, it would happen, he decided; if it wasn't, then it wouldn't.

He walked up to Steiner's desk with the black book in his hand. Doren noticed that he looked thin and haggard, as if he had been through a bad illness. Perhaps the dealer was sick. That might explain it.

"Well, Mr. Doren? You found something you want?"

"Yes," said Doren. He put the book on the desk and pushed it toward the old man.

Steiner opened it without curiosity and noted the price. "One dollar and seventy-five cents, please," he said, and when Doren had given him the exact change, he said, "Thank you, Mr. Doren."

Doren took the black book, knew it was now his, and was torn between the impulse to shout in triumph and, oddly, to cry in sorrow. He nodded at the old man and walked unsteadily through the shop. He paused at the door and blinked at the sunlight. It was too bright. It seemed unfriendly. He hunched his shoulders and went down the street, patting and stroking the book with his hands.

Steiner watched him leave. When Doren had passed out of sight the old man turned to look at the cat which perched calmly on the stall where the black book had been.

"All right," said Steiner wretchedly. "It's gone. Now you go."

The cat smiled broadly at the old man. It was a horrible smile. It was bigger by half than the cat's small head. The teeth were thick, white, and pointed like a shark's. The cat leaped gracefully to the floor and, still grinning hugely, left the shop in stalk of Doren.

Then the old man sagged in his chair, alone, completely alone, with his bleak awareness that he had gained no reprieve, after all.

M-1

een from across the desert, from miles away, the statue
had been dwarfed and easily understood, and Henderson
had smiled at its familiar outlines as he sat in the bouncing
jeep. Now, climbing from the jeep at the statue's base, he
found it unrecognizably distorted by its grotesque height.

Bentley, sweating in khaki, came up to him and shook
his hand.

"You'll break your neck if you keep gawking up at it like
that," he said, smiling.

They stood near the statue's left foot, a huge, gleaming
thing of curving yellow.

"Five hundred and thirty feet from here to the top of its
toe," said Bentley. "Sixteen hundred feet from the toe to the
heel. Four hundred and eighty feet across at its widest point."

The two men walked to the side of the foot, and Henderson
reached out to lay his hand flat against its surface. The Nevada

sun had made it uncomfortably hot to touch. He moved his hand back and forth over the gleaming yellow and marveled at its smoothness.

"It's like butter!" he said.

Bentley nodded, lighting a cigarette and squinting up.

"No damned traction possible, to speak of," he said. "Makes climbing around on the thing a real bitch. And you can't dig steps into it. You can't even drive stakes to hold ropes. Folger slid off its instep yesterday. Would have fallen to his death if he hadn't managed to grab the scaffold."

Against the side of the foot, and extending partway up the shank of the black leg, the towering scaffold looked absurdly small and unimportant next to the bulk of the statue. Henderson could see an army of men working at the top of it, slowly extending it.

"I can't decide if we're building another Eiffel Tower or playing Tinkertoys," said Bentley. "You get funny shifts in your self-image, living with this thing."

He dropped his cigarette and pushed it into the sand with his foot.

"You want to wash up and all that, or do you want to get on with looking it over?"

"Let's look it over."

"Right," said Bentley. He signaled to a man who detached himself from a group standing by the entrance to one of the scaffold's elevators and came walking toward them. The man wore curved sunglasses and a leather jacket. He was lean and had an easy stride. Bentley introduced him to Henderson.

"This is Captain Harry Grant. Captain Grant's on loan to us from the Navy, and how far away from water can you get? He flies us around the statue so we can all get a better look at it

and fully realize how little we understand it. He hasn't lost one
of us yet."

They shook hands, and the three of them began walking over to the helicopter which stood on a little pad of concrete. Like everything else next to the statue, it looked tiny
and delicate.

"Sometimes I like to get the layman's point of view, Harry,"
said Bentley. "What do you make of our wonder?"

Grant smiled and shook his head.

"I used to like him when I was a kid," he said, pointing up at
the statue with his thumb, "but now I don't know. Now I think
he scares me."

"I believe you've got just about as far with him as us scientists, Harry," said Bentley.

They climbed into the helicopter, and Grant started the big
blades turning. Henderson peered up at the statue through the
lightening blur.

The helicopter began to climb slowly. When it drew abreast
of the top of the scaffold, several of the men turned to wave at
them. Bentley smiled and waved back.

"I wish we could get that thing to climb as quickly as this
gadget," he said. "I figure with all the luck in the world we
might get up to its left tit by late August."

They had reached its midsection, now. Its red pants
sparkled in the sunlight, and the two vast yellow buttons
seemed to twinkle.

"The buttons are two hundred feet across," said Bentley.
"You get so you can really rattle off the statistics. They have a
way of burning themselves into your head."

"Have you tried digging into its upper parts?" asked Henderson. He'd never been in a helicopter before. It wasn't as

hard speaking over the roar of the propellers as he had thought it would be.

"Hell, yes," said Bentley. "Once, in a fit of pique, old Wellman even let fly at it with an explosive rocket. Didn't leave a goddamn mark."

Now they were up to its black, sprawling chest. One of its arms hung down at its side, the other was raised high in a titanic salute.

"We've had expeditions on the head and shoulders times past counting. We've drilled at it, lit fires on it, poured acid over it, and usually ended up kicking at it with our feet. None of it's had the slightest effect. I honestly don't think an H-bomb would dent it."

Suddenly they were opposite its face, and Henderson found the confrontation unexpectedly horrible. Somehow this nearness to the head was the thing which brought the monstrous enormity of the statue home to him. He had to look from side to side to follow the sweep of the inane grin. Sitting there in the helicopter, hovering feet away from the swollen bulb at the end of the thing's nose, Henderson had an abrupt and hideously convincing fantasy that the statue would come to life and crush them with a pinch of its tremendous yellow fingers.

The helicopter worked its way past a gigantic black eye set into the blinding whiteness of the face, around to the side of the head where it swung by one of the circular ears.

"The ears are quite thin, really," said Bentley. "Only average about seven feet thick. The flat surface has a diameter of more than one thousand feet. The point of attachment to the head is a piddling one-hundred-foot line around three feet thick. Gives you an idea of the structural peculiarities of our friend, here, doesn't it? We've mounted recording devices on the ears, just to see, and we've found they don't even wiggle in a high wind. If we tried to build something like that out of what we've got to hand in our advanced technology, you'll excuse the ironic tone I'm sure, we'd find we couldn't."

Henderson stared at the ear as the helicopter rose gently over its upper curve.

"Somebody built it," he said.

"That's right," said Bentley. "Somebody has. And they put it up here between National flight four-oh-five, which didn't see anything at all when it passed by here at four thirty-eight P.M., Wednesday, February the seventh, and five seventeen the same date, when the Reno air taxi flew right into the son of a bitch."

"Why didn't they see it?"

"My own theory is that they did see it," said Bentley. "They just couldn't believe it. Saw the damned thing smiling away at them with its big eyes with the little chips cut out of the sides, saw it waving at them in the moonlight, and there was plenty of moonlight, I checked, and maybe the pilot thought of a movie he'd seen once, or a Big Little Book, I don't know, and maybe he was screaming, and maybe he wasn't, and he just smashed into it."

They were over the top of its head now. Henderson looked down at the shadow speck the helicopter made moving across the shiny black dome of the statue's skull. Far, far down below he could see the long, thin, curling tail coming out of the rear of the bright red pants. Bentley followed the direction of his stare and smiled.

"Seven thousand feet, if you straightened it out," he said.

The helicopter began to descend. Henderson folded his

hands and looked down at his knuckles. He didn't want to see any more of the statue, not just now. He'd have plenty of time to study it in the months and weeks coming.

Bentley lit a cigarette and shook the match out carefully.

"It's still a rumor," he said. "But it keeps checking out better all the time."

He took a quick puff at his cigarette. Henderson was watching him.

"The last word I got on it came from Schillar," said Bentley. "He believes it. He said Brandt told him he'd seen photographs."

"What do you mean?" asked Henderson. "What's true?"

Bentley licked his lips.

"They say the Russians got Minnie."

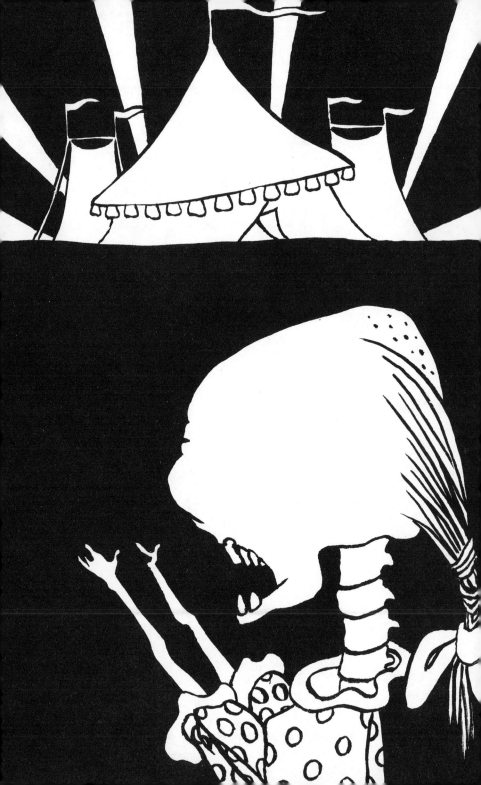

Come One, Come All

Professor Marvello tightened two guy ropes with an expert twist of his strong, pudgy little hands in order to make the poles holding the big canvas sign spread out above the platform stand a little taller, then he squinted upward at it with a slightly grim, lopsided smile of satisfaction.

The sign read:

* *MARVELLO'S* * *MIRACULOUS* * *MIDWAY* *

in ornate, gold-encrusted letters four and a half feet high—exactly the height of Professor Marvello, himself, by his personal instructions—and a multitude of spotlights helped each letter glitter proudly out at the silent, surrounding darkness.

Marvello regarded the effect with satisfaction as he carefully and neatly made the ropes' ends fast around their shared cleat, then he meticulously brushed a speck of Kansas dust off the lapel of his red and white checkered coat and adjusted the bright yellow plastic carnation in its buttonhole.

"A nice night," he murmured to himself softly, sweeping the horizon with a benign if slightly wary gaze, and taking a long, fond sniff of the warm, wheat-smelling night air blowing in from the dark fields all around. Professor Marvello had been plain Homer Muggins of Missouri in his youth and he still admired simple, farmy scents. "A helluva nice night."

Then, adjusting his straw boater, he turned to business, flicking his bright little blue eyes down to see if the light was glowing on the solar battery like it ought to be, jabbing back a switch to start the circus music whooping, and plucking the microphone from its metal perch on the banner-bedecked rostrum. That done, Marvello squared his small but sturdy shoulders, softly cleared his throat, and spoke:

"LADIES AND GENTLE——"

Too loud. You didn't need it that loud because there was no competition. No competition at all. He stooped with a slight grunt, bending to turn the knob down on the speaker system, then straightened his rotund little body so that it stood proudly erect as before, and spoke again.

"Ladies and gentlemen, boys and girls," he said, and the nasal drone of his voice swirled out from a baker's dozen of speakers and rolled over the midnight landscape of flat, dimly furrowed earth, sparse trees, and long-deserted farmhouses. "Come on, come on, come on. Welcome to the fabulous, most wonderful, undeniably, and by far greatest show left in the world. Come and see and be astounded by the one, the only Marvello's Miraculous Midway—the sole remaining sideshow in the world."

He paused, hacked, and spat over the edge of the platform

onto the dusty ground. He gazed at the dust, at its dryness, half reached for the flask of whiskey in his hip pocket, but then decided against it. Not yet. Later.

Did he hear a shuffle? His eyes guardedly darted this way and that. Not sure. Sometimes they stayed hidden just out of sight, watching you put up the show, standing on one foot and then the other, no idea what to do with their hands, hardly able to wait. Like kids, he thought, like kids.

"Don't miss it, don't miss it, don't miss it," he intoned. "Come one, come all, and bring your friends and loved ones so that everyone in this lovely area, in this beautiful county of this remarkable state, can be fortunate enough to experience the entertainment thrill of their lifetime, so to speak. So to speak."

Yes, yes indeed, there was a shuffle. He avoided looking in its direction, plucked a large polka-dotted handkerchief from his other hip pocket, the one not containing the flask, and wiped his brow in order to conceal his covert peering.

There it was, just by the popcorn stand. Raggedy, forlorn, and skeletal. It was dressed in torn blue denim overalls and the tattered remains of a wide-brimmed straw hat. There was no shirt, there were no shoes. It stared at him, mouth agape, and he could just make out the dull last remnant of a glint in its eyes and a vague glistening in its mouth.

"Good evening, sir," Professor Marvello said, giving it a formal little bow, an encouragingly toothy grin. "I observe you possess the percipiency to have been attracted by the sounds and sights of our outstanding exhibition. May I be so bold as to congratulate you on your good taste and encourage you to step a little closer?"

It swayed, obviously undecided. Professor Marvello increased the wattage of his grin and, producing a bamboo cane from inside the rostrum, employed it to point at an enormous depiction of a huge-breasted Hawaiian hula dancer painted in classic circus poster style on a bellying rectangle of canvas.

"Miss La Frenza Hoo Pah Loo Hah," he announced proudly, and leaning forward toward the wary watcher, winked confidentially and continued in a lower tone as one man of the world speaking to another, his S-shaped smile taking on a new chumminess and his voice growing increasingly husky and intimate.

"I am sure, my dear sir, that a man of your obvious sophistication and, if I may say it, *je ne sais quoi,* is well aware of the extraordinary sensual jollies which may be produced by the skilled locomotion of swaying hips and other anatomical accessories on the part of a well-trained and imaginative practitioner of the art of hula dancing. Permit me to assure you that the lovely Miss Hoo Pah Loo Hah is *extremely* knowledgeable in these matters and will not fail to delight the sensibilities of a *bon vivant* such as yourself. Come a little closer, there, my good man, don't be shy."

The figure swayed, its dark green, arms stiff and lolling, and then one large, bony foot pushed forward, stirring up a little puff of dust.

"That's the way, that's the way," said Marvello in an encouraging tone. "There's the brave fellow. Excellent. You're doing just fine. I trust, in passing, you've observed how plump the lovely Miss La Frenza Hoo Pah Loo Hah is, my dear fellow: how fat her hips, how round and fulsome her breasts, how meaty she is in all respects. I trust you've not let those aspects of our lovely dancer get by you, my good sir."

The overalled figure paused as if to study the poster with

increased intensity, or perhaps it was only getting its balance. There was a kind of gathering, a moment of staggering confusion, then it lurched itself forward with a series of crablike waddles until it had worked its way well into the brightly lit area before Professor Marvello's platform. This one had semi-mummified, its skin had dried more than rotted, and the dark green-brown of its bony, beaky head and face bore more than a slight resemblance to an Egyptian pharaoh's.

"Over here, over here, my wizened chum," said Professor Marvello with encouraging enthusiasm, indicating the tent's entrance with a wave of his bamboo cane. "Keep heading toward that welcoming aperture before you, spur yourself on with rapt contemplation of the sexual gyrative wonders the lovely Hoo Pah Loo Hah will perform before you as envisioned of in your most private dreams, and of course never forget nor neglect the generous pulchritude of her charms, which is to say the amazingly large amount of tender flesh which bedecks her frame."

When the mummy farmer paused at the entrance, Professor Marvello raised the tent flap invitingly with the tip of his cane.

"No need to pay, my good man," he intoned, though the thing had not made the slightest attempt to reach into its pockets, "The Marvel Miracle Midway is a rare phenomenon indeed in this hard world, my dear sir, being gratis, entirely free of charge. A generous, altruistic effort to brighten the, ah, lives of such unfortunates as yourself. Go right on in, do go right on in."

A few prompting prods from the tip of Marvello's cane between the separating vertebrae of its narrow, bony back, and the overalled entity finally committed itself and lurched on into the tent to be greeted by the soft throbbings of Hawaiian music issuing from within along with a gentle, perfumed wafting of the heady scents of tropical flowers.

"Almost looked happy for a moment there," murmured Professor Miracle thoughtfully, nudging the tent flap so that it fell softly back into place as the music and the scent of flowers ceased abruptly.

Nearly at once there was another timid shuffling, this from the far left, hard by the ring toss stand, and two figures edged sidewise into view. What was left of a mother and daughter.

They were dressed in faded, flowered frocks, which were frayed and torn and flecked with a multitude of dark, dry stains. The girl was missing her scalp on one side of her head, but a glistening gold braid with a large pink bow on its end grew from the other. Her mother held her hand tightly but mechanically, a habit which had somehow survived the loss of everything else.

"Fun for the entire family," Professor Marvello cooed into his microphone, essaying a fatherly wink which somehow slipped over into the lewd. "Let me assure you, Madame, and your precious little princess standing so trustingly by your side, that the Marvello Miraculous Midway fully satisfies both young and old. Both of you may positively and without reservation enjoy it to the full as we unhesitatingly guarantee to completely and entirely please folks from eight to eighty. Do come up, do come up."

He turned and waved his cane at the flapping portrait of a man whose mighty body bulged everywhere with layer upon layer of huge, rippling muscles, but whose calm, heroically moustachioed face radiated an almost saintly kindliness. With serene calm the man was carefully lifting a school bus packed full of laughing children high above a torrent of swirling water.

"Observe a true wonder of the world—Hugo, the Gentle Giant. He has the strength of a lion but within his huge chest softly beats the heart of a doting lambkin. Here we are privileged to witness him depicted performing his daring, legendary rescue of a group of innocent children from the raging waters of the Jamestown flood. That's right, dears, come a little closer. That's right. My, what a sweet little girl. You must be very proud, Mother."

They swayed closer and Marvello noticed that the girl's sharp, tiny teeth were constantly snapping, chewing on the air she walked through. He gave her an especially intimate grin.

"I'll wager Hugo has a lollipop or some other sweet edible possibly more to your taste, little missy," he confided. "Something chewy, something wet, something juicy, something nice! The gentle giant has never been able to resist the tender implorements of hungry little children, dear."

The child's eyes lost some of their glaze as she neared, tugging at her mother now. Marvello could hear her teeth clacking dryly. He reflected that it was a remarkably nasty little sound and gently prodded the tent flap up invitingly as he touched a hidden button which caused a deep, kindly voice to boom out from inside the tent amid the excited chirpings of happy children.

"It sounds like everyone's having a fine old time," Marvello observed, leaning over his rostrum and smiling gently down. "A fine old time. Why don't you go join them, darlings?"

He paused, furtively turned a dial, and then appeared to listen in happy surprise as the children's voices coming from inside the tent were suddenly amplified in a burst of avid glee, and enthusiastic crunchings and slobberings and gulpings became increasingly audible.

"Hearken," hissed Marvello excitedly, holding his hand cupped dramatically behind an ear. "Hearken at that, will you? It's my guess dear old Hugo has just now given his little chums inside some particularly tasty morsels—he has a whole tub full of them, you know—something ripe and gooey, something positively *dripping*, just the way I know you sweet things like 'em, eh? *Eh?*"

He leaned lower over his rostrum and leered openly at the two of them.

"Take a friendly tip from me, from your dear old Uncle Professor Marvello," he whispered, *"and hurry on in before it's all et up!"*

The girl's feverish pulling increased into a desperate frenzy of haulings and jerkings and the two of them were halfway into the tent when the mother balked stubbornly, her filmy eyes bulging up at Professor Marvello with slowly increasing interest, staring up at the smooth pink skin of his neat little double chin in particular.

"No, Mother, no," said the professor with a dry, friendly chuckle, firmly pointing at the entrance with his bamboo cane. "No, *non, nyet, nien* . . . the food's in there, sweetness. Inside the tent with dear old Hugo."

The mother's cracked lips writhed back, the lower one splitting slightly with the effort, and this brought her teeth entirely into view for the first time. They had been longer than the ordinary run of teeth in life to the point of deformity, but now, because of the shrinkage of her gums, they were of an appalling size and curvature. When she fully opened her mouth wide in Marvello's direction it looked like a man trap fitted out with yellowed boar's tusks. Quietly, without fuss, he placed the tip of his cane on the side of her shoulder, on the meatiest part so it would get a good purchase, then he shoved it with an efficient and expert brutality, timing his nudge with the haulings of her still tugging daughter, and sent the two of them tumbling clumsily into the tent's opening.

"Get inside there, inside with you, you grinning, rotting cunt," Marvello drawled softly, nudging the flap so that it rolled down smartly and pushing another button which caused the sounds of Hugo and the happy children to cease forthwith.

There was a faint sparking noise from within the tent and a wisp of acrid burning wafted outward. Marvello frowned slightly at this and consulted a series of dials set into the rear of the rostrum just to make sure all the readings were correct. It would never do to have a mechanical failure during a performance. It would never do at all.

He paused to give his face another wipe with his polka-dot hanky and to reponder the advisability of a sip from the flask. It was dry work; neither man nor beast could deny that it was dry work. He had allowed himself to pull the flask a third of the way out of his pocket when he froze at the sound of a persistent and complicated growling coming from the darkness to his left. He let the flask slip back into its hiding place and peered carefully in the direction of the growling, his hand screening his eyes from the spotlights overhead.

At first he saw nothing, but then he became aware of activity in the darkness outside the midway, an ominous black milling high lit with small metallic gleams. It stirred closer, then suddenly boiled out into the lighted area to reveal itself as a group of fifteen to twenty very large ones moving together as a unit.

They were a shaggy, snarling army of the night. Huge, all of them, built like bears and almost as hairy, and they all favored black leather outfits with bones and flames painted on them and lots of stainless steel rivets pounded in along the hems. Some wore visored caps, others Nazi helmets; the rest went bareheaded to show off bizarre shavings and haircuts, and a few had lost their scalps entirely. One of these last had a crude swastika hacked crudely into the top of his skull.

They were a group of bikers who had somehow, almost touchingly, managed to stay together after death. The gaudily terrifying tattoos on their skin might have faded or dimmed with mildew if they had not sloughed off altogether, and some of their bulging muscles and beer bellies might be lying exposed and rotting in swaying hammocks of flesh gone to leather, but their sense of being a group had survived into their new condition beyond a doubt. They all still glared balefully out at the world from a common center.

"Come this way, my dear gentlemen, do, for your pleasure's sake, come this way," Marvello intoned into the mike, upping the bass dial slightly to give his voice a little more authority. "I perceive without difficulty that you have wandered long and far—both in life and in your present status from the looks of you—and it is my considered professional opinion that you are all tired, very tired, very, *very* tired, yes, every one of you without exception, yes, and that you could all do with a little relaxation. Relaxation."

First they gaped vaguely around at the show in general, staring at the bright lights and flapping pictures and glittering words, but one by one their eyes began shifting in the same direction during Marvello's spiel until they had all zeroed in on the professor himself, the only living human in sight. Their stomachs began to rumble audibly and then they started to whine and bark, first one by one and then in a pack, like wandering wolves instinctively organizing at the sight of a lost and lonely child.

"Relaxation," Marvello murmured the word thoughtfully once more, seeming to be blissfully unaware any harm might befall him from his visitors. "And you have come to the right place for it, gentlemen, you couldn't have come to a better, because we have here on the premises of Marvello's Miraculous Midway one of the all-time expert practitioners of producing that enviable condition."

He turned and pointed with his bamboo cane at a large canvas rectangle bearing the painting of a thin, brown man wearing a turban and a loincloth, staring intensely with his large, dark eyes, and holding his hands poised weirdly out before him with all his fingertips pointed directly at the viewer.

"Allow me to direct your attention to this depiction of one of my most valued and trusted associates, the Swami Pootcha Ahsleep," intoned Marvello, beaming down at his guests in a friendly fashion, a man anxious to share a boon. "Pootcha Ahsleep."

The bikers steadily continued their sinister, shuffling approach and Marvello noticed that their odors preceded them and was interested to smell that the peculiar stench of tanned leather gone moldy had at last managed to completely dominate their other mingled stenches of decay.

"The Swami and myself," he continued, "both studied the occult arts at the very same Tibetan monastery during our childhood, but I am not ashamed to freely admit that Ahsleep, my old-time pal and fellow scholar, far exceeded me in a number of the difficult arts there imparted, particularly outshining me in the little understood and seldom mastered skills of *hypnotism!*"

As he uttered this last word with great emphasis, his hand moved smoothly under his rostrum and the Swami's eyes painted on the poster suddenly began to lighten and darken in a slow, even pulsing as the sound of a snake charmer's horn began to wail eerily from the tent's interior. For the first time the bikers paused in their meaningful progress toward the professor and shifted their large, jackbooted feet with the beginnings of indecision as they stared up with steadily increasing interest at the poster's throbbing eyes.

"I see you have noticed the irresistible fascination which the Swami's eyes inevitably hold for any intelligent observer," pointed out Marvello, lowering the bass even further and emphasizing the singsong quality which he had allowed to creep into his voice, allowing it to move in and out of the melody of the Hindu flute. "It is very hard to take one's eyes from their deep, hypnotic gaze, very hard. I'm willing to hazard you gentlemen even now are finding it increasingly difficult to look away even as I speak to you, that you are starting to discover that it is, in fact, impossible. Impossible. That you cannot look away. You cannot look away."

One particularly huge biker at the rear had rather worried Marvello from the start since for most of his hulking approach his head had been held at an odd, low angle and the professor had been unable to determine if the man actually had any eyes left with which to see the Swami's flashing gaze. But now, at the professor's last words, the biker's head had lifted with a painful-looking, sudden twist of his inflated purple neck, and Marvello was greatly relieved to observe it seemed he did have one eye left, after all. Not much of it, true, but enough for the purpose.

Gently, making as little fuss about it as possible, Marvello teased the tent flap open. The snake charmer music subtly increased in volume, grew more complicated, and the professor timed his commands to match its cadence.

"Walk into the tent, gentlemen," he intoned softly, intimately, close to the microphone. "Walk into the tent for peace at last, lovely, soothing peace. It's waiting in the tent, my wandering friends, my little lost sheep. All you need to do is stumble in any which way you can and take it for your own. Walk into the tent for peace. For peace."

With their various shuffles, staggers, and lurches in almost perfect rhythm, they began moving toward the opening with their gaze fixed dutifully on the throbbing eyes of Pootcha Ahsleep. They had almost got there when the large biker Marvello had noticed in particular, the cyclops with the faulty eye, hesitated and then halted entirely. He twisted his head this way and that in a mounting panic, and then he began to howl monotonously, to push and flail at his companions desperately in a sort of clumsy fit.

"Damn," murmured Marvello under his breath, for he saw that the fellow's piss-yellow, distended staring eye had chosen this unfortunate moment to explode altogether and that its slimy juices were even now slithering smoothly down from his now empty socket along the rough stubble of his cheek.

Now that he was totally blind he could no longer see Pootcha Ahsleep's hypnotic gaze, and since his retention span was almost nonexistent if not entirely so, he had forgotten that gaze completely and was no longer under the Swami's spell. As his pointless, panicky struggles and flailings increased, he began to seriously impede the steady, tentward drift of his companions.

"*All* of you must go into the tent, dear fellows," Marvello commanded, rising to the challenge. "*Every one* of you, with no exceptions, that's what the Swami wants. Recall that you are an organization of sorts, and press together proudly as you did when you thundered down the highway on your mighty machines, your fine black hogs. Keep the herd entire, keep the pack complete. That's the way, boys, that's the way."

The others had now crowded firmly around their blind companion, heaving a surrounding wall of hairy flesh up against him until they had actually lifted him so that the black toes of his boots scuffed the ground uselessly and he was as helpless as a small child hauled through a mall by its mother.

"Good lads," drawled Marvello, watching the bikers shuffle into the tent, carrying the struggling rebel along in the center of the group with the pressure of their rotting shoulders and bellies. "Good lads."

He lifted his cane, holding it at the ready, and when the last of the bikers had finally stumbled into the tent, he darted its tip at the flap with the speed and accuracy of a striking cobra, closing the opening instantly.

"That had a distinct and genuine potential of becoming downright unpleasant," he mused into the darkness, turning off the Hindu music abruptly.

Without bothering to enter into any further debate with himself, he plucked the flask from his hip pocket, unscrewed its cap with dispatch, and gratefully swallowed a good full inch of its contents. Perhaps he should altogether abandon this little hobby he'd developed of buck-and-winging the first stages of the scooping. Those damn bikers could have done him in. He replaced the cap on the flask and slid the flask back into his pocket, then took up the microphone.

"I believe," he said, smiling benignly around at the empty midway, "I believe the time has come for the Grand Finale."

What had happened up to now was, as Marvello would have freely admitted, a mere frivolity, a bit of harmless self-indulgence, a catering to his sense of whimsy. Now the evening was wearing on and he had his quota to meet and it was time for sterner stuff, it was time to really crank the midway up full blast, it was time to let her rip.

He bent to his rostrum with a faint sigh of resignation and began a major readjustment of the control board built into its rear and as he pushed its buttons and turned its knobs and slid its levers along their slots, a vast alteration began taking place along the abbreviated midway.

First the lights dimmed almost to darkness so that the towering silhouettes of the signs and tent peaks seemed a sort of Stonehenge; then, after a significant pause, the lights began to glow again, but changed from their former bright, bodacious white to sinister variations on the color red, ranging from burning crimsons to ominous scarlets, which were all of them so splashed and spattered with bright gouts of orange and rust that the whole place seemed to be suddenly soaked in gore.

Following that, the crudely painted, innocent carny posters of freaks and fire eaters and rounded women in spangled tights rolled out of sight while their places were smoothly taken by huge blank screens which rolled smoothly into view in order to receive the projections of three-dimensional, violently colored moving pictures showing freshly ripped-out bowels quivering in random loops, still-beating hearts exposed in chests newly torn open, and many such other anatomical wonders.

At the same time, the entire area was suddenly infused with the overpowering odor of fresh-spilled blood and the air was rent with a ghastly din of screams and shrieks mixed with the sounds of flesh being hacked and sawed amid the gurglings and splashes of spouting arteries and spilling guts.

"Very well, very well," murmured Professor Marvello softly, giving the ghastly effect his labors had created a steady, professional appraisal, carefully and critically observing all its grisly nuances.

"Not bad, not bad at all," he finally opined. "Perhaps a few more sobbing women, a little upping of the stench of newly opened innards."

He bent to turn a dial, then brightened and smiled as awful feminine gaspings and groanings joined the cacophony sounding about him and a new, tangy reek invaded his nostrils.

"Just the needed touch," he said to himself, adjusting his boater and bow tie contentedly.

He took up his microphone and spoke into it loudly and clearly so that his voice rang out resoundingly through the sea of darkness all around.

"Ladies and gentlemen, boys and girls. This is it, this is it. What you've been shambling around trying to find out there in those used-up fields and little bitty no-account towns, what you've been yearning for, hungering for, and likely starting to doubt to believe could possibly exist."

He pulled a lever and a thick, vomitous, charnel stench blew enthusiastically out of the four outlets of a tall pipe overhead, gouting forth its ripe, rich odors into each cardinal direction simultaneously.

"It's here, it's here, in Marvello's Miraculous Midway, my good friends, right here on this very sport where you hear the sound of my voice inviting you one and all. Inviting you all. Forget those friends and loved ones you've sucked dry so long ago, dear hearts, leave off trying to content yourselves with the wandering, shriveled cows and dogs and cats you run across less and less these days, and come on in, come on in!"

Marvello heard a faint, choking meep and turned to see a tiny shape crawling into the gory light of the midway. It was the corpse of a baby dressed in a long lacy dress which trailed along behind it as it hauled itself determinedly through the Kansas dust with what was left of its tiny, rotting fingers.

"Not much, but you're a start," said Marvello, observing the little creature with interest as it struggled toward the entrance. "If I'd have known the likes of you was out there I'd have lured you in during the preamble with Wally Mysto and his Edible Animal Puppets. Land's sake, I do declare this little nipper must have drowned in its baptismal font. Yes, I'd have sworn the likes of you would have shown up for one of the earlier shows, sweetness, yes I would, but there's no accounting for taste."

He made no move to close the flap as the baby cleared the entrance and entered the tent. He'd only done it with his earlier visitors because he liked the effect, the truth be told. A vague electrical sputtering, a curl of smoke, and perhaps the faintest hint of a tiny, cut-off wail were ignored completely by

Marvello because a surrounding murmur of activity had taken his full attention. He straightened and stared into the surrounding darkness.

There were so many of them, but then there were always so many of them. The first few rows now emerging into the ruddy light were distinct; you could read their separate forms, see their individual bodies, observe that one was little more than bones and shreds of leather, another was so ballooned with gas it could not bend its limbs but only totter, and that a third had the steel sutures the surgeons had clipped onto its arteries still dangling from its opened chest, but once you got past the first few rows of them, they all started to merge into one heaving thing moving at you. Steadily. Hungrily. Endlessly.

"Come one, come all," said Marvello softly, staring out at them. "Come one, come all."

He took a pull at the flask, replaced it, and leaned into the microphone, standing firmly on the balls of his little feet.

"Juicy, juicy, juicy," he crooned, watching the front curve of them filling in the midway. "Lots of blood, lots of blood, lots of blood. Lots of fresh, chewy flesh too, friends, *lots* of it. Sweet, sweet flesh like you haven't had between your teeth since god alone knows how long. Yummy, yummy, yummy."

He reached down to push a button and a soft red coiling of light began making its way round and round the opening of the tent, pulsing like a newly opened, still bleeding wound. They saw it, of course, they always saw it, and they headed for it just like flies heading for shit, as they were meant to.

He'd often noticed those among them that reminded him of people he'd known and he'd wonder *was* that old Charlie Carter he just saw stumble in there? *Was* that whatsisname who used to sell papers at that newsstand on the corner of

Dearborn and Washington? Was that *Clara*? She had a great laugh, did Clara. He could remember just how it felt when he held her shoulders. He'd sure as hell hoped that thing hadn't been Clara.

They started cramming themselves into the entrance. Somehow or other they always managed it. There were snarls and struggles and so on, but in the end they always somehow managed it.

"That's right, dear hearts," he said, smiling down at them, but he knew there weren't any of them listening to him now, not after he'd turned on the doorway lights. "Have a fine old time, enjoy yourselves to the fullest."

At this stage of the game he could sing old sweet songs if it struck his fancy, and he sometimes did, just for the hell of it, or because he was feeling mellow. From here on in, the midway did all the work. From here on in, it was purely automatic. But the old habits die hard.

"Let that one-legged gentleman through, folks," he said after he'd observed a hopping fragment get pushed aside by the eager multitude for the fourth or fifth time. "There may not be all that much left of him, but I absolutely guarantee that what there is is just as hungry as the most complete among you. I absolutely guarantee it."

He smiled quietly and took another pull from his flask. What the hell, he thought, what the hell, the night's work was drawing softly and successfully to its close, so what the hell.

The damnedest thing was that once he actually *had* seen someone he knew go into the tent, really and truly had, no doubt about it, but the whole thing had given him a real hoot, a genuine kick in the ass, praise be, because it'd been a man he'd truly hated, Mr. Homer Garner, one-time proprietor of the Garner Hardware Company of Joplin, a real revolting son of a bitch who'd done him dirty back when he was just a kid and really needed the money and didn't know any better way to get hold of it. It had given Marvello undiluted joy to observe the even uglier than usual, pus-leaking remnants of Mr. Homer Garner shamble helplessly into the tent.

He was glad, you might even say genuinely grateful, that he'd never seen anybody he liked go in there since he was certain he would not have enjoyed that in the least. Of course the danger of such a thing happening had diminished considerably through the years. He didn't suppose there were all that many left in either category, those he'd hated or those he'd liked, when you came right down to it. He supposed most of them were dead by now, *really* dead, not just shuffling around dead. Dead and buried dead, the good old-fashioned way.

Marvello leaned over the rostrum, propping himself on spread fingertips, and sized up the midway. The crowd was down to the final stragglers now, the really timid ones, wandering in at last from wherever they'd been shyly hiding their bones. It wouldn't be long at all, now. The show was almost over.

He glanced down at the glowing readout, watching how the number was growing at a slower and slower pace now the big rush was over. They kind of relaxed when there weren't so many of them around. They almost sort of strolled in when you got down to the last little trickle.

The readout showed a good score, of course. It was always a good score.

"You don't want to miss it," he called out softly to the final, staggering arrivals; then he took another pull, washing the booze around his teeth before he swallowed it. "Nossir, you don't want to miss it."

One left, now, just one. Standing out there in a cockeyed stance, swaying, looking around with its dim eyes, pawing the air with its shriveled little hands. A tough one to turn, this baby. A real hard sell.

"All your friends and loved ones are in there, my handsome fellow," he said, smiling out at the solitary figure.

On an impulse, he turned off the lights moving around the doorway, the lights that pulled them in no matter what. He felt like bringing this one in himself.

"Why be lonely?" he called out, cooing, first waving his cane in the air to get the thing's attention, and then, when he'd caught its eye, pointing the cane at the entrance and giving its tip a tiny, emphasizing twirl. "Come, come, your solitude serves no purpose, and it's self-inflicted to boot. Cut it short, old chum, cut it short. All those near and dear are but a few short steps away, a mere totter or two. They are all eagerly awaiting your august presence inside. They're all inside."

It looked up at Marvello, aware of him for the first time. Rags of skin swung from its forearms, blowing slightly in the night breeze. It took a step or two forward. It lifted its head and sucked the odors coming from the tent through its nose hole.

"Smells even better *in* the tent, friend," he said. "Say, don't be a spoilsport, don't be a party pooper. You only lived once."

It wavered idiotically for another half minute and then, its jaws starting to work, starting to wetten, it began to shuffle steadily ahead. Marvello nodded down at it, finishing off his flask as it passed by him and stepped into the darkness of the entrance. There was a final electrical crackling, a last wisp of smoke.

Marvello carefully slipped the flask back into its pocket, threw a series of switches, then hopped gracefully off the platform just a moment before it began to pull itself smoothly back into a slot which had opened at the bottom of the tent.

The showman stood on the hot, dry, dusty ground, his hands in his pockets, and watched, interested as always, while the entire midway slowly started to fold in on itself. Marvello never failed to enjoy this moment. Sometimes he felt it was, in a way, the best part of the whole show.

First the poles shortened, smoothly telescoping, then the wires and ropes rolled back in perfect synchronization onto hidden spools as the fabric of the main and smaller tents sucked inward, begining with large tucks, then working down to smaller and smaller ones, all of them tidy, all of them precise, and soon the whole thing had reduced itself to a neat rectangular block which confined and sculpted itself still further until, when it had neatly resolved itself unmistakably into the shape of a huge truck, highly polished panels rose from all around its base to form the truck's sides and top and wheel guards, and shiny bits of chrome and glass rotated into view to make up its grille and headlights and trim.

There on the side of the truck, in proud, tall letters of glistening gold, a bold sign read:

* MARVELLO'S * MIRACULOUS * MEATPIES *

Marvello regarded the truck with satisfaction for a long moment before he walked to its side, opened its door, and made himself comfortable in the driver's seat. He turned the waiting ignition key and when the engine instantly began a strong, steady purring, he reached forward to the glove compartment, extracted the full bottle of whiskey waiting there, pulled its cork, and took two long, slow, deeply satisfactory swallows.

He rolled down the window, looked out in a friendly fashion at the empty space which had been the midway just a little while before, and gave it a companionable wave. He drove smoothly across the soft bumpiness of the field until he reached the straight, flat Kansas highway, and there he turned northward, following the beams of his headlights onto his next gig.

Best Friends

God, love you to death, darling! Always forget *completely* how much, how deeply.

What an absolutely adorable hat.

Isn't this *hideous* rain totally ghastly? Poor Muffin has positively given up because of it, you know. Just sits there brooding by the window, glaring out at all those silly drops thumping down on the terrace and *won't* listen to a single word I say about cheering up.

Here we are.

Stop here, driver. *Here!* By that little green awning with the fat doorman, damn it! Only now it's way back there. You may keep the change, not that you deserve it.

Christ, it's absolutely beyond belief the sort of people one finds driving cabs these days! Did you see that shitty, third world glare he had the nerve to give me? He's probably got the makings of some idiotic bomb stuffed into his trunk with the explosives cooked up out of cow crap or whatever it is the papers say they use. I suppose we should all be grateful the bastards can't afford proper dynamite.

Let's for God's sake get inside before we're both soaked.

Oh, dear, now I get a look at it I really do wish I hadn't suggested this restaurant. I'm afraid it's caught on altogether far too well. Will you just look at all these ghastly *people*, for God's sake. Do you know *any* of them?

My *God*, honestly, do you *see* the hair on that woman?

It slipped my mind one's actually starting to read about this place in the *papers*. Who was with whom and where they sat and what they ate and was it well prepared and did they look adoringly at one another and did they fuck at the end of the day?

Well, high time, here somebody comes to look after us at last.

Yes, Andre, so good to see you. Yes, it has been too long. Yes, that table will do quite nicely; you've remembered it's one of my favorites. I'll sit on the banquette and Miss Tournier will sit on the chair. Thank you, Andre.

As if he'd dare give me anything but a satisfactory table, darling. Just let him try and he'd see the fur fly and doesn't he know it!

God, it's been *years*, hasn't it? Positively *ages*, for heaven's sake! Now you *must* tell me all that's happened and leave absolutely nothing out. For instance: You *did* leave him, didn't you? Charles, I mean?

Good! I knew you'd come to your senses, given enough time. Just *knew* it. You're a sensible girl, Melanie, darling. Always have been. I don't care what they say.

Yes, Jacques. Good afternoon. Yes, I'll have my usual but I don't know what Mademoiselle Tournier will have. What would you care for, darling? Kir Royal. There you are, Jacques. No, I think we'll have the menu a little bit later, thank you just the same.

I simply can't believe it. Did you see that, darling? Did you see how he positively *pushed* that damned menu at us? Honestly, it's gotten so this is almost a fucking Greek restaurant. I feel as if I'm sitting at some greasy *counter* with *workmen* and things like that all over the place, for God's sake. The staff will be walking around in their shirtsleeves wearing aprons the next thing you know. Really!

Anyhow, enough of that. It's not worth our time, let's go on to something that *matters.*

What happened with Charles, darling? Did you get rid of him on your own, or was it Cissy's doing?

Oh, good for you! Did it all by yourself, did you? Cissy must have been that proud. He wasn't worthy of you, darling, but of course you know that. How absolutely marvelous of you to kick him out on his ass, the bastard, the shit.

I only wish I could say the same about the way I handled things between Howard and myself. I suppose you've heard something of it, most everyone seems to. Unfortunately.

Of course, the whole business has been profoundly embarrassing. I'm usually pretty good about finishing off entanglements, as you know, but not this time. I'm afraid poor Howard really had my number.

God, did you hear that?

Did you hear me *say* that?

Poor Howard, indeed! He still *has* my number, or would

have if he were still alive. I might as well face it, it'll be months before I manage to work that son of a bitch completely out of my system. Positively months. I just know it.

It was those sad eyes of his that always did me in, darling. I couldn't help it, no matter what unforgivably stinking, crappy thing he did, those goddamn sad eyes of his always managed to get right through to me. *Always,* damn it! Honestly, he was *such* a waif.

Anyway, when Muffin saw I was floundering she came to my rescue and made a quick end to it. She was marvelous, of course, simply marvelous.

Honestly, you really should have seen the look on Howard's face, I tell you it was a perfect scream! I don't think I've ever *seen* anyone so completely and absolutely astonished.

No sad looks from him *then,* darling—no time for that act with Muffin coming at him from every direction like a little white blur—only bulging eyes and a gaping mouth and his hands flailing every which way trying to bat her off!

The astounding, the absolutely remarkable thing is that she never actually touched the bastard! Didn't leave so much as one tiny scratch to get people thinking.

And it was such fun, you see, because I knew just what she was up to. It was like watching a movie on the late show that I'd seen before in a theater.

She maneuvered him so neatly, darling! She positively *herded* him just as if she were a dear little sheepdog. All the way from the bar across the carpet to the terrace and over the railing and down he went to land, kerplunk, on a taxi parked in front of our building.

I just hope its driver was like that clod that bungled us over here, I really do. The impact mashed the cab's top in completely and set that quaint sign on its roof to blinking over and over and over like a yellow Christmas tree ornament. And there was Howard gaping up at me from the middle of the ruin.

Of course now his sad look was playing on *my* side, darling. That was sweet, I can tell you. They asked around and learned how gloomy poor Howard had always been, how blue, and of course they saw how sympathetic and understanding I'd been to him, and death by suicide it was!

If only all life's problems could be solved so simply.

So it's over, and so is he. Over with a vengeance. Over in spades. Thank *God* for Muffin is all I can say.

We are so lucky, aren't we?

Oh, shit, here comes Jacques with his bloody menu again. Are you sure you're up to it, dear? Very well, then. Actually I don't even need the damned thing because I know exactly what I want.

I'll have the grilled turbot, Jacques, with that nice mustard sauce. You know the one I mean.

Well, if it doesn't happen to be on your precious menu to-day I'm sure you can have the chef make it up, can't you? Would you like that, darling? Good. You'll enjoy it. And a nice bottle of Meursault, Jacques. And would you like a nice little salad, darling? And a nice little salad, Jacques. Yes, for both of us. Of course for both of us. Something light, naturally. Thank you, Jacques.

Muffin still hasn't quite *entirely* forgiven me for my lapse. Her brooding isn't altogether because of the rain, I'm afraid, but I don't blame her. After all, it hasn't been a full three weeks since it happened and, besides, she *is* starting to soften. She even gave me really rather a sweet look this morning just before I left the apartment to meet you. We'll patch things up. Muffin and I always patch things up.

Of course, there are some that can't.

You've heard about Maddy and Clara.

You really haven't? My God, where have you *been,* darling? I thought absolutely *everyone* knew about it. Oh, of course, you were in the south of France. And it's obvious you haven't read this morning's *Post.*

Well, I hadn't expected I'd have to do it, but I'd better bring you up to speed before I can tell you about what happened last night. Then I'll tell you about what I'd like us to do.

Actually it's really something we absolutely *must* do, as I'm sure you'll agree once you've heard the story.

We really must do it.

It seems poor Maddy went head over heels for this man she met vacationing in Rio last winter. She fell absolutely and *hopelessly* in love with him, poor dear, and couldn't get over it no matter how hard she tried. Just went totally silly over him, gaga as a schoolgirl.

God, you should have seen her with him; it was horrible, absolutely ghastly, to see a grown-up female like Maddy gaping at this perfectly ordinary man with an unbelievably adoring simper spread over her face. I mean it positively made you want to puke, to throw up right then and there, all ov~ two of them.

Clara put up with it for quite some time agreed completely that she really was extrem~ very, *very* understanding, but the damned ~ ing on and on and getting worse and wor~ falling deeper and deeper in love, and creasingly obvious that Clara was running

a bit
thoughtle~
ful business
course, that's rea~
I shouldn't have be~
Have some more wine.
Better?
Well, I tried again to talk se~
though it seemed perfectly hopele~

completely and set that quaint sign on its roof to blinking over and over and over like a yellow Christmas tree ornament. And there was Howard gaping up at me from the middle of the ruin.

Of course now his sad look was playing on *my* side, darling. That was sweet, I can tell you. They asked around and learned how gloomy poor Howard had always been, how blue, and of course they saw how sympathetic and understanding I'd been to him, and death by suicide it was!

If only all life's problems could be solved so simply.

So it's over, and so is he. Over with a vengeance. Over in spades. Thank *God* for Muffin is all I can say.

We are so lucky, aren't we?

Oh, shit, here comes Jacques with his bloody menu again. Are you sure you're up to it, dear? Very well, then. Actually I don't even need the damned thing because I know exactly what I want.

I'll have the grilled turbot, Jacques, with that nice mustard sauce. You know the one I mean.

Well, if it doesn't happen to be on your precious menu to-day I'm sure you can have the chef make it up, can't you? Would you like that, darling? Good. You'll enjoy it. And a nice bottle of Meursault, Jacques. And would you like a nice little salad, darling? And a nice little salad, Jacques. Yes, for both of us. Of course for both of us. Something light, naturally. Thank you, Jacques.

Muffin still hasn't quite *entirely* forgiven me for my lapse. Her brooding isn't altogether because of the rain, I'm afraid, but I don't blame her. After all, it hasn't been a full three weeks since it happened and, besides, she *is* starting to soften. She even gave me really rather a sweet look this morning just before I left the apartment to meet you. We'll patch things up. Muffin and I always patch things up.

Of course, there are some that can't.

You've heard about Maddy and Clara.

You really haven't? My God, where have you **been,** darling? I thought absolutely *everyone* knew about it. Oh, of course, you were in the south of France. And it's obvious you haven't read this morning's *Post.*

Well, I hadn't expected I'd have to do it, but I'd better bring you up to speed before I can tell you about what happened last night. Then I'll tell you about what I'd like us to do.

Actually it's really something we absolutely *must* do, as I'm sure you'll agree once you've heard the story.

We really must do it.

It seems poor Maddy went head over heels for this man she met vacationing in Rio last winter. She fell absolutely and *hopelessly* in love with him, poor dear, and couldn't get over it no matter how hard she tried. Just went totally silly over him, gaga as a schoolgirl.

God, you should have seen her with him; it was horrible, absolutely ghastly, to see a grown-up female like Maddy gaping at this perfectly ordinary man with an unbelievably adoring simper spread over her face. I mean it positively made you want to puke, to throw up right then and there, all over the two of them.

Clara put up with it for quite some time. Everybody's agreed completely that she really was extremely tolerant and very, *very* understanding, but the damned thing just kept going on and on and getting worse and worse and Maddy kept falling deeper and deeper in love, and it was becoming increasingly obvious that Clara was running out of patience, and naturally we were all becoming quite worried about what she might do.

We all know you can only push them just so far.

Maddy called me up and asked if we couldn't have tea at the Pierre, you know, in that funny room with the trompe l'œil walls and ceiling? Because she wanted to talk about what was happening and of course I jumped at the chance because, like everybody else, I was dying to know all the gory details.

God, she was so *pale,* poor dear, so *frightened.* I hate to see a pretty woman so distraught, don't you? I mean she was actually chewing her lips and plucking at her fingers, for God's sake! And her eyes never stopped darting, looking up along the balcony and the staircase, shooting quick, searching looks at the floor and the doorways.

She was wearing a long-sleeved dress and it wasn't *like* Maddy to wear a long-sleeved dress. Not with her beautiful arms, certainly not during a heat wave. She must have noticed I'd noticed, because after she'd done all this peering around the room she rested one arm on the table and then pulled its long sleeve back and showed me a crisscrossing of white bandages and nasty red scratch marks stretching out from under them.

She glared down at her arm with this perfectly *fierce* frown on her face—something right out of *Medea,* I can assure you—and said in a perfect hiss: "*Clara* did this to me! There will *always* be scars!"

Then she positively jerked her sleeve back down over those bandages and things and went on and on about how unfair Clara had been and how she wasn't going to take it anymore and about how she was a grown-up woman and could do what she pleased if she wanted to and all the rest of that tiresome garbage.

I did what usually works in situations like this: I let her go on until she'd run down a little and then I tried talking sensibly to her. I told her how much she owed Clara, how much we *all* owed our darlings, and I was even unkind enough to ask her flat out in plain English how she thought she would manage if she *did* leave Clara for the man she'd met in Rio.

"I mean, is he rich, darling?" I asked her. "Is he *that* rich?"

She turned and pouted at me.

"No," she said. "He thinks *I'm* rich."

"Of course he does, darling," I told her. "*All* the men do. That's how come we get our choice of them, don't you see?"

But she didn't see, and all my advice did was to set her off again on a new tirade, which ended with her leaning close to me and whispering the most appalling thing! The most perfectly awful thing!

But here are our salads. Thank you, Jacques. Yes, the wine is excellent, Jacques.

Wait a second, darling, until he's out of earshot.

The silly bitch told me she planned to kill Clara!

Oh, I'm sorry, dear, I can see now I should have led up to it a bit more. Padded the approach. Please do excuse my thoughtlessness, but it's just that this has been the most *awful* business for me and it's got me thoroughly upset. Of course, that's really no excuse.

I shouldn't have been so abrupt.

Have some more wine.

Better?

Well, I tried again to talk sense to her, even after that, though it seemed perfectly hopeless. She had that crazy, glazed look people get when they're absolutely determined to do the stupidest, silliest thing possible, so in the end all I asked of her was not to do anything drastic for at least a little while and—after what seemed hours—I wore her down and she agreed she'd think things over once or twice again and call me in a few days and then we'd have another little talk about it all.

So I felt rather smug when we parted.

This wine isn't really all that good after the first few sips, is it? I do believe Jacques is losing his touch. I think I really might permanently cross this place off my list, don't you think?

Anyway, it was over a full week when a call came, but it wasn't the one I was hoping for, to say the least.

I was profoundly asleep as it's just possible I'd had a touch too much to drink, and the ringing of that pretty bedside phone Andre gave me—you do remember Andre, don't you? He was a count and I've never had anything to do with counts since—hauled me out of the depths of some god-awful dream so that I was really only half awake when I'd managed to put the receiver to my ear so at first I couldn't make any sense of what I was hearing and I suppose I kept saying "What is it?" in this slurry, muzzy voice a half-dozen times until it dawned on me at last that it wasn't a human voice at all on the other end of the line!

It was a mewing, darling, the saddest, sweetest little mewing you ever heard. Going on and on in the most pathetic way possible. It wasn't a few more seconds before I recognized it, and then the most ghastly chill ran through me from my toes to the crown of my head because, of course, it was Clara. Maddy's little Clara.

But after that I thought: My God, she's calling me for help!

and I knew I'd *never* been so touched. It was—I'm afraid I'm getting quite teary-eyed just talking about it—positively the most wonderful thing that ever happened to me in all my life.

The trust.

The idea that she thought of me first.

Excuse me but I've positively *got* to dab my eyes.

That's better.

"Don't worry, sweetness!" I said into the phone, gently as I could. "Don't worry, little dearest! I'll be right over!"

I was as good as my word, darling. I got up and dressed though it was the middle of the night and taxied right over to Maddy and Clara's building where I proceeded to bully the doorman and then the building manager in turn when the doorman woke him up—great sleepy hulks, both of them—and we finally all took the elevator to Maddy and Clara's apartment, after ringing it God knows how many times, and opened the door.

Well, you simply wouldn't believe the smell, dear. Totally extraordinary. The whole place reeked, simply reeked. It moved out at you like a wall.

The doorman took one choking gulp of it, then turned and puked his guts out on the floor of the hall. The manager just kept saying "Jesus, Jesus, Jesus," over and over again until I ached to slap his silly fat face until he shut up.

But then I heard that little mew and Clara stepped timidly into the light coming from the hallway and trotted right over to my feet looking up at me in the most pathetic way, and I leaned down and picked her up and kissed her poor, sad little face right on its nose in spite of the terrible, *terrible* stench of her which she hadn't been able to lick away in spite, I'm sure, of the most heroic attempts to do so.

I barged right into the living room while the babbling manager staggered along behind me as there wasn't any doubt where the smell was coming from and there was Maddy sprawled out on the carpet like a swastika right in the middle of an impossibly huge splash of dried blood that they'll never, *ever* manage to scrub away.

What was left of Maddy was lying there, that is, because it was obvious that poor Clara had been forced to eat quite a bit of her over the last week or so.

I simply can't imagine why someone hasn't had the brains to come up with cat food packed in a container the poor dears could open themselves in case of an emergency, can you? Then so many of these distasteful things you hear about simply wouldn't have to happen.

Anyhow, Maddy had absolutely no face left and her lovely slip had been reduced to red ribbons all gone stiff. I suppose poor Clara had been forced to tear it apart so that she could get at the rest of her after she'd finished off all of the exposed soft parts.

Absolutely ghastly.

Of course, I knew perfectly well it wasn't just hunger that made Clara take away *all* those bits and pieces. Hunger wouldn't explain why the whole throat was completely missing, darling, even those tough, rubbery chunks that must be *hideous* to chew and swallow if you've only got tiny teeth and a little pink mouth to work with.

I'm sure it will never dawn on those stupid policemen that if there'd *been* a throat then there would have been its original wound for all to see and it might have given them a problem with their theory that Maddy had sliced her neck open with the chef's knife clutched in her hand because she'd been so sad about her friend from Rio.

It's not likely, but one of them might have even been smart enough to take a good look at that wound and wonder if a certain little pussycat had been very angry at her mistress for trying to chop her up with that same knife.

But there was no original wound to look at because Clara had eaten it all up, clever little thing.

Ah, good—here's the fish at last. Yes, of course we want it boned.

Thank you, Jacques. We'll do our very best to enjoy it, never fear.

My God, the lazy bastards will be asking us to *cook our lunches* the next thing you know!

Now, then—as to why I asked if you were free today, darling.

There's a girl I've spotted working in that small perfume counter at Bergdorf's. You know, the little discreet one they've tucked in a corner far away from that cabash they've got spread over all those other rooms?

I've chatted with her quite a bit and noticed her looking sidewise at my jewels and my furs. She loves the way I buy the most expensive stuff without a thought and I know she'd give *anything* to be able to do it herself.

Absolutely anything.

Of course you remember how *that* felt, don't you, dear? God knows *I* certainly do!

Why don't we go over there after lunch and you can look at her and we can sort of feel her out together?

She's very pretty.

She's like us.

I think she'd be absolutely perfect for Clara!

Campfire Story

There were four boys in all, gathered up close by the fire, their fronts curled toward the light and warmth of the flames, their backs crouched away from the growing nighttime cold which was seeping in from the forest all around them along with the drifting smells of leaves and earth and ancient, patient bark.

"You said you were going to tell us the scary story after we ate," said Bill, wiping marshmallow stickiness from his fingers on a rumpled paper towel and turning to look at Eddy with a challenge in his eyes. "The one that's so terrible awful to hear we might none of us live through listening to it! You still going to tell it?"

Ted snickered as he cuddled up to his knees, pulling them closer into his chest for the snugness of it, and Bill glanced angrily in his direction.

"What do you think you're laughing at?" he asked.

"Come on, Bill, don't be such a dummy," Ted said scornfully. "Don't you know Eddy was just putting you on? Don't you know there isn't any story that can kill you dead?"

"What's that?" said Arthur, his head suddenly popping up from a long, thoughtful study of how differently his shoelaces looked in the firelight. "Did you say Eddy was just kidding about that story? Hey, Eddy, were you just kidding?"

"No," said Eddy, after a pause, speaking in his soft, quiet way. "And I didn't say the story killed people. What I said was it ended them. And it does."

"Baloney," Ted snorted, but then a stick in the fire snapped and he jumped and Arthur grinned.

"You're just as scared as any of us to hear it," Arthur said with a laugh, and then he turned to Eddy. "Tell the story, Eddy, and let's see if we all die or end or whatever!"

Eddy waited, as any good storyteller should, until his listeners had settled themselves down and gathered their attention. Then he placed his elbows on his knees, rested the point of his chin on his knuckles, and stared solemnly into the flames.

"There were four boys in the woods, sitting around a fire," Eddy began, speaking in a solemn, measured way, speaking in a gentle kind of chant. "They were all alone. There was nothing around them but a lot of tall old trees, and it was so dark between those trees you couldn't see a thing. But now and then, from way out there, you could hear an owl hoot."

At that moment, as if it came at Eddy's bidding, the soft hoot of an owl floated out from the surrounding blackness.

"Wow!" said Arthur, grinning with delight from ear to ear. "Just like in the story! Wow—it's *working*!"

Eddy looked at him, a long, knowing, steady look, and then he gazed back at the fire.

"There were three boys sitting around a fire," he said, "And a cold wind blowing through the leaves made them shiver."

Then, sure enough, the trees did rustle with a chiller new stirring as Arthur and Bill both moved in closer to Eddy, and all three of them stared across the fire at some leaves scuttling across the empty space opposite them.

"Something's wrong," said Arthur in a whisper. "I don't know just what it is, but something's wrong!"

"There were two boys sitting around a fire," said Eddy.

Suddenly Arthur stood, almost springing to his feet, and stared all around with his eyes as wide open as he could get them, but he knew somehow, deep, deep down inside of himself, that he wasn't seeing whatever it was he was trying to see.

"How come none of the others came with us?" he cried out, looking down at Eddy. "Ted and Bill said they'd come, didn't they? How come we're out here in these darn woods all alone?"

Eddy looked at him thoughtfully with his big, dark eyes.

"We aren't alone, Arthur," he said. "I'm alone. Just me."

It was true. Then there was a pause and a moment of great stillness passed through all the forest as if every living thing in it down to its softest chick and smallest mouse had frozen in their tracks for fear.

"And pretty soon even I won't be," said Eddy, going on with his story. "Pretty soon there'll only be this fire, burning lower and lower because there'll be nobody around to add any wood, and it'll burn down to ash and fall in on itself and die, and in the morning Mr. Knudson will wonder who lit it and never know."

Eddy curled his toes inside his running shoes and smiled a secret smile as the owl hooted again, and when Eddy hooted softly in return the owl hooted a third time.

But Eddy never hooted back because he wasn't there, and after a moment or two of cocking his big, round head this way and that to listen the owl grew discouraged and flew away soundlessly on his thick, soft wings, and pretty soon he found a mouse and killed it and ate it.

The Power of the Mandarin

Aladar Rakas gave a wicked grin and raised his brandy glass.

"To the King Plotter of Evil. To the Prophet of our Doom. To the Mandarin."

I joined the toast willingly.

"May he never be totally defeated. May he and his vile minions ever threaten the civilized world."

We drank contentedly. Rakas leaned back, struck a luxurious pose, and wafted forth a cloud of Havana's very best.

"How many have been killed this time?"

Rakas tapped an ash from his cigar and gazed thoughtfully upward. I could see his lips moving as he made the count.

"Five," he said, and then, after a pause, "No. Six."

I looked at him with some surprise. "That's hardly up to the usual slaughter."

Rakas chuckled and signaled the waiter for more brandy.

"True enough," he said. "However, one particular murder of those six is enough to make up for hundreds, perhaps thousands, of ordinary ones."

His dark eyes glinted. He arched his thick, sable brows and leaned slowly forward.

"I have given the Mandarin a real treat this time, Charles," he said.

"You have, have you?"

I took a quick, unsatisfying puff at my cigarette and wondered what the old devil had been up to. I tossed out a guess.

"You haven't let him kill Mork?"

The brutish Mork. The only vaguely human emissary of the insidious Mandarin. He was, in his apish way, ambitious. Perhaps he had gone too far. It would be a shame to lose Mork.

Rakas waved the idea aside with an airy gesture.

"No, Charles. I have always liked Mork. Besides, he is far too useful as a harbinger of horrors to come. No, I would never dream of killing the dreadful creature."

Belatedly, a grim suspicion began to grow in me. Rakas was making quite a production out of this revelation. It would be something very much out of the ordinary.

"As a matter of fact," he continued blandly, covertly watching me from the corners of his eyes, "the only one of the Mandarin's henchmen to die in this particular adventure is a Lascar. A low underling hardly worth mentioning."

The suspicion hardened into a near certainty, but I tried a parry.

"How about the Inspector? Have you let him kill Snow?"

"Why bother? Inspector Snow. The poor blunderer. No, Charles, this murder is one of the first magnitude. This murder is the one which the Mandarin has burned to do since book one."

He looked at the expression on my face and grinned hugely.

"Of course you've guessed."

I gaped at him unbelievingly.

"You're joking, Aladar," I said.

He continued to grin.

He'd let the Mandarin kill Evan Trowbridge. I knew he'd let him kill Evan Trowbridge. I swallowed and decided to say it out loud and hear how it sounded.

"He's killed Evan Trowbridge."

It sounded like a kind of croak. Rakas gave a confirming nod and continued to grin.

I won't say that the room swam before my eyes, but I did wonder, just for a moment, if I was going to faint. I sat in my chair building up a nervous tic and thinking about Evan Trowbridge.

Who was it who stood between the malevolent Mandarin and his conquest of the world? I'll tell you who. Evan Trowbridge. Who was it who foiled, again and again, in book after book, the heartless fiend who plotted the base enslavement of us all? None other than Evan Trowbridge.

And now he was dead.

I wiped the palms of my hands carefully with my napkin and cleared my throat. I could think of nothing else to do, short of leaping over the table and crushing in the top of Aladar Rakas' skull.

He looked at me with some concern. I suppose I looked like a man trembling on the verge of a fit. I may have been.

He sighed.

"You must understand, Charles," he said. "If only you knew how often I have ached to let him do it."

"But why?"

His eyes shown dreamily.

"Evan Trowbridge," he said. "Pillar of the Establishment. Pride of the Empire."

He had turned deadly serious.

"Do you know where the strength of a Trowbridge lies, Charles? I'll tell you. It lies in his sublime conviction that he and his kind are superior to all other men. That anyone who is not both white and English is automatically not quite a human being."

He ground out his cigar forcefully, yet precisely, as if he were sticking it into a Trowbridge eye.

"It's different here in America," he said. "Do you know what it was like to be a poor Hungarian in London? Speaking with a foreign accent? Looking alien? Liking garlic and spicy foods?"

He looked down at his huge white hands and watched them curl into fists.

"I dressed like them. I even thought of changing my name. Then I realized I would only make myself more ridiculous in their eyes."

He looked at me, and then his expression softened and he chuckled.

"Wait until you read how the Mandarin kills him, Charles. It is a masterpiece, if I do say so myself. It takes an entire chapter."

I bunched up my napkin and tossed it on the table.

"So what happens to the series, Aladar? Have you thought about that? Who the hell is going to fight the Mandarin?

He brushed it away.

"Somebody will, Charles. The series will continue. We will continue. I have several possibilities in mind. I have thought, maybe, a Hungarian. Maybe someone rather like myself."

We finished our coffee and parted in widely divergent moods.

I took the manuscript to my office, informed my secretary that I was strictly incommunicado, and read *The Mandarin Triumphant* from its first neatly typed page to its last.

I discovered, thank God, that it was good. Really one of his best.

I had been afraid that the hatred for Trowbridge which Rakas had just confessed would show through, and that he might turn him into some kind of villain, or, much worse, a quivering coward, but none of this had happened. The brave Britisher fought the good fight to the end. The Mandarin, after having committed what really was a masterpiece of murder, even spoke a little tribute to his redoubtable foe just before boarding a mysterious boat and vanishing into the swirling fog of a Thames estuary:

"He was a worthy opponent," said the Mandarin in the sibilant whisper he adopted when in a thoughtful mood. "In his dogged fashion, I believe he understood me and my aspirations as no man has done."

Slipping carefully from the plastic coverall which had protected him from the deadly mold, the towering man bent respectfully to the nearly formless heap which lay at his feet, and with great solemnity, he made an ancient Oriental gesture of salutation to that which had once been Evan Trowbridge.

I closed the manuscript feeling much for the better.

After all, I figured, Rakas had managed to make the Mandarin series into a very successful enterprise with Trowbridge, and there was no reason to see why he couldn't go right ahead and carry on without him. It was the Mandarin who really counted, and if the heroic Englishman irritated the author all that much, I couldn't see why he shouldn't be allowed to go ahead and kill the bastard. There were a few bad moments with some of the other editors, but in the end, we all sat back with smug little smiles playing on our faces and waited to see how Rakas's new champion fared in the struggle against the vast criminal campaign of the diabolical Mandarin.

One very comforting development was the unexpectedly large popularity of *Triumph.* The critics who had rejected the previous books as being too much loved it. They liked the idea of the superhero getting horribly murdered. It moved the whole thing into a campy sort of area where they could relax and enjoy without being embarrassed.

We worked a series of TV and radio slots for Rakas, which was something we'd never done before, and he clicked. The public liked his sinister presence. They relished him in much the same way as they did Alfred Hitchcock. There is something very reassuring about a boogeyman who's willing to joke about his scareful personality. It eases all sorts of dim little fears and makes the dark unknown seem almost friendly. This sudden celebrity pleased Rakas.

"It is very nice," he told me. "I was walking down the street the other day and a beautiful woman came up to me. 'Are you Aladar Rakas?' she asked me. And I told her I was. A perfect stranger, and that very night we went to bed. I like this being famous."

I asked him how the new book was going.

"It's coming along nicely," he said. "My hero is a Hungarian, as I warned you he might be. I have not given him a name yet. I call him Rakas, after myself, for now. Later on I will figure out some name for him. I want it to be just right, of course.

"He is not a bullhead, like that Trowbridge. He is a man who thinks. The Mandarin will have his hands full with him, you will see. I think the only real problem will be to make sure that this new hero of mine doesn't finish him off in the first three chapters."

Then he laughed, and I laughed with him.

It was just about two weeks later, about four in the morning, when the telephone rang. I knocked over the alarm clock and upset a full ashtray before I managed to bark a hello into the receiver's mouthpiece. I expected to hear some fool drunk blurting apologies, but I got Rakas, instead.

"Charles," he said, "could I come over? I'd like to talk to you. Now. Tonight. I'm worried."

I told him he could. I slipped on a bathrobe and groped my way into the kitchen. I'd just finished brewing a pot of coffee when the doorbell rang.

He looked bad. He was pale and I think he'd lost weight. I noticed his hand shook a little when he lifted his cup.

"What's wrong, Aladar?"

"It's the book. Here." He had a manuscript in a folder and he passed it over to me. "It's not going well."

I considered giving him a little lecture about office hours and then decided to hell with it. I turned through the pages. Everything looked fine. A man killed by a poison dart on a misty wharf. The new hero narrowly missing death by scorpion-stuffed glove. A brief meeting with the Mandarin himself in a dark Soho alley.

For an instant Rakas saw the huge forehead, the glittering eyes, the deep hollows of the cheeks, and then the light snuffed out, leaving only a skeleton silhouette.

"You are confident, Rakas," came the harsh, icy whisper. "You consider me a puppet, a marionette."

Suddenly Rakas felt his shoulder grasped by a merciless talon which seemed hard as steel. He grunted in pain and tried to twist free.

"There are no strings on this hand, Rakas," continued the chill muttering of the Mandarin. "It kills when I want and releases when I wish."

Then the talon wrenched away, and Rakas found himself alone.

I lit a cigarette and read on happily. It was around the end of chapter 8 when I saw the beginnings of the drift.

The awful spasms of his dying had twisted the face of Colonel Bentley-Smith's face into a grotesque grin, and this look of dead glee seemed to mock the perplexed frown of Aladar Rakas.

"I don't understand, Inspector Snow," he snapped, "didn't you deploy your men as I asked you to?"

"I did that, sir," replied the puzzled policeman, "but they got through to him without one of us having the foggiest."

Rakas snarled and ground his teeth together.

"Then we have sprung our trap upon a corpse!"

I looked up at Rakas.

"How did they get through?" I asked.

"That's just it," he said. "I don't know!"

He pulled out a cigar, started to unwrap it, and then shoved it back into his pocket.

"You've read it," he said. "In chapter seven I show how I, or rather I show how Rakas, has made absolutely sure that the Colonel's study is inaccessible. Every window, every door, all possible means of approach are under constant observation. There is no way, no conceivable method, for the Mandarin or his minions to have snuck in with the cobra."

He sat back and spread his hands helplessly.

"And yet they do get in, *and* out, and no one the wiser."

I flipped an edge of the manuscript and looked at Rakas thoughtfully.

"Let me show you," he said, leaning forward and taking the folder from my hands. "Let me show you how it happens again." He thumbed through the pages. "Yes, here it is. Here is something just like it."

"Would you like some more coffee?"

"Yes. Sure. Here Rakas has rigged the mummy case in the museum so that there is no feasible way for anyone to open it and remove the body of the sorcerer. The slightest touch on the case's lid and an alarm goes off and cameras record the event. A fly couldn't land on the damned thing without setting off the apparatus. And yet the Mandarin does it. I don't know how, but he pulls it off."

I began, "Aladar—"

"No. Wait," he said, cutting me off. "That's not all. Here, in chapter fourteen, here's one that really gets me. I absolutely defy you to explain to me how he manages to poison the—"

This time I cut him off.

"Aladar, it's not my job to explain how he does it. I'm merely the reader. You, Aladar, are the one to explain it."

"But, how?" he asked me, flinging his hands wide. "I would like you to explain to me how?"

"Because it's a goddam story, Aladar, and because you're the goddam author. That's how."

It took him by absolute surprise. It seemed to stun him. He sat back in his chair and blinked at me.

"You are the one who's making this up," I said, waving at the manuscript which lay, all innocence, on the kitchen table. "You made up the Colonel and the Mandarin and the whole thing. It's you who decides who does what to who and how they do it. Nobody else but you."

He reached up and squeezed his forehead. He shut his eyes and sat perfectly still for at least a minute. Then he let his hand fall to his lap.

"You are right, aren't you?" he said. He sighed heavily and reached out to touch the manuscript gingerly with his fingertips. "It's only a story, isn't it?"

He looked up at the clock on the wall.

"My God," he said. "It's the middle of the night."

He took the manuscript in his hands and stood.

"I'm sorry, Charles. I'm a fool. I can't understand how I let myself be carried away like this."

"It's all right, Aladar," I said. "You just let yourself get too wrapped up. It happens."

We said a few more things, and then I walked him to the door. He opened it and stood there, looking dejected and foolish. I put my hand on his shoulder.

"Remember," I told him, "you're the boss."

He looked at me a little while.

"Sure. That's right," he said. "I'm the boss."

Then the preparation for that year's Christmas rush got underway, and I found myself up to my hips in non-books to lure the prospective festive shoppers. It is a busy season, this pre-

Yule observance, and Aladar Rakas got crowded out of my mind along with everything else except the confused and frantic matters at hand. At least that is my excuse for not getting in touch with him for a good month and a half.

In the end it was he who got in touch with me. I was plowing through a manuscript we'd bought on the archaeology of ancient Egypt, wondering what the copy editor was going to say about the author's ancient use of commas, when my secretary came in to tell me that Rakas was in the outer office. I went out, covered my shock at the way he looked, and walked him back to my sanctuary. He was so thin he had become gaunt.

"It has proven more difficult than you thought," he said. "I believed you, that night, but now I am not so sure."

He had an attaché case with him. He opened it and took out an enormous manuscript. He hefted it and then laid it on my desk.

"Is that the new book?" I asked.

"It is."

I squeezed its bulk, estimating the probable wordage.

"But, Aladar," I said, "the thing's easily three times as long as any of the others."

He smiled ironically.

"You are right, Charles," he said. "And it is not yet finished. If I go on like this I will end with a *Gone with the Wind* of thrillers."

I pulled the thing to me and went through the opening pages. It was obvious he had done a lot of work on them; the changes were considerable, but the story line remained exactly the same.

"You remember the scene where the Mandarin, or Mork, or whoever it is gets in and kills the Colonel?" he asked. "Well, it keeps on happening, Charles. No matter how I rearrange the constabulary of the good Inspector Snow, no matter if I, myself, remain on the premises, even in the room itself, it keeps on happening. The Colonel always ends up being killed by that damned cobra."

"But that's mad, Aladar."

"Yes. Possibly it is because I am going mad. I sincerely hope that is the case. I was sure of it in the beginning. But now I am not so sure. The terrible possibility is that I may be sane and the thing may actually be happening."

I looked at him with, I think, understandable confusion. Rakas lit a cigar and I began to go through the manuscript quickly, skimming, turning several pages at a time when I felt I had the direction of the action.

"It goes that way all through the book," he said. "I increase the protection. I double and redouble the guards. It is all to no avail. The Mandarin wins. Again and again, he wins."

He had a weird kind of calm this time. He even seemed to be amused at his plight. He leaned forward and pointed at the manuscript with his cigar.

"At least a dozen times in there he could have killed me, Charles. Always he lets me go. Just in the nick of time, as we say in the trade." He paused. "But this last time, I am not so sure, I think he is getting tired of the game. I think he almost decided to do me in."

I turned quickly to the end of the manuscript. I found the scene easily.

Despite the almost unendurable pain, Rakas could not move any part of his body, save his eyes. In particular, he could not move his hand. He stared at it, watching it become ever more discolored under the flickering ray from the Mandarin's machine. It felt as though a thousand burning needles were twisting in his flesh.

The cadaverous form of the Mandarin arched over him, lit by the infernal rainbow of color emanating from the device. Rakas had the momentary illusion that the creature was not flesh and blood at all, but a kind of carved architectural device, like a gargoyle buttress in some unholy cathedral.

"Your thoughts of rock images are most appropriate, Rakas," hissed the Mandarin, casually employing his ability to read men's minds. "Perhaps your unconscious is attempting to inform you that you, or at least your right hand, is undergoing a process unique in the history of living human flesh. It is turning into stone."

Rakas stared in horror at the graying, roughening skin of his hand. When his bulging eyes traveled back to the Mandarin he saw that the face of the evil genius was now inches from his own. He could feel fetid breath coming from the cruel slash of a mouth.

"Shall I turn you into a garden ornament now, Rakas? Or should I spare you for a time? What do you think?"

Rakas was smiling at me.

"Shall I show you my right hand, Charles?"

It had been hidden behind his attaché case. He pulled it out and held it before me. It was bluish pale, and stiff.

"It is flesh, not stone," he said. "But it cannot move."

He touched the back of it with the lighted tip of his cigar.

"It cannot feel."

He removed the cigar and I saw that the flesh was still smooth and unbroken.

"It cannot burn."

He chuckled and slid his hand back behind the case.

"You see it is not as bad as in the story. Not yet. But it is getting close, is it not?"

I closed the manuscript without looking at it. Then I threw a part of my professional life out the window.

"Kill the son of a bitch," I said.

"What?"

"Kill the Mandarin. Get rid of him. End the series."

I took a deep breath.

"Look, Aladar, I'll admit the books make a nice bundle of money for us all, but to hell with them. They just aren't worth the damage they're doing to you. This hand business is awful but it's explainable. You can do things like that under hypnosis. But it's a goddamned frightening symptom."

I pushed the manuscript away from me. I didn't want to touch it anymore.

"I'm telling you as your editor, Aladar, that you have absolute carte blanche to slaughter the Mandarin and wrap up the whole business. As a friend, I suggest you do it quickly."

He chuckled again. It was a fair imitation of his usual one, but it didn't have the depth.

"You don't understand, do you, Charles?"

He took the manuscript back and put it into his case. He closed the case and brooded over it for a while.

"Don't you see? I am trying to kill him. Desperately."

He looked at me and his gaze made me uncomfortable.

"With Trowbridge it was altogether different. It was a sort of chess game. Check and counter check. It was safe. Contained. But now I have removed Trowbridge, and the Mandarin is getting out. The only thing that kept that fiend in the books, I realize this now, was that blasted Englishman. Now I have killed him, and now there is nothing to stop the evil from slithering off the pages I have written."

"All right," I said. "Resurrect Evan Trowbridge. Bring him back from the dead. Conan Doyle did it with Holmes."

This time Rakas actually laughed.

"You have cited the perfect example why I cannot, Charles. Was Holmes ever really the same after Doyle killed him? No. Not except in the adventures Watson remembered from before the event. Even the most convinced Sherlockian must admit in his heart that Holmes never truly survived the tumble into the Falls."

He rapped his knuckles on the case and frowned.

"You see, Charles, that is the thing. These creatures are real. They exist. I did not create the Mandarin. I came across him. Do we ever make anything up? I doubt it. I think we only make little openings and peer through them. And openings work both ways."

He stood.

"Doyle was infinitely wiser than I. He respected what he created. He respected the vile Moriarity. He made bloody damned sure that Holmes took the devil with him when he died. He knew that no one else, least of all himself, would have been able to stop him. And so we are presently safe from the baneful doctor. But I have loosed the Mandarin."

Then, without another word, he turned and left.

I don't know how long I sat there cursing myself for not having done something before, such as keeping in touch with Rakas after that early morning visit, before it occurred to me that sitting and cursing was hardly likely to help. I told my secretary to plead with Rakas to come back up if he decided to phone in, and then I left the office.

I figured the best possibility was that he'd head for his apartment. It was east off the park in the sixties. I knew he seldom took a cab but always walked if he had less than fifteen blocks to go. It was a good bet that he was walking now.

He might go up Fifth, and then he might cut over; there was no way of telling. I decided that a man in his state of mind would probably take the simplest route, the one that needed the least attention, so I crossed my fingers and bet on Fifth. I hurried along and when I drew abreast of the fountain in front of the Plaza, I saw him. He was heading into the park.

My first impulse was to dash right up to him, but then I realized I'd probably just dither, so I slowed to match his pace and tried to get myself calmed down. He needed a doctor, he needed help, and it was going to take some fancy persuading. I followed him and mulled over possible gambits.

When he got to the zoo he began to walk idly from cage to cage, looking at the animals. I stopped by a balloon-and-banner man and bought a box of Crackerjack. It helped me blend in, and I figured the taste of the homely stuff might bring me a little closer to earth. Rakas had stopped by a lion cage and, with slow turns of his head, was watching the beast walk back and forth.

I was standing there munching my Crackerjack, creating and rejecting openers, when I caught a flicker of movement out of the corner of my eye and turned to see, or almost see, someone dart back under an archway. I stared hard at the empty place. The someone had been very squat and broad. His suit had been a kind of snake green.

I looked back to check on Rakas. He was still standing in front of the lion's cage. I backed, crabwise, to the arch, keeping one eye on it and the other on Rakas. When I reached the arch I darted through it and looked quickly to the left and right, and I got another glimpse of the squat figure.

He'd slipped around the corner of the monkey house. He'd done it so quickly I wouldn't have seen him if I hadn't been looking for him. I remembered a film strip I'd seen demonstrating the insertion of subliminal images. Just one frame, maybe two, edited in so that you weren't sure if it was something you'd really seen up there on the screen or a passing thought in your own mind.

Green clothes, ape-like, and quick as a lizard.

Mork.

The Mandarin always sent Mork on before.

Then a kid's balloon burst and he gave out a squawk of fright and I found myself standing in Central Park Zoo with a box of Crackerjack in my hand.

I went back through the arch and saw that Rakas was no longer standing in front of the lion's cage. I looked in all directions, but he was nowhere to be seen. I wondered what Evan Trowbridge would have done in a situation like this, and then I shook my head and tossed the fool Crackerjack into a Keep Our City Clean basket. Aladar Rakas had gone mad; it was important to remember that. He had gotten lost in his own lunatic fantasy.

I left the zoo and hurried along the path leading uptown. It was logical to assume he had gone that way. In spite of myself, I found I kept looking from side to side to see if I could spot Mork. Of course there were only young lovers walking, women pushing baby carriages, and old men lost in their smoking.

Then, as I stopped to catch my breath on the hill overlooking the pond where children sail their toy boats, I saw Rakas sitting on a bench. He had the manuscript open, resting on his case, and he was writing with furious speed.

I walked up to him carefully. He was absorbed in his work, and it was only when my shadow fell across the pages that he looked up and saw me.

"Charles! What are you doing here?"

"I was worried, Aladar."

"Oh?" He smiled. "That was very thoughtful of you. I am really quite touched."

He looked down at the manuscript.

"I am sorry to have left your office so rudely, Charles. But you know," he looked up at me suddenly, "just as I was leaving, I got an inspiration. A real inspiration. Sit down, please."

I did as he asked. I could see that he had several pages of close scribblings before him. He must have been writing at an incredible speed.

"I think I have figured out a way to get him, Charles. I really believe I know how to get the necessary leverage."

He smiled at me benignly.

"How do you propose to do it, Aladar?"

"Drag him out ahead of schedule. Manifest him before he is strong!"

I only looked at him blankly, but he was far too excited to notice.

"The Mandarin has been trying to get out, you see, attempting to push his way into life. He has been, you might say, pursuing me into existence. Well, I am going to fool him. I am going to turn and face him and pull him, willy-nilly, into reality. That should put him off his balance!"

He grinned and waved at the scene about us.

"I am going to write him into this actual location, Charles. And on my own terms!"

He rubbed his left hand over his stiff, pale right hand and cackled to himself.

"I began writing it, not on paper, but writing it nevertheless, while at the zoo, watching a lion prowl in his cage. I decided I would begin with Mork. I would not break the tradition of the stories. I had Mork pick up my trail there. I had him follow me," he pointed, "along that path."

I looked back at the path. It was, oddly enough, empty. Only dry leaves blew along it.

"Do you see that boulder?"

I did. It stuck out of the ground like the nose of a huge, gray whale.

"At this moment Mork is hiding behind it."

He tapped the manuscript.

"I have written it here. I have put it down in black and white. He cannot get away. He is trapped. He knows I know. It's all here."

He tapped the manuscript again.

"And now I am going to go over there and kill him, Charles."

He put the manuscript and the case on the bench beside him and then he stood. I opened my mouth, trying to think of something or other to say, but it all got stuck in my throat when I saw Rakas reach into his coat and calmly pull out the biggest revolver I had ever seen in my life. I hadn't known they made them that big. It was terrifying and, at the same time, ludicrous.

"I have been afraid for a long time now, Charles," he said. "Now wait here. I will be right back."

I sat and watched him walk over to the leaning rock. His

black coat fluttered about him and the leaves swirled where he walked. He reached the rock, held the revolver straight before him, and walked out of sight.

I waited for the sound of the shot, but it never came. Eventually I stood and followed him. My legs felt rubbery. When I got to the rock I had to lean on it for support. I felt my way around the rock to its other side and saw him lying on the ground, partially covered with a drift of dirty city leaves. He looked up at me.

"How stupid," he said. "I couldn't bring myself to kill him."

Then he closed his eyes. I bent down, close to him. A thick, dark rivulet of blood ran from one of his ears. I brushed through the leaves until I found the revolver, and then I lifted it with both hands. I stood and walked around the rock and looked back toward the bench.

The Mandarin stood there, weirdly tall and thin, like the statue of a mourning angel in a graveyard. He held the manuscript clutched to his breast. Leaves scudded and broke at his feet. I began walking toward him.

"Not yet, you don't," I said.

I came closer.

"The manuscript isn't finished," I said, "not even if the author's dead."

I was closer. His eyes caught the gray autumn light and glinted.

"I'm the editor," I said. "It's my job, it's my right, to see that the book is properly finished. That's the way it's done."

A leaf blew through the figure's head. I was very close. I could see the long nails on his fingers.

I dropped the gun and held out my hands.

"That's the way it's done," I said.

And then I held the manuscript.

I turned away. Some playing children had discovered Rakas and they were shouting excitedly. I put the book into the case and took it away.

Now this, what I have written, is part of the book. I have added it to Rakas' terminal scribblings and now I am going to finish the book.

I have selected this place carefully. It is miles from any other habitation. Its destruction will not endanger any bystander.

I have soaked the walls and floors with gasoline. I have piled rags around my desk and the chair facing my desk and they are also saturated with it. Everything in this room is wet except for the folder of matches which lies beside me within easy reach. The matches are dry and ready.

Aladar Rakas discovered the Mandarin, but he couldn't quite believe in him. Even at the end he was unable to convince himself that such evil could really exist. He was too civilized a man. Too kindly and too generous.

But I am different. I have seen Rakas in the leaves and I, like Evan Trowbridge, believe in evil.

And I, like Evan Trowbridge and unlike Aladar Rakas, believe in and respect the power of the Mandarin. The devil may know what vile knowledge coils in that huge and unnaturally ancient brain, but I have only the faintest of glimmerings. I know only enough to realize that there is no question of my outwitting the monster.

I will attempt no subtleties. I will use the power I have as author to bring him here, and then I shall destroy everything,

the entire hideous fabric of the pattern which made this situation possible. The book, the author, and the creature spawned—
all shall be burned cleanly away.

Now I am going to finish the book.

He is outside the door, now. He does not want to be but he
must because I am writing it.

Now he has put his hand on the latch. Now he is opening
the door. Now he stands there, in the twilight, looking at me
with hatred in his eyes. That hatred takes a hater like myself to
meet it.

He is here. Really and truly here. Not a near phantom, like
the last time, but a solid, breathing being.

He is moving forward carefully, stepping high to avoid the
soaked rags, but gasoline stains the hem of his gray, silken
robe all the same.

Now he sits and glares at me.

He cannot move. He cannot budge, try as he may.

His eyes glow. They shimmer like fire seen through honey.

He cannot move.

Now I have lit a match and set the pack aflame.

He cannot

I hope I shall never forget the extraordinary expression of astonishment on Charles Pearl's face when he realized he had
committed suicide to no purpose.

He remained conscious for a remarkable period of time,
considering the damage the fire was doing him, staring at me
with utter disbelief as I gathered up the manuscript, including
this last page torn from his typewriter.

The idiot had discovered Evan Trowbridge's strength, which
was implacable hatred, but he had shared, and therefore

missed altogether, his weakness, which was a lack of sufficient imagination.

Trowbridge always failed to bring me down altogether because he never quite managed to foresee the final trick of my science, the last fantastic ingenuity, the climactic trapdoor.

It would never have occurred to him, for instance, that I can live invulnerable in a pool of fire.

And so I, the hero of the series all along, have the opportunity to bring this final volume to, it pleases me to say, a happy ending.